Casey Chaplin

# Necromancy… And Other Mystical Things

PUBLISHED IN CANADA.
ISBN 978-0-9919967-1-1
Photo credit to John Reed.

# CHAPTER 1

The intensity in his eyes would generally suggest that he was a focused and determined individual; a person with the utmost intelligence and determination. He could have been a doctor, or a lawyer, or a doctor lawyer in space even. Unfortunately, in the case of Mortimer Blake, that simply wasn't true. In fact, he was a rather dimwitted and passive individual, but in his mind, he was that astronomical defender of justice doing surgery. He took a deep breath, and held it for a moment to build up his nerve, he then exhaled slowly and meticulously. Narrowing his eyes he brought it into focus, it was all he could see, it was all he could think about, and at that moment it was all he could care about.

"Alright excessively large Tostito, it's between you, me, and this jar of salsa now," Mort said. He took another breath. "You WILL fit. I'm not losing another good chip to this jar... too many innocent have fallen already to this plight. No more I say, no more!" Mort glanced down to his feet where hundreds of broken tortilla chips lay. It was a right snack food massacre.

Another breath and another internal pep talk and Mort was ready to conquer his demons. He raised his hand with the chip high above his head, holding it there for a second; the anticipation was building like a train steaming along a track, and Mort could hardly contain himself. He must succeed, there couldn't be any failure... Do or do not, there is no try! He swung his arm downward towards the jar of salsa with a far too small opening and –

"What the crap are you doing?" A voice rang out. Mort looked up in a panic like he was just caught masturbating causing him to lose control of the chip, and in the surprise of the moment, he crushed it in his own hand. The air in the room became so tense it could be cut with a knife. Mort stared down at his hand in a saddened disbelief. He closed his eyes and breathed heavily for a few seconds, and then he raised his glare. If looks could kill...

"What the hell, man? That was my last good solide-uh, chip," Mort said shifting his gaze around the room now. "Too many good men lost..." He whispered under his breath while looking at the fallen crumbs at his feet.

Chip's seen Mort do a lot of strange things over the years, so nothing really surprised him anymore... however, that was unique, to say the least. All he could do was stare blankly as Mort glared at the ground and whispered something. He shook loose the cobwebs and sat beside Mort on the couch, who immediately perked up, sniffed the air, and looked over at Chip with an expression of curiosity and disdain. He looked rather like a prairie-dog sitting atop its mound on the watch for predators – or something to fuck. Instead, he only found his smelly roommate, which was sort of like a predator and something to fuck.

"Dude... you smell like..." He leaned in closer to Chip, uncomfortably close, and sniffed again.

"Man, you smell like death. What the hell?"

In a flash of frustration Chip jumped from the couch, landing on many of the broken chips, Mort looked down and let out a slight whimper of pain.

"Goddamn! That is me, isn't it?" Chip said looking at Mort who appeared to be mourning the loss of his own mother.

"Mort!" Chip shrieked.

"Huh, oh yeah, you smell like a corpse man, what were you doing all day?"

"Nothing! I got up, went down to work at the bookstore, stood there for six and a half hours and now I'm home, nothing out of the ordinary happened." Chip confessed.

"Well man, you reek. When did it start?" Mort asked.

"I dunno man, around one, one-thirty people started giving me this look like...like..."
"Like you smell?" Mort finished. Chip shot him a look, returning the *if looks could kill* favour.
"Yes, like I smell... Did I become the smelly guy everybody avoids like over lunch or something?" Chip questioned.
Mort stood up and got even closer to Chip than before. He sniffed the air and moved nose to nose with Chip.
"Yes... yes you did," Mort said and pulled away, "You should seriously leave the apartment now... I can't concentrate on anything with that stench. Please... go... now," Mort said as he began to usher Chip towards the door.
Chip, while being pushed along by Mort stopped and turned around. "Ok, ok. Geeze I'm going... Subtlety was never your strong suit, was it?"
"Nope, now go on stinky, air yourself out. I've got an enemy to conquer," Mort said as he fixated his gaze on the salsa jar sitting on the table.
"Mock me will you...I will win," Mort said aloud. Chip tilted his head and raised an eyebrow. He wanted to say something, he truly did, but there were no words. Chip stood in the doorway dumbfounded. He just blinked, shook his head and walked out of the apartment. Mort, in turn, sat back on the couch and folded his hands on his lap. He leaned back and started to contemplate his plan of attack. He reached down and grabbed the last corn chip from the oversized party bag. All its comrades had fallen; will that one be the hero? Surely, it must be.
Mort hoisted his hand up high, muttered a few words of encouragement, and struck the chip down on the rim of the jar. In an almost slow motion effect, the chip shattered into a hundred small pieces and fell to the floor like a whole grain thunderstorm. Mort's eyes opened wide and his jaw hit the floor in disbelief.

“NOOOOOOOOOOO!” Mort yelled out before burying his head in his hands. “Why God, Why...? He was a good man! HE WAS A GOOD MAN!”

The echo of an epic *NOOOOOOO* rang through the hallway outside of the apartment. Chip stopped and glanced back at his door. He thought about turning back, but used his better judgment; that and he had other things to worry about... like smelling of a dead body. He couldn’t comprehend it, he noticed the smell too, but it didn’t seem that intense to him; at least not as pungent as the reactions he received warranted. But still, it was a pesky stench that came from nowhere and didn’t seem to want to leave.

Chip and Mort’s apartment happened to be on a pretty quiet street as far as they were concerned. They lived in a lower-class part of the downtown core where the foot traffic was rarely more than a local, sometimes a bum wandered through, but it was mostly squirrels, which Mort fed causing them to stick around. It was annoying when the clamoured against the balcony window, but God damn if they weren’t just the most adorable things.

Chip couldn’t be more relieved that they lived in an area where foul smelling creatures and people frequented – like rodents and the homeless. New York City. The Big Apple, but like any fruit, it was complete with worms and rot.

Though Chip lived in a pretty low-profile part of town, he did indeed live downtown, which meant it *is* busy in other parts, parts close to where he was situated. In fact just two blocks up there was a street riddled with small shops and cafes; and with shops and eateries comes homeless people and garbage filled back alleys, a place he might be able to wander around unnoticed: blend in with the stench if you will.

It was a warm day, too, which didn’t help. With every step Chip took he felt more and more sweat bead up on his forehead, only making him feel even dirtier and ranker than he already did. He felt a slight wave of anxiety pass through him when he strolled by a certain shop. Any other day of the week Chip wouldn't give this place a second glance. It was the weirdest store; they sold all sorts of weird crap: voodoo dolls, *magical* incense, spell books... If it were odd, strange, or queer, they sold it. *Pssh, magical incense... what crap. Who the hell gets conned into buying that junk.* Chip always thought to himself as he walked by.

As creepy as the store was, the guy who owned it was creepier - Older fellow with a beard riddled with salt and pepper and a bit of grey and white. The salt and pepper was surely from the sandwich Chip always saw him eating. There was often a dash of mustard too. Nevertheless, Chip felt even more uneasy than ever. Flavour-saver took notice of him as he walked past. Of course, the man had to be standing outside his shop when Chip meandered on by, and he must have caught wind of poor ol' Chip. The way he just dropped his sandwich and bolted inside, all the while fixating his gaze upon him was just rude, Chip thought. But as over exaggerated as it was, it was indeed understandable. Chip smelled like death, there was no way around it.

After scuttling past the creep-show shop, Chip felt excessively uneasy. It was bad enough that he felt he was drawing attention to himself, but now there was proof; he had to get off the busy streets. Why he wandered that way was a mystery; after all, why would he want to hang out in a busier part of town than where he lived. There were plenty of alleys with dark shadowy nooks and crannies for him to duck into. He could have stayed home and had a shower, which in retrospect, seemed like the best idea in the world.... Nevertheless, he felt drawn to the area he happened across.

Chip and Mort's apartment was a cozy little place that had just enough room for the two of them. Since neither of them were really social butterflies, the apartment worked. They lived in a sort of odd couple harmony, though they weren't really a couple. Chip was the ever-present conscience, and Mort was like the retarded kid who had to be reminded not to stick a fork in the wall socket. Regardless of his intelligence, Mort was a wholeheartedly good person who would never harm anybody. He was a good friend, if not a little too honest at times.

The apartment in question, however, still reeked of Chip's death cloud, but Mort didn't seem too bothered. He had other things to worry about at that moment, like giving his fallen soldiers a proper burial, even if they did fail miserably at their mission. Mort couldn't lay all the blame on them, however; he couldn't have been a very good general if everybody under his command bit the dust, so to speak.

"Yeah, I know, it's weird right... wait, did you... you did know... You clever sonofa... Yeah, sorry, I keep forgetting she actually was... sorry. Yeah, ok. I gotta go; I've got some stuff to do. Bye," The ending of every phone call was so ominous, Mort thought. If you lingered too long on the line everything was punctuated with dread. The infamous clicking of the receiver switching off, and then the alarming dial tone, which sounded suspiciously like a flat line on a heart monitor, Mort always thought put the perfect stamp on the end of a diabolical conversation. The stuff that went through that lad's head was incredible. Like the time he locked himself in his room to contemplate why *Playboy* was for boys, and *Playgirl* was for girls. It didn't make sense to him, and the amount of energy he spent thinking about it scared the crap out of Chip. He never did come to a conclusion.

Nevertheless, he did have something to do, and he knew exactly how to go about it. Mort threw the portable phone on the couch and scurried into his bedroom, once there he set his sights on his closet. He rifled through it looking for something like a bloodhound sniffing out drugs; he wasn't going to give up until he found it...

“FOUND IT!” he squealed out his excitement. From the closet he produced a brown box with a lid and rushed to the bed, dropping the box and ripping off the lid as if it were the first Christmas present he’d ever seen. He tore through that box with a purpose; he had to do it just right.
He had to be dressed as a soldier himself to properly perform the ritual of passing… for the tortilla chips – it only seemed right in his mind. It was the purpose his great grandfather had for his World War II uniform, surely.

Chip thought about calling Ellie, the girl with whom he was entirely enamoured, and lucky enough to call his girlfriend, to see if he could go there for a little while, but he used his better judgment. After thinking about his situation for the briefest of moments, he figured she would dump him at first sniff. But, he didn’t know where else to go, he didn’t even know if he still smelled, though he assumed he did. It had been a while since he passed anybody on the street, and he didn’t really smell anything anymore, although that could have just been a tolerance he built up. He needed to test his stench level; he wanted to know if he was still an olfactory assassin, so he took a right down an alleyway. He noticed a bum slouched over on his first lap of the block, and if it affected him, then it would hit everybody.
He eyed the bum from around the corner of a building, making sure he didn’t make himself come off too obvious when marching in front of him waving his stank around. Everything seemed kosher, so Chip went on his way. He started off slowly, somewhat tentative at first a little nervous about being in a dark-ish alley as the sun was beginning to set. It was like the start of every good vampire movie (Good being the key word – not these sparkly vampire movies...). Nevertheless, there were much more real threats to be weary of, like muggers, rapist...rats; oh how Chip hated rats.

And so he trudged on, passing by the slumping homeless man, he made sure to slow down as he moved by to give him the full effect, but he didn't react. The bum didn't even flinch. The smell must have dissipated as quickly as it appeared. But, just to be sure, Chip stopped and stood right in front of the man, pretending at first to tie his shoe, and then with a fake yawn and stretch, lifting his arms high above his head, armpit pointed directly at the guy. Nothing, not even so much as a cough or a deep breath, Chip figured he was clean and ready to head home. Little did he know however was that the homeless guy was already dead... but even worse than that, Chip still smelled...bad.

Chip never knew what he would find when he walked through the front door of his apartment, most times it was nothing, sometimes it was something, but this time, well not even Chip was ready for what he was about to see.

As Chip walked through the threshold of the door, he was totally unaware that he would be standing on the precipice of reality, about to fall into the realm of the totally insane. Approximately fifteen feet to Chip's right stood Mort, dressed as a World War Two soldier saluting to nobody. Chip needed a better look. As he circled around, he noticed an abundance of tiny little crosses erected from toothpicks on the floor.

"What the hell...?" Chip said in astonishment.

"Shhhh!" Mort turned and motioned with his finger over his lips. Chip stopped dead.

The two stood in silence for a moment or two longer; Chip confused and Mort solemn.

"Annnnnd.... OK," Mort said and turned to Chip. "What's up?"

Chip was dumbfounded, "Uh – err...what?" Was all he could muster, though he did manage to make a motion with his hands towards the make-shift graveyard.

“What, oh, this? It’s a monument to the fallen. The brave that sacrificed so much for the cause of my hunger; poor little fellas,” Mort answered; Chip just blinked.
“How are they standing there...the little crosses that is?” That was really the only question Chip could think of that would have a reasonable answer.
“Glue,” Mort said before turning and marching into his bedroom.
“Right, glue, of course,” Chip said to himself. He walked over and plopped himself on the couch, eyeing the mess of crumbs and crosses on the floor. It was like a freaky little shrine to snack foods.
“Hey, Mort... What happened to the salsa?” Chip yelled out.
“Assisted suicide!” Mort yelled back from behind his bedroom door.
“Assisted suicide...?” Chip whispered to himself. “What?!” He yelled out.
“Yup, he couldn’t handle the onslaught anymore. Victory was mine and he knew it.” There was a pause, Chip didn’t respond as he was still trying to make sense of the situation.
“I threw it out the window,” Mort said as he emerged from down the hall.
“Ahh... Wait, why?!” Chip said as he jumped to his feet and rushed to the window. He peered out and saw an explosion of salsa on the concrete below; it looked like a crime scene with broken glass and chunky red stuff smeared all about like somebody threw a head in a glass jar from the roof.
“You are one strange dude,” Chip said as he turned from the window and walked back to the couch.
“Yeah, and you’re one stinky dude,” Mort said as he held his sleeve over his face.
“What!?” Chip said jolting sideways to look directly at Mort. “Still?”
Mort nodded his head feverishly, afraid to leave the stink protection of his cotton sleeve.

"What the hell, man? I have no idea what it is. The homeless guy didn't react," Chip said as he stood up.
"Homeless guy?" Mort muttered, confused, from under his arm.
"Never mind, I'm gonna have a shower, maybe that will help," Chip said as he made his way down the hallway toward the bathroom.
"Can't hurt!" Mort yelled to him. "Goddamn, he stinks," Mort said to himself while waving the air around him like a crazy person.

Chip turned the off the water and stepped out of the stall and into the fog steamed room that awaited him. He sniffed both his armpits and smelled nothing. He wiped off the mirror, which caused a squealing sound, a sound which Chip hated. He proceeded to check himself out in the mirror looking for anything out of the ordinary. He didn't notice any weird things in the shower; no green-tinged water from some dead rat-sized parasite that attached to his back, silently numbing him while it leeched off his lifeblood. Nope, nothing like that anyway.
Chip had an overactive imagination, but he could never have imagined what was happening to him.
Satisfied with his shower, Chip dried off and re-clothed – with fresh clothes of course. He contemplated burning the garb he had on earlier. He was certain he smelled like a corpse no longer; well, he at least prayed he didn't smell like death anymore. And if there was a God, he would have to listen to that request, right? Starving kids in the world, or a smelly man – surely the stink was much, much worse.
Chip opened the door of the bathroom, only to be met by Mort standing inches from the threshold; Chip jumped back, and a small yelp may or may not have escaped his lips. The two exchanged an awkward glance after the possible yelp, and then Mort leaned in and sniffed Chip's personal bubble.

"Nope, still stink," Mort said and backed away, making his way to the living room.
"Are you kidding me?! It's no better?" Chip pleaded.
"Well, now you smell like fruity death; does that help?" Mort asked as he sat on the couch, looking for the TV remote. "Speaking of fruity, what kinda shampoo are you using? It has potential to smell awesome... ya know, as long as the rot smell goes away..."
"Oh shut up," Chip said, following Mort to the couch. "I just wish I knew why this happened," Chip finished by plopping down beside Mort.
"You and me both man..," Mort said sliding to the opposite end of the couch.
"Well, too bad, you're stuck with me for the night," Chip stated.
"Oh, no I'm not. You have a girlfriend, and said girlfriend has an apartment, I think you should go spend the night with her. I mean, what I have I done to upset you? Why torture me?" Mort asked.
"Are you nuts?" Chip started. "I can't see her like this. She'll dump me on the spot."
"Welp, she chose you, now she has to deal with the consequences.Get out, go, now. Go see her," Mort said grabbing Chip under the arm, ushering him off the couch.
"Great, I touched you. Now my hand's gonna fall off or something," Mort joked.
"Haha, very funny...But you can't be serious, I can't go see Ellie like this man," Chip added.
"Sure ya can! What if this smell never goes away, hmm? I mean, what, you're never gonna date again? That means there will never be any little Chip's running around. She has to accept you for who you are, and what you smell like, or ya know...it was never meant to be," Mort said as he exhaled his last breath. He was wearing it kind of thin near the end.
"Yeah, I guess you're right..." Chip conceded.

“I know I’m right. And if it doesn’t work out, I know a girl... Latisha. Wonderful woman, no sense of smell as far as I can tell, and she’s black...” Mort paused and met Chip's eye, a small smirk crept onto his face. “That way you guys can have...”
“Don’t say it...” Chip implored.
“Little chocolate Chips!” Mort finished, looking rather satisfied.
“I hate you, Mortimer Blake,” Chip said.
“Eh, I try. Now go, before I yak all over you.”
“Fine! Jesus, maybe I’ll just sleep in a dumpster or something.”
“Couldn’t hurt. Now go. See ya when you don’t smell like death anymore,” Mort finished and closed the apartment door. He somehow managed to guide Chip out of the dwelling during his diatribe on Chip’s stench.
When the door was closed, Mort flipped out his cell phone and dialled a number from his contacts. He waited while it rang for a moment.
“Yeah, he’s on his way..,” Mort said, and then slipped the phone back into his pocket.

Chip had only been home about an hour before Mort kicked him out, but in that hour it had become wicked cold, though just being out of the shower didn’t help either. Chip swore he would blame Mort if he froze and died during the night, after all, he didn’t really have a place to go. There was no way in Hell he was going to head to Ellie’s house, and he was pretty sure no hotel – scratch that – no reputable hotel would let him stay there smelling like a dead horse. Chip figured he’d probably end up walking the streets until the early hours of the morning in anticipation of Mort fell asleep, then he’d just sneak his way into the apartment unnoticed, like a super ninja. The smell couldn’t possibly wake somebody up; after all, the homeless guy didn't wake up... even if he was already dead, but Chip didn't know that.

Wandering the streets alone in the twilight hours on a weekend was always unnerving to Chip. He didn't exactly have the alpha-male, macho tough guy mentality. He was often afraid of being out at night, especially alone. The streets were deserted at that hour, even if it was only about 9:30 pm. Most, if not all the little shops were closed, and the cafes didn't have too many occupants. It was a far-cry from an hour or so ago when Chip had been standing in the exact spot he is was. The streets weren't bustling with people, the lights in the windows were dim, and the occasional street lamp flickered announcing that it's about to die. Everything was totally different...except for one thing. The homeless guy in the alleyway remained.

The grizzled old man hadn't moved. He was still perched against the wall of a building; his head slumped over with a hood covering most of his face. Chip thought this to be rather peculiar, even hobo's move once in a while, right? Against his better judgement, Chip slowly lurked down the alley, making sure no muggers or rapists hid in the shadows waiting to pounce on some helpless prey, like himself.

With every step taken, Chip argued with his conscious; one side argued it was his humane duty to check on the geezer, the other side protested saying it was just an old bum and the world would be a better place without him. Chip didn't much like the logic of side B, no matter how sound it was – he was just too good natured.

As he approached the seemingly lifeless man, he noticed something change within him, and beyond him. The smell seemed to disappear clearly proof of God and miracles. Chip thought it was his imagination, but regardless, it still seemed to be dissipating with every step. When he got within about five or six feet, he felt a strange sensation within him that he couldn't explain; it was like a butterflies in the stomach feeling, but times a hundred. Chip felt like they would burst out of his stomach *Alien*-style and fly away. Of course, that didn't happen. That would be impossible. Instead, Chip raised the dead, which was totally plausible, apparently.

Upon closer inspection by Chip, he noticed the man was deathly pale, motionless, and if he had a mirror, he would have stuck it under his nose just for good measure. Chip determined that the man simply died of old age or some other natural cause. But what wasn't natural was what happened a second or two after Chip checked the bum's pulse, he gasped for air like a maniac.

Chip jumped backed, shocked and scared – he may or may not have yelped again. All he could do was clinch to the adjacent wall like it was his mother and watch the dead become undead. The old not-so-dead guy clawed at the air in front of him, gasping and groaning for any bit of oxygen that would agree to flow into his lungs. And then, out of nowhere, he stopped just as suddenly as he started. If a corpse coming to life wasn't confusing enough, the glowing green eyes definitely put the situation into the realm of mystification.

The thoughts that flowed through Chip's head were many: Did he merely miss the pulse; was it just really faint because the old guy was nearing death; did he crap his pants when the bum gasped for air; or most importantly, did he just raise the dead? He couldn't have, that was foolish. He dismissed the thought... but how could he explain the glowing green eyes? Chip's mind was playing tricks on him, he was sure of that.

"Your mind wasn't playing tricks on you, I'm sure of it," A voice rumbled from down the alley.

Chip's head shot to the side so hard, he swore he heard something rip. "What the hell?!" Chip yelled half to himself and half to nobody, "Who are you?" He said with his voice cracking on *who.*

"Bill. And yes, you just raised that guy from the dead, as I thought you might do," Bill said, "Follow me."

"Follow you? I don't even know you, why would I follow you?" Chip pointed out.
"You know me, I'm Bill," Bill refuted.
"Well, yeah, I know your name. But still, I don't know you; you're stranger Bill, that's all."
"Shut up, Chip and come here. You've seen me before."
"Wait, what – how do you now my name?!" Chip said sounding very demanding; he was quite proud of himself.
"Just come here!" Bill shouted in his husky voice.
"No, you come here!" Chip shouted, realizing the poor choice he had made as he finished saying it. Why in Hell would he want *Bill* to come to him in a dark alley with a dead-ish body laying beside him?
"Fine," Bill said.
"Damnit!" Chip muttered under his breath, but before he could make a break for it, Bill was standing just to the left of him.
"OK, I'm here, now can we go? This alley gives me the creeps... and the dead bum doesn't help either," Bill said and Chip jumped. That time he yelped.

And so they were off, Bill guiding chip from under the arm – a lot of people seemed to be grabbing him there lately, must be an easy point of access or something. Once out of the darkness of the alley and into the dimly lit street, Chip recognized his escort; it was none other than the creepy creepstore owner that always creeped him out. The familiarity would usually make things better, but in this case, it made them much, much worse.
Chip's imagination ran wild. He was certain, 100% that flavour-saver would add him as one of the delicacies in his beard. Chip was about to be eaten... well in his mind anyway.
"Relax, kid... I'm not gonna eat ya," Bill said in a humoured tone.
"What... err, who, why?" Chip sputtered out. He felt that was good enough to get his point across.

“Boy, you have A LOT to learn. Your world’s about to be turned on end,” Bill said.
“Wonderful,” Chip stated. “Still didn’t answer my question.”
“That’s ‘cause you didn’t ask one... as I recall, all you mustered was something along the lines of *what...err, who, why?”* Bill smartly remarked.
“Smartass,” Chip said under his breath, Bill shot him a nasty little look as he dragged him to the front of his store.
“Well, here we are, kid. We’ll answer everything you’ll ask... in there,” Bill said.
“We...?” Chip questioned as Bill opened the door.

The door swung open slowly, revealing a well-lit little shop, and a familiar figure standing at a bookshelf.
“Hey Chip, still smell like death?” Mort said with a goofy smile on his face. Bill wasn’t lying, Chip’s world was about to be turned on end, and it started with Mort... as was often the case when something odd happened in his life.
“What?!” Chip shouted in disbelief. “What the hell are you doing here, Mort?”
“Eh, ya know... browsing ol’ Bill’s wares?” Mort responded nonchalantly.
“Browsing his wares?! What the hell is going on here?!” Chip yelled, spinning around to look at Bill, and then shifting back to Mort.
“Sit down, kid... You’ve got a lot of learning to do,” Bill said putting a hand on his shoulder.
“Kid? I’m 24, how old are you, 40, 50 max?” Chip said in defence of his age.
Bill chuckled and gave an oddly compassionate look to Chip. “I’m four-hundred-and-twelve.”
Chip sat down. In fact, Chip nearly fell down. He looked over at Mort for some kind of assurance, but he just stood there and shrugged and continued to pretend to look at the crap scattered throughout the shelves.

"How the hell can you be four-hundred-and-twelve? That's impossible," Chip said trying to rationalize the situation, and then another thought entered that frazzled noggin of his. "And how is it you know what I'm thinking?"
Bill let out a deep belly laugh. His bushy beard bounced out of turn with the rest of him, it swayed right, while his rotund gut bounced up and down. It defied physics. That greatly disturbed Chip.
"Son, I can read your mind; it's *impossible,* right? But I know your every thought, sometimes before you know it."
Chip glared at Bill hard, as if to say *I'm calling your bluff, what am I thinking old man.* Bill caught on quickly.
"You reallllllllllly need to get laid, kid if you're thinking about that," Bill said with a snarky tone.
Chip's eyes widened, and then he sunk into the chair, hoping it would open up and swallow him, which at that point in the day seemed entirely possible.
"Ok...fine," Chip said quietly all the while turning increasingly red. "But what's going on?" The question was more directed to himself more than his counterparts.
"Well, Chip. You're a necromancer," Mort said, turning to look at Chip in a dramatic fashion. He thought that was pretty epic and felt pretty darn good about himself.
"Oh, yeah. A necromancer," Chip started off calmly, but that was about to change. "WHAT!? Alright, what kinda crap are you guys smokin' 'cause I don't want any. Like really, a necromancer? Mort, I didn't even know you were into Dungeons and Dragons," Chip fumed.
"No, seriously buddy...you are. Did you touch that homeless guy outside? Did he touch that homeless guy outside?" Mort asked Chip than Bill. Bill nodded and Chip didn't say a word. He may have been having a small heart attack at the moment. He wasn't sure; it was probably just a mental breakdown or gas. Either seemed far more likely - especially gas. That can sneak up on a guy. Regardless, Chip didn't even believe what

these two were saying, so why would he be having a mental breakdown? More likely than not, it was just being in the shop that weirded him out.

"And he came back to life, didn't he, just for a second?" Mort said, sounding slightly excited.

"Aye," Bill chimed in. Mort sauntered over to Chip, trying to look calm and cool. It didn't work, it just looked like he had gas. It's contagious.

"Dude, you just raised the dead!" Mort exclaimed, hugging Chip.

Chip pushed him off and stood up from the stool (It hadn't swallowed him after all), and he began to back away slowly, but bumped into Bill.

"Where ya going?" Bill asked rhetorically, "We're not done here." Chip felt as big as an ant and slithered back to the stool.

"It's still impossible. The guy just had a bit of life left in him is all..." Chip tried to reason, more to himself than to Bill and Mort.

"Nope, sorry Chip. He was long dead, a few days anyway," Mort said.

Chip raised an eyebrow, "And you know that how...?"

"Well..." Mort started, but Chip interrupted, "Oh God, you killed him didn't you?!"

"What, oh, hell no. I just borrowed the body," Mort corrected.

"Oh, that's fine then..." Chip paused, "Wait, what? Borrow from who...where...what?"

"I know a guy at the morgue. He's been dead, well, undead for years. He owed me one."

Chip felt weak in the knees, it was a good thing he was sitting down. He wondered if he could faint while sitting...

"We used him as a test for you. Bill here knew, somehow that you were...special," Mort said, as Bill grunted with content to Chip's left.

"A test...well, it didn't work. Coroner made a mistake, sorry to disappoint," Chip stood up again, took one glance at burly Bill and sat back down looking like a scolded dog.
"Were the eyes glowing green?" Mort asked.
"No," Chip lied.
"Yes," Bill corrected.
"Traitor," Chip blurted.
"Wimp," Bill said. Chip stood, but remembered what happened seconds earlier, and sat down.
"Touché," Chip said quietly.
"And the smell, God damn, Chip, you've smelt like death since I put that guy there. It's kinda like radar...a deadar, if you will." Mort felt clever for coming up with that, Chip was also rather impressed, more so with the grammar, though. Deadar was kinda lame.
"Deadar, like...I can sense the dead? Really...you're not telling me this, it's ridiculous." Chip stood by his point that everything happening in that moment was impossible.
"Well, it started as soon as I dropped that body there, you started to stink," Mort said.
"But it went away the closer I got..."
"That's the aura releasing into the body. The smell is like a hormone. When you get close to a dead body, your body reacts the same as a horny dog walking past a bitch in heat. So when you get close, that hormone releases and enters the next closest dead thing. It's kinda like how my mom met my dad," Bill chimed in.
Chip and Mort both look horrified; eyes wide and jaws gaping.
"So I orgasm bodies to life?!" Chip said when he snapped out of the trance of gross.
"Sure, and soon enough – with the proper training, you won't even have to touch the bodies to bring them back... Like how it is with your sex life," Bill said with a chuckle.

"HAAAAAAAAAAAAAAAA. So funny. Where the hell did you find this guy, Mort?" Chip said.
"Oh God, don't ask. It's a really long story, one that gives me nightmares for a week. Remember that night you caught me with the blanket and the fake plastic sword?" Mort said.
"Yeah..." Chip answered cautiously.
"That was the night we met." Chip raised an eyebrow at that. He didn't bother to dive deeper into Mort and Bill's history. In fact, the less he knew about the entire situation, the better off he would be. All Chip wanted to do was get out of this creepy shop, away from the creepy owner and his increasingly creepy friend.
"Anyway, well, it was a nice meeting fellas but I think it's time I take my leave." Chip stood up again from the stool, took another look at Bill, thought about sitting down again, but instead took a step or two backwards. He was desperately hoping there was a back door to the place.
Bill looked at Chip with a degree of intimidation, Chip looked at Mort with a large degree of fear, and Mort looked at Bill with a degree of contempt. Bill rolled his eyes and stepped aside motioning that the way was clear for whomever to pass.
"Chip, this isn't like Columbine or something. You're not our prisoner, you're my buddy, who happens to have a special power, and now, has a really weird life. It's all good man," Mort paused and motioned to the door, "You can go. I'll see ya at the apartment."
Chip looked quizzically at Mort than fearfully at Bill as he wandered towards the front door. Bill eyed him the entire way, and Mort gave a goofy little wave. Chip slowly opened the door, gave a fake little smile, then bolted out of the door and into the street – Before the door closed a crash of garbage cans clattered, and the screaming of a cat echoed through the night. Mort turned his head and looked at Bill.
"Well...that was cliché, wasn't it?" Mort asked.

“Yeah..,” Bill started, and Mort narrowed his eyes. “I dunno about this kid, Mort... I mean, he’s like a wiener,” Bill said honestly.
“Oh come on, give him a break,” Mort said in his friend’s defence, “He just found out he can raise the dead, what did you expect? *Oh Mort and Crazy Beard Guy, thank you so much for changing everything in my world and turning me into a freak,*” Mort said sarcastically.
“Well, technically, we didn’t turn him into anything. He is what he is,” Bill stated.
“Beside the point!” Mort snapped, “He would never have known about this, he would have just gone on his whole life with this hidden...thing-“
“Ability,” Bill interjected, Mort raised an eyebrow, that was apparently the theme for the day.
“Yes, ability. He would have lived a normal life... I mean, how often does somebody hang around a dead body? Two or three times in a lifetime? He would have been normal,” Mort said, sounding remorseful.
“We need him, Mort. You know that..,” Bill said, sounding strangely sympathetic.
“Yeah, I know... he’s too valuable an asset. But he’s still my friend, and I don’t like this at all,” Mort said before walking out of the storefront and into the back.
“Where are you going?” Bill yelled out.
“To get some Tostitos!” Mort yelled out; Bill raised an eyebrow.

*A Necromancer?* Chip thought to himself as he walked down the cold dark street. The thought was rubbish, and he couldn’t quite believe it, though the alone time was beginning to sway him slightly. It still appeared to be more like a really well thought out practical joke. But then that would mean Mort was the mastermind behind it; he instantly dismissed the intricate joke scenario, but that only left one option.

Chip always felt he was special, or at least different. But he always thought it was his divine ability to fold underwear perfectly; not the ability to raise the dead.

The wind blew sharply and Chip accordingly shivered; he looked up in hope of some answers from some celestial source, but to no avail. All he got was momentary blindness from a street lamp that hung directly above him. He looked away and rubbed his eyes. It just wasn't his day. Maybe he needed to call Ellie. After all, he didn't smell anymore. Actually, that sounded like a wonderful idea. A little foreplay always cheered him up.

Chip pulled out his cell phone and realized it was on silent, unfortunately, the biggest clue was the six text messages and one voicemail. Chip skimmed over the texts, at first they were nothing, just simple *hey, how are you?* messages from Ellie, but then they took a turn for the vicious. Hell hath no fury... The messages progressed from cheery to volatile exponentially - Chip was afraid to listen to the voicemail – it was left after all the text were sent, and based on the anger portrayed in the in last text by various emoticons, the voicemail would surely be much, much worse.

He dialled the number and the automated voice came on; Chip never realized how cold and ominous the recording sounded, like Stephen Hawking if he were a she, and she happened to be on the rag.

Chip dialled in his password, selected one as prompted by the demonic recording on her period, and listened. The tirade was epic; filled with accusations of infidelity, questioning Chip's honesty and reliability, and ending with a blubbering incoherent mess of words that sounded like a long string of curses and profanities. All in all, it was a very mean message. But it took Chip's mind off the whole Necromancer thing for a while. He had more dangerous things to deal with: A pissed off girlfriend.

On his way to Ellie's house, Chip had to come up with an excuse. Clearly, he couldn't walk into her apartment and say: *Hey, I have the uncanny ability to raise the dead. Mort and some guy with a crazy ass beard told me so.* That might not go over too well; actually, castration might be on the menu if he told her that. The news of becoming a Necromancer would have to wait for another day, preferably when she's either asleep or drunk, or both.

Ellie lived approximately thirteen minutes and twenty-eight seconds from Chip's apartment. It was a rough approximation that Chip very thoroughly timed out over three weeks when they first dated. Ok, so it wasn't so much an approximation as it was an exact measurement. But he wanted to know how long it would take to run there in case of an emergency, so he merely cut a minute or two off his thirteen minutes and change and came up with eleven minutes and six seconds. Although he never actually ran it, he was sure, it was all very scientific. However, on this occasion, it took a bit longer. Chip was both scared and confused, so he slumped along at a very pedestrian pace; he was in absolutely no rush to get to Ellie's place. Why was it that bad things always came in droves? The smell, the whole raising the dead thing and having your best friend know about it... Actually, how *did* Mort know? That was one question that slipped Chip's mind at the time. Amongst all the confusion and the denial, Chip didn't bother to ask how either Bill or Mort knew about his condition. It was just another headache for Chip Adams. He told himself that he was going to stop thinking about this whole supernatural business and focus on fixing things with his girlfriend. Priorities.
Ellie's apartment was located in a very upscale condominium, well upscale for the area: It had a buzzer to get into the lobby. Chip, for some reason, found this very uppity. His apartment didn't have one, Hell, his apartment barely had a front door.

Chip's gut turned to knots when he approached the intercom on the door. He had to call up to her before she could open the door, thusly, she would know it was him. Based on the messages left on his phone, that can't be a good thing.
Chip hit the buzzer and the waiting began. He stood there transfixed on the small speaker-like panel on the wall, his body language had nervous written all over it. His arms were crossed, and his shoulders shrugged; a passerby could have easily mistaken him for somebody with a bad case of explosive diarrhoea. He looked pained and distressed, and then the speaker let out a lowly little voice.
"Hello?" Ellie's soft and sleepy voice said into the intercom.
Chip paused for a moment, frozen in time contemplating his next move.
"Shit," He said louder than he wanted.
"Excuse me?" Ellie's voice said from the little box on the wall.
"Sorry, it's Chip, can I come in?" Chip waited, but nothing came from the other end. She wasn't going to let him in, he knew it. It took all he had to go to her apartment, and even more to actually go through with calling up to her room. He hung his head and decided it would be best to leave.
"Sorry, who's there? I left the kettle on the stove." Chip's heart dropped. He had to go through it again.
"It's Chip," He mumbled into the speaker, and without any words from the other end, a buzz sounded and the door clicked signifying its ultimate unlocking. Chip's heart sunk even lower than he thought possible; it was no longer in his torso, but rather on a string on the ground in front of him which forced him to kick it with every step. It was much like some odd Greek mythological punishment. He endured that imaginary punishment up six flights of stairs. Sure, there was an elevator, but today felt like a stair taking day: Whatever delayed the inevitable at that point.
The door at the end of the hall always seemed daunting, it just so happened that this was also Ellie's abode making the terror

multiply by 2.3, that seemed like a proper number in Chip's mind. He was certain what waited beyond that door was more horrifying than anything he could imagine. He pictured chains hanging from the ceiling equipped with a devilishly devastating meat hook, and an uber pissed off Ellie in a leather Dominatrix outfit. He more or less envisioned much of the movie *Hellraiser* as what laid beyond that door, but sexier. Ellie as a dominatrix was a pretty hot thought.

He approached with caution, even contemplated turning tail and running like a scolded dog, as he was sure Ellie would devour his soul. It's a well-known fact that scolded dogs lose their souls. However, before his imagination could run even further, the door swung open and there stood a silhouette of somebody who may or may not have been glaring down the hallway; it was safe to assume she was probably staring down the hallway. Chip froze on the spot; he felt a bead of sweat form on his forehead.

"Shit," He muttered very quietly to himself. The form just hung in the doorway for a moment, as if the atmosphere would not allow it to move until Chip either ran, moved closer, or screamed like a girl. The latter being the most likely of the three.

It was at the ultimate moment of suspense that the shadowy figure in the doorway moved out into the light of the hallway. It was only Ellie, it was always Ellie. Chip knew that, of course, but that was exactly what he was afraid of.

"What the hell are you doing just standing there like an idiot?" Ellie shouted from the doorway. Chip snapped out of his trance, he shook his head and tried to speak, but nothing came out. He moped his way down the hall.

He started off slow, to kill as much time as possible, but it was a futile act as it just made Ellie more irritable.

"Hurry the hell up!" She yelled again, not caring if her neighbours could hear or not. Chip broke into a jog.

"Sorry," he muttered when he broke the threshold of the apartment.
"Why didn't you call me to tell me you were coming over?" Ellie asked from the comfort of her oversized couch. Chip loved and hated that couch. It was like a big comfortable trap that Chip always wanted to get caught in, but never leave. No other couch could live up to the standard of that couch. He hated it for that. He did not sit on said couch.
"I didn't feel like being yelled at over the phone...again?" Chip said, just standing there like an idiot.
"Stop standing there like an idiot," Ellie said. "And what do you mean again?" Chip found an armchair in which to take solace.
"Well, your messages...?" Chip said frightened.
"Messages, what messages? I didn't leave you any messages," Ellie said very matter of factly.
Chip raised an eyebrow at her. "Yes, you did." That was the best refute he could come up with.
"Did not," Ellie said in an equally weak attempt.
"I have them right here!" Chip jumped from the armchair; he was really grateful now that he didn't sit in the Big Comfy Couch. He fumbled around his front jean pocket looking for his cell phone – it took a fraction of a second longer than it should have, which induced a cock-eyed reaction from Ellie. Chip returned the look as he produced his cell phone; it was nearly a moment of eureka for him.
"See, look... I have it right..." Chip flipped through his inbox, but nothing. He checked everywhere in his phone but couldn't find the texts. Ellie got up from the couch (with ease, which Chip could never understand) and wandered over to Chip to comfort him. He was clearly losing his mind.

"No, El. They're here, and they were mean! The voicemail! Here, it's gotta be there still," Chip pleaded.

Chip held down the *1* key as was customary to when one was dialling his voicemail. The wonderful lady who sounded like an evil female Stephen Hawking on her rag asked for his password, which he produced granting him access to the world of missed calls. There was one saved message; Chip hit play with great excitement. This truly was the eureka moment Chip had been longing for, but it was short lived... The message produced nothing but static.

Chip's eyes widened and Ellie's eyes turned sad.

"NO! Goddamnit, somebody's fucking with me. It's like a Mission Impossible tape or something. *This message will self-destruct in five seconds*, or something like that," Chip said.

"Honey, it's just static... not the end of the world." Although, it may well have been as far as Chip knew.

"No! It was you before, I swear to it. Why would I lie?" Chip said.

"I dunno, long day... hearing things maybe?" Ellie replied. Chip thought about that for a moment, perhaps a moment too long as Ellie noticed how deep in thought he actually was.

"No!" Chip snapped out of the thought process, "I'm not that far gone," He said. Ellie reeled back slightly in surprise but shook it off with a shake of her head.

"Aww, maybe you just wanted to see me that badly that you thought you heard my voice in that static," Ellie said sounding overly sweet, no doubt on purpose.

"Yeah, yeah..." Chip paused and processed the thought for a second. "YEAH!" He shouted out, spooking Ellie a bit. "That's exactly what it is!"

"Huh?" Was all Ellie could muster.

"Somebody wanted me to come here so they could follow me... follow me right to you! Oh fuck, I lead them right to you didn't I?" Chip said frantically.

Ellie shifted her eyes once or twice, "What? Lead who here, honey?" She said as calm as humanly possible. Chip couldn't figure out why she wasn't freaking out like he was. Chip freaked out a lot.

"No, Ellie, we have to get you –" The front door produced a knock. Both Chip and Ellie looked towards it. One terrified look, the other curious, yet calm (guess who was who.).

"Hmm, I wonder who that could be?" Ellie said as she wandered over to the door.

"NO!" Chip yelled out and grabbed her arm with enough force to spin her around to look at him. "You didn't buzz anybody in. You have to buzz somebody in before they can come up, right?" Chip asked, but made it sound more like a statement.

Ellie leaned in nice and close to Chip's ear. He loved when she did that, regardless of the situation. "And if it's somebody who actually *lives* in the apartment...?" She stated. Chip leaned back with a puzzled look on his face.

"But... if they live here, why would they need to follow me?" He asked in what Ellie thought was a very adorable way. She caressed his cheek with her hand and walked towards the door, "It's probably the super or something. Relax." At her touch, Chip melted and so did his worries for a moment. He did what she asked and just relaxed. She was right; it was foolish to think that somebody would follow him to her. Why would that even be the case? Sure, he was a newfound necromancer, but *he* just found this evening, how would anybody else know? And the bigger and better question, why would anybody care? Chip totally had nothing to worry about.

He watched with caring, and of course, relaxed eyes which drifted to Ellie's butt for a moment, as she sauntered over to the door to open it up. The handle clicked its quiet click as it turned releasing whatever it was that held doors shut. But a fraction of a second later, the door flung open, sending Ellie reeling backward to the ground.

It took Chip a second to realize what had just happened. He stood there like an idiot.

Two men burst through the door and stood over Ellie, looking excessively daunting. They look to be identical twins or something like it. They both had huge sloping foreheads, much like a Neanderthal; they both had huge bulging biceps that looked sort of cartoonish, as well, and their legs were teeny tiny little things. In any other situation Chip probably would have laughed at these too, but in that situation, he nearly crapped himself.

Following the two goons through the door was this well-dressed man in a dark red suit with slicked back hair and...a cape? Chip looked stunned, but more so at the cape than anything. The man stopped and guided the two buffoons aside so he could stand in between the two. He looked down at Ellie and smirked, she returned the smirk with her middle finger.

"Ooh, feisty," The man said, "Grab her!" He said in a British accent that Chip missed the first time. They seemed to be totally ignoring Chip, though he didn't exactly make his presence known.

"Ahem?" Chip coughed. He realized too late that it was a weak attention getter.

The man looked up however and over at Chip. "Yes, yes, I'll get to you in a moment, please don't interrupt." The man rolled his eyes. "How rude," he said to no one really.

"Oh, sorr-" Chip was about to apologize, but thought better of it. "Wait, no, what are you doing? Who the hell are you?"

The man shot him a look that nearly did kill him. It was such a powerfully evil glare that Chip stumbled back a step or two as if hit in the chest with a violently thrown beach ball. Nothing too crazy or anything, it was *that* evil a stare.

"I said wait your turn, runt!" The man yelled out and threw his hand towards Chip. A weird gesture, Chip thought, and then he realized he couldn't really move. He was frozen on the spot, but not by ice or anything, he was being held by some unseen force. Chip thought that to be really unfair.

"Mmhmm mmmmh," he couldn't speak either.

The evil British guy in the red suit smiled then turned his gaze back to Ellie who still sat on the floor; she looked more pissed than anything. The evil Brit took a knee and crept awfully close to Ellie's face before whispering to her, just loud enough for Chip to hear.
"Thanks to your idiot boyfriend, we've found you. You're not an easy lass to track down, must be your new aura." The man stood up, "Take her to the car," He said to his own private Neanderthals.
The two oafs grabbed her under either arm and carried her out of the apartment. Once they left, the Brit turned his attention to Chip. He casually strutted over to the statue formally known as Chip.
"Foolish boy. You don't know who you've just led me to, do you?" Chip tried to respond, but with no luck; he was frozen, and there were no two ways about it.
"Oh, right; frozen. I don't think you'll be any sort of a problem, besides I want to hear what you have to say. I do enjoy a good whiner. You lot are all the same: *No, don't take her, she's my everything, I'll kill you, etc...*" He mocked, snapped his fingers, and Chip became an animate object again.
"You sonofabitch. I swear if you don't let her go I'll..." He realized he was saying exactly the same thing the Brit had just said. Chip tried to think of something else to say to him, "Well, what the hell else am I supposed to say?!" He said giving up on a clever comeback. The Brit paused to think on that for a second.
"Fair enough. But no matter how you say it, or how many times it's said, it never comes true. Just do what's best for you, kid and leave it alone... It's for the best." And with that, the British asshole in the dark red suit walked out of the apartment, and Chip just stood there, reeling with anger, confusion and dread. He needed to sit to calm himself down. He plopped into the Big Comfy Couch; he always expected a creepy little puppet to crawl out of a crevasse or something, but it never

did, thankfully. If it happened at that moment, Chip probably would have just accepted as it would have fit into the theme of the day, which seemed to be: The day of Weird Shit.

All he could do was sit there. He felt useless, even more so than usual. He felt weak and powerless, and worst of all, he had no idea what just happened. He didn't know where to start. He couldn't exactly call the cops; what would he tell them? It would be utterly ridiculous – they would probably throw him in jail, or at least the loony bin. So with the cops out of the question, there was only one person he could go see: Mort.

There was one important detail, however, at some point after the Evil Brit's tirade; Chip's eyes had turned a bright glowing green that appeared to be smoking slightly. He had no idea.

In the fashion of Kramer from *Seinfeld*, Chip burst through the door of Bill's shop. He was extremely grateful it wasn't locked, as he ran into it at full steam. On the other side sat both Bill and Mort. Chip had only been gone a little over an hour, so Bill and Mort were sort of surprised to him back so soon. Mort had figured he went back to the apartment to lock himself in his room for a few hours and cry. He'd done it before after watching *The Notebook*. Bill, on the other hand, thought he would have killed himself, well tried to. It's a tricky thing for a Necromancer to kill himself, what with the whole bringing things back to life ability. However, after the initial shock of having somebody, especially Chip, burst back into the shock, it was hard to reach another level of surprise; but somehow the two pulled it off when they noticed Chip's eyes.

Chip opened his mouth to tell them about what had happened at Ellie's apartment. He had it all planned out; he would tell them about the two brutish ogre type characters, and the jackass Brit. But he had to pause and raise an eyebrow at Bill and Mort sitting there dumbfounded and slack-jawed.

"What...?" He said very inquisitively.

Bill and Mort looked at one another, exchanging the awkward *you tell him – no you tell him looks.* And then Bill narrowed his eyes at Mort and nodded furiously as if to say *He's your friend, you tell him or I'll squash you into a puddle so fine not even the necromancer would be able to bring you back.* Mort rolled his eyes and stood up from the stool on which he sat.
"Well, Chip old buddy... Don't freak out..." Mort slowly approached hold out his hands in a calming gesture.
Chip's eyes widened. "What... Why would I freak out?" He asked cautiously.
Mort took a deep breath and said, "Well, your eyes...they're green." Mort reared back, bracing for a shit-fit, but got quite the opposite. Chip merely tilted his head like a curious dog.
"Haha, Mort you fool, my eyes are brown," Chip said very matter-of-factly. Mort looked back at Bill, who ushered him towards Chip with his hands. Mort looked around the room and found a mirror. Chip watched him closely trying to figure out what he was doing. When Mort returned with the mirror, he held it up in front of Chip, who was sort of smirking at the situation. He stopped smirking when he saw his reflection.
The shit-fit Mort had anticipated duly came.
Chip threw his arms in the air as if to say *I give up; you win,* and slowly backed away from Mort and the mirror.
"I give up, I just give the hell up man. You win, I... I...Damnit, I don't even know what the hell's going on man," Chip confessed
"You're a necromancer," Mort said so nonchalantly like he was saying Happy Birthday. It was really nothing for him. That annoyed Chip slightly; why and how could Mort be so calm? The even better question is how in the name of all that is sacred and holy did Mort know what a necromancer was? He still thinks the moon is made of cheese and that all cats are girls.
"He wants to know how you know all this, Morty boy," Bill chimed in from the back of the room. "And you really think

all cats are girls? Wow...just... wow." Chip peered around his friend to stare at weird beard.
"Yeah, I know right?!" Chip blurted out. "Wait...You...stop doing that...whatever that is. What is that anyway?"
Mort took a deep breath and put a hand on Chip's shoulder. "Well... he can read minds due to the fact that he's a Djinn who's about three or four hundred years old." He paused for a reaction, but Chip's expression was just a simple glazed one.
"And I'm –" Chip interrupted, "A three-thousand-year-old sex demon," He said very sure of himself.
"Yeah- what, no, Chip. I'm twenty-four...But I have an uncanny ability to use the art of Voodoo."
"Voodoo?" Chip questioned.
"Yes, voodoo," Mort responded.
"But you're white."
"Racist. But, if you must know, I'm 1/24th Colombian on my adopted grandfather's side."
"What the hell does that have to do with voodoo?"
"Nothing. I'm just stating facts here, Chip. C'mon, keep up!" Mort finished with a clap, which startled Chip.
"Right. And he's a...?" Chip asked motioning towards Bill.
"A Djinn," Mort finished. Chip's glazed expression returned as it had moments prior. He had no damn clue what a Djinn was.
"Djinn are a very rare and very clever bunch. They've been in almost every cultural story out there...they're kinda like a badass genie." Mort checked over his shoulder and then leaned closer into Chip, "Just don't ask him for wishes. He'll kick you in the balls and say *bet ya wish I didn't do that.*" Chip pulled back to meet his friend's eyes, which were very wide at the moment, as if to say *yes, seriously, I know from experience.* Chip eyed Bill. Bill eyed Chip. There was a mutual eyeing going on and Mort was caught in the middle.
"Oh yeah!" Mort blurted out, "He can read minds, too... or did I already say that? I should really get this short term memory

thing check out." Chip's eyes widened, and widened, and widened, Mort thought his eyes were gonna pop out of his head or something. Bill smirked, looking satisfied.
"Anyway..," Chip said, "I came here for a reason..." Chip started searching his memory banks for the reason, which he knew was of great importance.
"Well you burst in here like a snowball falling out of hell," Mort said.
"I know... What?" Chip said.
"You're girlfriend was kidnapped by a...sexy maid?" Bill said with a perplexed look on his face.
"What?" Mort asked.
"NO! What, sexy maid? No, a crazy evil British guy with two cavemen looking guys took her. They knocked, she opened, he froze me, and they grabbed her and left." Chip decided it was best to give the Coles Notes version of the story. Regardless, it caught the attention of both Mort and Bill.
Chip knew instantly that something was up, and it wasn't Mort's intellect. Mort only had this kind of look on his face when something was awry. He raised an eyebrow yet again and looked over in Chip's direction, "okay, Chip I need you to tell me everything that happened exactly as it happened."
Chip looked at Mort with a look of confusion, "I just did."
"No no, we need every detail down to the last."
And so Chip told him everything, about the knocking, about not feeling right about the situation, about the evil British guy, and the other two Neanderthals he brought with him. Mort and bill hung on Chip's every word, however, they looked somehow unsatisfied.
"And..," Mort said expecting more.
"And? What else do you want from me, I've already told you everything I know," Chip explained
"But that's just what you told us 10 minutes ago!" Mort argued
"I know. Because that is exactly what happened."

"Well... That's sorta useless." Mort stroked his chin as if he were in a state of actual thinking; Chip knew this was just for the dramatic effect. Mort spun on his heels and looked directly at Bill, which had somehow produced a sandwich. Both Mort and Chip had the same look on their face when they noticed the magical sandwich appear from nowhere. Mort shook his head and got back on topic, "Bill, I don't like where this is going. How the hell is he here, I thought you got rid of him."
"Well..," Bill paused to take a bite of his sandwich, "I thought I did," Bill said with a full mouth.
"You thought you did?" Mort exclaimed. Bill just shrugged and took another bite of his sandwich, "well he's a tricky bastard to get rid of, you know being supernatural and all."
"Wait, what?! You know this guy? How the hell do you know this guy? He just stole Ellie, and you know this guy?" Chip said, beginning to act frantically. He began to pace without even realizing it, this was something that Chip did often and Mort had noticed, he figured it was some sort of neuroses; Mort didn't even know what neuroses was. He saw it on a word of the day calendar, but couldn't be bothered to read the meaning, it just sounded cool.
"Well, when you've been around as long as I have; you meet a few unsavoury characters," Bill said.
"Oh, just a few unsavoury characters, eh?" Chip said, the *eh* must of come from some latent Canadian he had in him. Chip suddenly felt a little uneasy being around Bill, not that he had felt particularly good before; there was something about his familiarity with the evil British guy that made him even more so uncomfortable. Chip narrowed his eyes and took a step towards the front door.
Bill merely nodded at Chip's sarcastic comment, Mort shot Bill a look and then shot Chip one, shooting looks and raising eyebrows continued as the theme of the day.

"Okay, okay, okay first things first - where the hell did you get that sandwich, Bill?" Mort said, pointing a finger at Bill, "why didn't you get me one?”
“Wait, what? Forget the magical sandwich for a minute! I think there are bigger issues at hand right now,” Chip stated. Mort shook his head and snapped back to the topic, but still looked over his shoulder at Bill, who was smiling a shit-eating grin. Mort really hoped the sandwich wasn’t of the shit variety. You can never know with Djinn.
"Yeah, you’re right. We have to find this British ass and get Ellie back, and I think that sandwich eating prick behind me knows where to find him." Chip peered around and narrowed his eyes at Bill; Bill rolled his eyes and took a deep breath. "Fine,” he said swallowing the last bit of sandwich. Mort looked sad at the departure of the final piece of said sandwich.
"Well, where are we going to start?" Chip said with a sense of urgency.
"Yeah, Bill, where *are* we going to start?" Mort said, but what he really meant was *don't think you’re getting off the hook for the sandwich.*
Bill stood up and walked over to the bookshelf on the far side of the room, he stood there for a moment studying its contents, until finally after spining all the books with his finger, he picked one out.
Chip and Mort stood with anticipation of what Bill was about to say. Suddenly, the fact that he had a book in his hands made him seem wise. That thought was short lived.
Bill opened the book and pulled out another sandwich. Chip and Mort’s excitement dropped exponentially.
"Really? You really just did that?" Chip said in a state of shock. Mort looked rather impressed, but looked back at Chip and saw his disappointment; he thought he should do the same. Mort was the happiest depressed guy in the world at that moment.

"What, I was still hungry," Bill said taking a bite of his sandwich, "a guys gotta eat." Chip closed his eyes and took a deep breath, "can you help or not?"
Bill sauntered over towards Chip and Mort; he passed Mort who followed the sandwich with his eyes like a starving dog and got close to Chip's face. Chip felt that this was a total invasion of his personal bubble. He leaned back to avoid the arterial like spray of Bill's chewing. His beard didn't catch everything.
"Well..," Bill said taking a bite of his sandwich, "I can help you help her."
"Help me help her? What the hell does that mean?" Chip said taking several steps backwards.
Bill smirked and took yet another bite of his sandwich; Chip wasn't even sure he had swallowed the first one. He questioned where it could have all gone if not his stomach.
"The dead know a lot," Bill said forcing Chip to squint and glance over at Mort who happened to be drooling.
"Great, helpful, thanks," Chip said sarcastically, "How about we stop talking in riddles and enigmas for just a second, Bill, and you tell me with one-hundred percent clarity what in the crap is going on here?"
Bill sighed and looked back at Mort, who still had that starving dog look to him; he even began to shake with excitement over the prospect of some scraps.
"Okay lad, I'll tell ya. The British guy, he's called Mephisto," Bill said ominously.
"Wait, you mean like the guy from Diablo II?" Chip questioned.
"Right on! Sweet ass game!" Mort yelled from across the room while looking for another magical sandwich.
Bill sighed and looked back at Mort and shook his head, "You won't find one, kid... And yes, not too different from the character in the game. In demon form, he looks more like a Devil, though. It was his idea, actually, the cocky prick. He

has that kind of power, ya know; he planted the idea in the head of some game developer, and next thing ya know..."
"He made himself a video game boss?" Chip finished.
"Sad, innit?" Bill said.
"Yeah... I mean, he's not even the end boss..." Chip replied.
Bill raised an eyebrow at Chip as if to say *That's what you find sad?*
For a moment or two, there was an awkward silence, each of the three had a different thought flowing through their heads. Chip was filled with dread, fear, and an overwhelming sense of incompetence. Mort shared Chip's feelings of dread and hopelessness for he was a good friend of Ellies too, but his urge to find the magical sandwich trumped everything. And of course Bill, the Djinn knew what both were thinking.
The old man pondered over the situation for a moment. He was too old to be of any use to these two, he'd just get in the way and end up like Obi Wan Kenobi... or would he? Was there still some kick left in that old dog? He felt immortal, although he knew he wasn't – he was just very, very old – and even though he'd probably outlive the two other people in the store, he still felt his age catching up with him.
But he couldn't sit idly by with Mephisto out causing havoc again. He put that good-for-nothing Brit in his place once, he can do it again. It was Bill's stubbornness that got him where he is, and it would surely be the end of him, too.
A few moments passed without even the hint of a murmur, and then Bill felt something deep within, something he had to let out, and with the roar of a mighty lion, Bill belched. Oh, did he ever belch. It was so large in fact that Chip would swear he saw a bit of magic sandwich fly from his gaping mouth and land on the wall behind him.
Chip looked shocked... and slightly impressed.
From across the room, a slow clap began. Mort, standing there was a proud smile on his face was so impressed with the burp

that the only way to express his admiration was through a round of applause.

“Enough! Ok, Bill... Tell me what I need to do,” Chip shouted forcing Mort to cease his cheering. Bill smirked at the new necromancer and said, “We need information, lad.”

# CHAPTER 2

It's funny, isn't it? You know, how things can change instantly; like how one second your slightly winded boyfriend shows up at your apartment going on about some voicemail that you didn't leave, and the next second well, you're kidnapped by a British guy with two semi-evolved men. Oh yeah, and the British guy left your boyfriend seemingly frozen in time when he tried to rescue you. Suffice it to say, it'd been a strange night for Ellie McDonald, and to make matters worse, she had awoken to a bland, grey room shackled to a chair bolted to the floor. Her first thought was to scream, her second thought was that she didn't want to be *that* kind of hostage. Screaming seemed so cliché, besides screaming was probably pointless. A person who commits grand theft person is most likely not going to keep the package in an apartment with paper thin walls so the neighbours could hear everything.

She squirmed, though, that was inevitable. The wiggling and shimmying didn't do much, she had chains around both her ankles and wrists which were both looped through a ring also bolted to the floor. It seemed a little overkill for a 5'2, 110lbs girl... okay, 115lbs, but she had a big lunch. Nevertheless, the thought crossed her mind that her prison probably wasn't intended solely for her, it was probably used before on much bigger and stronger captives. Though, she couldn't quite understand why every link and every inch of the ring on the floor had some sort of inscription inscribed on them.

Ellie leaned in for a closer look, but just as she was able to make out some kind shape, the door crashed open, and strutting through was that pompous looking Brit who took her from that awkward and peculiar conversation with her boyfriend. Thinking back, that conversation may have had something to do with what was going on. This guy had impeccable timing, what with the conversation interruption and breaking Ellie's concentration whilst investigating the shackles which bound her.

"Hello, luv," he said in a sickly smooth English accent. Ellie hated that she thought he sounded really, really cool.

She refused to respond. The two locked gazes for a moment or two, maybe even three before the Englishman took a breath, sighed and knelt down to meet Ellie on the same level.

"It's been a while, sweetheart. How've you been?" He asked. Ellie had no idea what the hell he was on about. She just raised an eyebrow.

"Hmm. This is indeed interesting, innit..," he said in response. Clapping his hands on his knees, he stood back up and began examining her from a higher angle, as if it would reveal some new secret about his prisoner.

"No, you're definitely the right girl. I think..," he said half to himself, half to Ellie, and half to nobody. Yes, three halves. Deal with it.

Ellie, however, began to grow tired of his little game of one player *Clue*, and finally said something.

"Who in the crap are you... Also, what in the crap do you want with me?" Covering all the important bases of crap.

"Me? Luv, I'm ashamed and honoured that you had to ask. I'm Mephisto. You can call me Meph, though."

"Rather not, really. I'd really just rather you let me go," she said in response.

"Well, I mean, what kind of kidnapper would I be if I just let me victim go when she asks politely?" He said. "To be fair, I do appreciate the politeness. I didn't know you were a Canadian."

"I'm not," Ellie responded quickly. "But since you won't let me go, how about you tell me what you want? I don't have any money, so you're out of luck on that one."

"... Did you say aboot?"
"No."
"I think you did."
"Shut up."
"I don'-"
"Shut up and tell me why I'm here."
"Well, so much for the politeness. And here I thought we were going to get along. Tsk, such a shame," Mephisto said as he began circling her around the small, grey room.
"You're here, Treacle because you're special. Apparently, you've forgotten just how special you are, and that I'll have to figure out. But in the meantime, you just sit here and try to remember." He finished as he opened the door. Ellie tried her best to sneak a peek around him to see if anything outside the room could clue her into where she was. She didn't see anything but a dark hallway.
Mephisto slunk out of the room, yet he did so with as much pompous pizzazz as when he burst in. He certainly had a flare for the dramatic and leaving situations on a cliff hanger. He left Ellie with more questions than answers. How was she special? Well, she knew she was pretty awesome, but who doesn't think that? More to the point, that's probably not what he meant. And what did she forget? Chances are, if she knew something, even if lost in the deepest recesses of her mind, that was important enough for her to be kidnapped over, she would remember it.
The whole situation was bizarre, to say the least. But perhaps strangest of all was how Ellie felt. Taken in the middle of the night from her own apartment by a strange man, being chained, not tied, but *chained* to a chair and then interrogated should send most people into a panicking frenzy. She figured by this point, she should have choked on her own tongue or something out of pure fear. But she wasn't afraid. Her heart didn't race, her blood pressure didn't boil over, Hell, she wasn't even trembling. That was freaking her out the most, she should

be terrified by normal, human standards, and even though her calmness was worrisome, she wasn't even that worried about it. What a confusing train of thought.
However, Mephisto barging into the room did one thing to her mind, it took her attention away from the inscriptions upon the steel chains and the ring in the floor. She had totally forgotten about them, her mettle had a new riddle to figure out, and as her brain raced, her body slunk back in the chair. So distracted was she that she didn't even notice the small green stem sprout beside the bolted ring.

Down the hall of blackness, the suave Mephisto was also trying to solve a riddle of his own. He slowly paced down the corridor until he reached the end, where there happened to be a door. He paused briefly in front of said door and rested his right palm against it while his left hand was counting out something unknown. He shook his head as if he gave up on whatever it was he was trying to count and looked at the door in a confused manner. He tilted his head and gave the door a swift kick causing it to come awake, no - alive. Lines of light began to spread from where Mephisto's hand lay like a spider's web. They shot out in an orangey glow with spots of yellow sprinkled through it. It was almost as if his hand was the heartbeat to this doors being…thing, and the orange lines were its veins bringing life to every corner of the barricade.
Mephisto looked much more satisfied now, and it culminated in the door groaning a strange growling groan before vanishing completely. Out of the darkness of the hallway walked Mephisto into a well-lit room filled will all sorts of oddities, and those two Neanderthal guys from Ellie's apartment. The room was unlike your typical bungalow living room. It had jars filled with yellow tinted fluid, most likely formaldehyde with various pieces of flesh floating in them. It wasn't human, in fact, most of it was unidentifiable. Things that looked like talons and tentacles floated side by side with

beaks and feathers of sorts, yet nothing looked of this world. That probably had to do with Mephisto not being of this world, and the things in the jars were probably from some kind of Hell. Regardless, they fit the mood of the house, that mood being serial killer - very Jeffery Dahmer chic.

The two Neanderthals were playing a game where they would consistently smack each other on the back of the head and blame it on everything but themselves. One blamed the couch, the other blamed the cat. There was no cat. Mephisto walked on by and shook his head, wondering to himself how this was the best help he could get for his task. It's not easy to be exiled, turns out you end up losing all the resources you once had at your disposal and end up with the only two morons you could trick to come with you.

Candy: Candy was the trick. They came with him for bloody candy... They don't even eat candy. They didn't eat anything for Christ's sake. He should have known that he would have been better off alone, however, he probably wouldn't have been able to get rid of them anyway. They kept asking for the damn candy. Nevertheless, they could prove useful one day.

Across the room, beyond the couch where the brothers *played*, sat a desk. The desk itself was covered with a multitude of books and scrolls, which were messily strewn about it. Old books, too; one of a kind books; expensive books, nay, priceless books. Books that were so important that the information held within could change the world forever. Mephisto sat down in front of the desk and began to read from an open page, but something caught his eye right away.

"Bloody Chinese food?! Really guys? C'mon. Where did you even get this? You never leave here, and you can't even eat!" He said crumpling up and throwing the plastic like menu at the Neanderthal brothers causing them to scatter. "What's the bleeding point." He finished, going back to his book with an epic sigh.

Besides the fact that Ellie couldn't remember who she was, there was one other thing was scratching at Meph's brain. The boy from the apartment, the one who tried to intercept, there was something different about him. He stank, but not a usual human stink, it was a smell he hadn't smelt in a very long time, but it was one that was truly unforgettable. It just took him a little while to remember what it was. The young man was a necromancer, of that he was certain. But what Ellie was doing with one, that is something the mighty Mephisto couldn't quite comprehend - and he usually could comprehend everything, what with being a former General in Hell and all.

Still, a necromancer was troublesome to him. They broke all sorts of laws, natural, spiritual, and metaphysical. They were a rare breed, and often chosen by Death himself to be gifted with such power, but as far as he knew, there hasn't been once in centuries. They always end up causing more trouble than they're worth, and the mess, oh God, the messes they made were Biblical. Even if this rookie seemed a few cards short of a full deck, he still had to worry. Not even the king of Hell could raise and control the dead. Demons, sure - they were a piece of cake, but bring a spirit back from the Ether, now that was something else. Hopefully, Mephisto could complete his plan before the kid could figure out his true power. It would also be handy if the ancient book in front of him had *any* information of use. Apparently, just because it's old doesn't make it smart. Stupid book.

"I don't get it. Why is there nothing in here I can use? I mean it's the..." He picks up the book and flips it closed and reads the title aloud, "A Grimoire of... Fairies?! Alright, which one of you swapped the books?" Mephisto said spinning to face the brothers.

One pointed at the ceiling. The other pointed up his nose. And then he stuck his finger up his nose and proceeded to presumably dig for a lost treasure. Mephisto shuttered and turned back to his desk.

"I've seen some gruesome, horrible things in my time... but that..." He choked back some vomit and shuttered again. He shuffled around something on his desk, but with no avail. If one of the brothers did bring out the fairy book to read if they could read, what would he have done with the other one?

Several hours later, Mephisto's plopped down in the middle of the floor with books open all around him, surrounded by crumpled pieces of paper. He was sobbing. Uncontrollably. How could he have been outsmarted by a couple of imbeciles? He had looked everywhere in the room that it could have possibly been. He flipped the couch and the cushions; he took everything from his desk and threw it around the room; he even upturned their beds, which he also found out they used as bathrooms; then he threw up for a while. He eventually gave up when he saw the mess in he'd made. He started crying again. Crying, a demon general from the pits of the underworld had been reduced to tears, and that was when he felt a tap on his shoulder. Reluctantly and almost desperately he looked up with tears running down his face and a snot bubble forming just under his nose to see one of the brothers standing there with a book grasped in his hands. Mephisto grabbed the book frantically and looked at the cover:
*Mother Nature and how to Destroy Her.*
His tears dried up in an instant, mainly because flames erupted from his eyes. He let out a loud laugh, which was unfortunately accompanied by a gigantic snot bubble, which the Neanderthal could help but pop. He giggled.
"You great big lummox!" Meph exclaimed. "I could kiss you, you know that... Ah, bugger to it!" He said before grabbing the giant by the cheeks and landing a great big kiss on his forehead.
Near instantly Mephisto yakked, again. The oaf tasted like the smell of his bed, or bathroom, or whatever it was.

After he was done throwing up, Mephisto turned to the brother who remained with his dumbfounded look and asked him the simplest of questions, of which he would receive the simplest of answers.
"Where was it?"
The seemingly smarter brother pointed to the bookshelf. Mephisto's eye twitched. The Moron put the book back where it was supposed to go. How in the hell was he supposed to know that? These idiots use their beds as toilets for Christ's sake, yet they know where a book should go when it's not being used. Remarkable, truly, deeply remarkable.
The book Mephisto held in his hands could quite literally change the world, and not for the better either - after all, he *is* a demon, they don't often want to change the world for the better. With the excitement of a schoolgirl getting a text from her crush, Meph rushed over to his now empty and rather spacious desk and threw the book on it. He went to sit and fell flat on his arse. He had overturned his chair and ultimately forgot about it. Usually, he was quick to anger (Again, demon...), but he brushed it off, picked up the chair and sat down, as his original plan intended. He opened the book which made a very satisfying creaking noise; now that's the sign of an old book, and if it's old, surely it's good.
However, his joy was short lived when he heard a loud slam and a scream from down the dark hallway. Instantly, Mephisto's head shot up and snapped around in a half circle, much like that of an owl's head. His jaw clenched as he eyed the door.
The brother's ducked out of sight, one hiding behind a lamp, the other playing dead. Whatever happened down that hallway had the brothers spooked. After a few seconds of waiting, Mephisto slowly rose from his chair, he crept past brother one behind the lamp who made a feverish attempt to use the shade to cover more of his face.

He continued towards the door, stepping over Brother two, who flinched and squeaked ever so slightly as Mephisto breached his personal bubble. Closer to the door Mephisto crept. Something big had happened, and he didn't want to rush in... Then again the foolish girl could have somehow tipped the chair over...even though it was bolted...and chained...and...poop, she didn't fall over.

Just as he reached the door and put his hand on the middle of it, an even louder crash occurred. So loud was it that it made the previous bang sound like a pew pew girly laser gun noise. Frantically he raced down the hallway once the disappearing groaning door faded away. He barged into the small grey room where Ellie had been held. The first time he barged in he was filled with warm fuzzies and a strange tingling sensation. This time, well, not so much.

The Neanderthal brothers struck up a bit of bravery and slowly approached the hole left behind by the strange door, which still confused the two of them, and peered down the hallway.

"NOOOOOOOOOOOOOOOOOOOOOOOOOOOOOOOO OOOOOOOOOOOOOOOO!" Ricocheted and echoed throughout the hallway. The noise hit the Brothers causing them to cover their ears and mimic the noise the boss had just made. Then they fell to the ground in the foetal and rocked nervously back and forth.

# CHAPTER 3

"This is what he meant by gathering more information?" Chip asked Mort as they walked down a long spiral staircase.

"Yup," Mort humbly responded.

"And you knew about this place?" Chip continued.

"Yup," Mort said once again.

"Are you gonna say anything else?" Chip inquired.

"Yup," Mort echoed.

"Like wha... Holy balls," Chip said as he and his pal entered quite possibly the largest - and coolest - library Chip had ever seen. He was, of course, witnessing for the first time *The Library of Everything Unknown.* The not-so-clearly- named building stood about 200 feet below the Church of the Holy Trinity, which was like most churches, a cover for something else. The library was old, very old, perhaps even older than Bill, and as the name indicated held all kinds of information and secrets on things that the average person wouldn't know. If Bigfoot is of interest, there's a section for that. How about mermaids, dragons, aliens, or even what they put in the soup in the 48th street diner. It's all held within the walls of the massive library, and for Chip's sake, some information on Mephisto, besides what Bill already told him.

Chip remembered it well. He should, it only happened a few hours ago, to be fair.

"He's a what?!" Chip exclaimed.

"A general from Hell. Well, a former general. I believe he was exiled a few centuries ago, or something," Bill answered as if Hell General's were commonplace to Chip.

"And he's got Ellie? Why, what's he want with her? Is she still alive? Oh God, please tell me she's not been sacrificed to the

Devil. I couldn't live with myself if..." Chip was blabbering. Bill hated that, so he shut him up with a finger over his lips. Though, to be fair, he probably held it there longer than needed and the situation became slightly awkward.

"Look, mate, you need to get one thing straight here. Your idea, the common idea of Heaven and Hell is not real," Bill started before plopping down on a stool. "Right now, Christianity and Catholicism reigns supreme in the world of the religious folk, well in the west anyway - don't even get me started on that Muslim jazz. But anyway, Christianity is a bastard religion," Bill said causing an eyebrow to rise on Chip's face, and Mort to... well, Mort may have already dozed off.

"Look, what I mean by that is it's just a conglomeration of a bunch of other religions. It takes from ancient Egypt, Greek, and Pagan beliefs and throws it into one neat and tidy book. So, there is no singular Devil, and there is no singular God either. But," Bill continues, "There are some aspects that are true. There is an underworld and afterlife - the latter you've experienced for yourself when you raised that poor bloke out in the alley. Let's see... Oh, there's also a King of Hell, which would explain the General status of Mephisto, and his name is Lucifer, or the first of the fallen, or any one of those nonsensical names. He's a powerful sonofadog too, but he doesn't care about sacrifices or anything like that. He's quite content doing what he does down there," Bill eyed Chip, who seemed to be hanging on every word. He smacked Mort in the face to wake him up. Poor Mort's head bounced off the table he happened to be leaning on.

"Want me to continue, lad?" Bill asked Chip, while eyeballing Mort.

"Holy crap, yes!" Chip said with the enthusiasm of a fat kid getting asked if he wants seconds on dessert. Bill smiled at that energy, there may be hope yet.

"Well, A lot of things in this world exist that you probably just thought of as rubbish. Faeries for one, Djinn, like myself, VooDoo, when used done by a select few... How this moron got that power is beyond me, but hey, I don't choose 'em. What else... There are all sorts of things, lad, and we don't have time for me to list 'em all. You'll find out what's out there on your own in due time.

But at the moment, we have to focus on why Mephisto wants your girl. I'd imagine she's still alive; she must be important to him in some way, and there's nothing she can do for him dead," Bill ended and began to ponder with one hand rubbing his filthy beard. A crumb of a sandwich long eaten fell out into his lap, he picked it up and put it back in. Chip choked back some puke.

"Bill..," Chip said.

"Hmm?" Bill responded.

"You're gross."

"Thank you."

"Not a compliment."

"Ah."

"Bill?"

"Hmm?"

"Why was Mephisto kicked out of Hell?"

"He was up to no good, lad. It's none of your concern now. It's best to focus on the here and now," Bill answered in a low grumble.

"Bill?" Chip said again.

"Hmm?"

"Are unicorns real?" Chip asked with the wonderment of a five-year-old girl.

"Aye, son, they are," Bill said with a smile.

"Cool."

As Chip and Mort walked under the giant archways that was *The Library of Everything Unknown*, Chip stopped and just

took it all in. The golden shimmering ceiling was a work of art. He couldn't quite make out what everything was, but it looked a lot like the constellations, and it sure was pretty. The pillars that lined the main hallway and every offshoot was just as intricate. It was embossed with golden patterns and markings, some of them even looked like a language, but Chip had no idea what. It was then that the grandeur of his situation hit him. What had he gotten himself into this time? Would Ellie be alright, what was really going on, and why was Bill being a bit vague about Mephisto's past? There were so many questions, and even if all the answers were in the gigantic library, it would take him forever to find them all. The weight of the state of affairs finally took their toll causing his knees to buckle. He propped himself up against a pole and slowly slide down it on his back.
"This is useless." He muttered to himself.
"Get up; you haven't even started yet." A disembodied voice whispered into Chip's brain.
"What? Who said that?" Chip said, not seeing who said it, being a disembodied voice and all. That would be impossible.
"Said what?" Mort said, "And what are you doing down there? Did you drop a contact?"
"You didn't hear that?" Chip answered, "And I've never even worn glasses, why would I have dropped a contact?"
"I dunno, first thing that came to mind."
Chip sighed and got to his feet. He brushed off his pants, despite there not being any dirt around him. He crept towards Mort, who had walked a short distance from where Chip had a moment of giving up, and as he did so he checked over his shoulder, half expecting to see an angel, or some other new previously non-existent thing lurking behind him. But alas, there was nothing, just a giant void beyond the pillar. He met up with Mort, who put his arm around his shoulder and assured him that they can find another contact lens on their way home.

Just in front of them sat a reference desk which was built out of mahogany and laced with gold. It rose to just above the waist, making it a kind of awkward height for anybody under five foot four inches, really. Behind the desk sat a surly looking woman, at least, it looked like a woman. Her hair plumed outwards in a crazy mess of grey tangled curls, like a perm job gone awry. She wore glasses that nearly covered her entire face and bright red lipstick that took up every inch of lip real estate she could offer. Although everything about this person, if it even was a person, screamed woman, in Chip's new life, he really couldn't be certain of anything.
"Hello!" Mort said with a great deal of enthusiasm, which kind of took Chip by surprise.
"Yes, hello." The woman said with a raspy, sort of gnarled voice. Surely she wasn't human, not with a voice like that.
"History section, please. Preferably the history of Hellspawn and Demon Armies," Mort said with a Cheshire Cat grin.
"Thirty-eight rows back, in the Cassiopeia section. Here, you'll need these." The librarian said handing Mort a pair of flashlights, and a little brown bag.
"Thanks!" Mort said with even more enthusiasm.
"Take your time, kids. And keep an eye out back there." The woman-thing said with an air of danger to her voice. Chip eyeballed her as he and Mort walked on past the desk.

"So, Mort... The Librarian lady... What kinda creature was she?" Chip asked when they were well clear of the desk, walking through the empty - and creepy - halls of the ancient library.
"Hmm? Whattya mean?" Mort responded.
"C'mon, was she a Gremlin, or a Goblin or something?"
"What, no, she's a person," Mort explained.
"No freaking way... The hair, and the glasses... and that Godforsaken voice..." Chip blabbed.

"Yeah, she's old and smokes a lot... What do you want from her? Geeze, Chip, I didn't know you were so heartless," Mort said, shaking his head in disapproval.
"Wait, what... No, I mean... Huh."
"Never mind, Chip, c'mon, we've got a long ways to go yet," Mort said trudging on in an apparently bad mood. Chip also felt sort of bad, he felt like he had racially profiled somebody based on their looks. In his defence, there are a lot of things that could be a lot of different things now, and how was he to know? He's not even sure that he, himself, is human now, let alone some scraggly old woman in a library that shouldn't exist. The world made no sense anymore, but in a strange sort of way, that made sense. As with Ellie's life, things were very confusing.
The pair walked, with Mort leading the way by torchlight. Chip had always figured his roommate and friend as a bumbling buffoon who tried to jam party sized tortilla chips into a single serving jar. He never even hinted at a glint of intelligence behind those dull eyes, yet here he was following the great imbecile through the hallways of the world's largest unknown library. It was sort of poetic in an ironic kind of way, and as strange and backwards as it was, Chip was glad that he had to go through this ordeal with his best friend.
The longer they walked, the darker their surroundings began to feel. In fact, the darkness seemed to be alive, which was a terrifying thought before Chip knew that monsters and demons existed. With what he knew now, it was downright spooky.
"The darkness is alive, ya know," Mort chimed in, the first words he said since their discussion of the not-so-gremlin-receptionist.
"'Scuse me?" Chip replied in a state of disbelief.
"Yeah, not usually, but down here it is. Nobody knows exactly what it is, but if you sit quietly for a while you'll hear a heartbeat, almost like you're in the pulse of the thing. I don't know, call me crazy -"

"Crazy," Chip interrupted.
"Shut up," Mort shot back. "Call me crazy, but I think it's the library itself that's alive. Like it's some kind of being with near infinite knowledge, and somehow, some long freaking time ago somebody found a way to harness it, or maybe even work with it," Mort finished. Chip had never heard something so profound and extraordinary from Mort before, and it startled him even further. He stood there dumbfounded for a minute, and Mort seemed to take offence to that.
"I know, I know - It's stupid. Let's move on, we're nearly there, I think... I always get lost down here." Mortimer Blake - always just beaming with confidence.
"How will we know when we get there, exactly? I mean, we can't exactly see anything. I mean, there's nothing down here but the darkness and emptiness," Chip added.
"Aww, must feel like your heart then!" Mort jabbed. It was a joke, but it struck closer to home than he knew.
"Shut up," Chip said before he had a thought. "Oh, hey Mort... What was in the bag the Grem... Uhh, lady at the front gave you?"
"You'll see soon enough," Mort answered all ominously like. Chip thought he relished that moment.
"Fine, keep your secrets,"
"I will! Besides, we can't give you all the answers on your first day. Your head might explode or something. I've seen it before."
"Oh, ok... Wait, what?!"
"Hmm? Oh, nothing. Never mind," Mort said ignoring the last thing he said, which seemed rather important. "I think we're here," He finished, completely taking Chip's mind off the head exploding comment.
"Now you'll see what the bag does," Mort said as he unravelled the leather lace that looped through the rings keeping whatever was inside safe and secure. When he did so, a brilliant golden

flow erupted, like a dormant volcano that had been waiting centuries to blow its load...
That came out wrong.
Regardless, the light was overwhelming to the point that Chip had to look away and shield his eyes from the intensity of the glow. From the depth of the light shot an even brighter ball of light, it was so bright that it appeared to be nothing more than a white blur as it shot from the bag. It ascended at such a rate that it had only been visible for a split second, but it was enough to send Chip into another state of wonderment. He was easily amused, apparently. Up and up the light went into the darkness that may or may not have been alive, but wherever it went, it was gone for no longer than it appeared. Mort stayed almost exactly where he was when he let the ball loose, and he did so with the bag open so it could promptly plop right back into place.
The second it landed in the bag without a noise, Mort spun the leather lace rapidly around the top, as if it would just fly away again unless it was procured in place.
"What in the Hell was that?" Chip cried.
"Hells," Mort corrected. "That was the information we needed. Nobody knows how it works, but this little light flies up into...wherever...whatever? Anyway, it disappears for a few seconds and when it comes back it contains the answers to whatever you were looking for, which in our case is Mephisto... and how to make the perfect sandwich," Mort saying the last bit really fast and under his breath hoping Chip wouldn't hear it.
"Sandwich, really?!" He heard it. "Ellie's God knows where, and you're thinking about the perfect stacking of meats, cheeses, and breads?" Chip complained, again.
"First, it's Gods. Man, when are you gonna get the hang of this. And yes, we'll need some sort of celebratory treat when we kick this Mephisto guys ass," Mort said trying to justify his food obsession.

Chip rolled his eyes, and Mort figured he had another tongue lashing coming his way. "Mort... Damn it, you know the perfect sandwich, no matter what it is, has just the right amount of mustard. C'mon man," Mort blinked. That was unexpected.
"Anyway, do we have everything? I mean, can we just like... leave now?" Chip asked.
"Yup. We take this back to the front, the little ball of light goes into something and it turns into a book for us to understand. I mean, whatever info this little guy now holds can't be heard by human, or really any ears. This whole process is very mysterious. Some say it's the voice of a god, and if we heard it our puny heads would explode," Mort said with a smile.
"Great, more exploding heads. Does that happen a lot?" Mort thought for a moment before answering.
"More than you'd expect; less than you'd hope." The perfect answer Mort thought.
Chip blinked, "Right. Can we get outta here now, though? It's starting to get creepy in here."
"Starting?" Mort said, "I've been creeped out since we starting talking to the librarian. I mean, did you hear her voice?"
"Yeah... Wait, you sonofa-"
"Time to go!" Mort said skipping on past Chip into the abyss from which they came. Rather than arguing, Chip decided to just follow along, like a puppy at the heels of his master. Chip still felt overwhelmed, but it was getting better, at least he thought it was. Besides, he has a long walk back to civilization to think about the new element to his unique situation. What did this ball of light mean, and what kind of information will it hold. Is there a weakness to Mephisto? Did he have an army? What was he after? Is there really such a thing as the perfect sandwich? So many questions to be answered. Maybe it'll become clearer the more he thinks about it.
Or maybe his head will explode. He couldn't quite be sure, but he was certain of one thing: This whole thing *is* mysterious,

and adding to the mysteriousness of the situation was that voice he heard when they first got to the library. Who was it? It didn't sound like Bill, though he couldn’t be sure, and that bothered him slightly. Okay, maybe more than slightly. Nevertheless, Chip felt it was best to keep it to himself for now, after all, he's got enough to worry about; he doesn't need both Mort and Bill thinking he's crazy. Hell, he wasn't sure just yet that he wasn't.

# CHAPTER 4

Was it just a dream? Ellie couldn't be positive one way or another, all she knew is that when she woke up in what looked like a sewer she had one mess of a headache. The last few hours were nothing more than a blur to her, and rightfully so really. What she could remember didn't make much sense, like a creepy Brit kidnapping her, freezing her boyfriend, and then chaining her to a chair. The very last thing she remembered though made the least amount sense. She couldn't see it, but she swears she could smell nature. Nothing specific, it wasn't the freshness of a pine breeze, nor was it the quaint essence of a lily flower in the air, but rather it was just... nature. She couldn't explain it to herself in any other way.

What she would give for a spot of nature now, though. Surrounding her feet was the sludge of brown water that was so murky it hid her toes even though it sat barely ankle deep. It smelled like, well, like a sewer would smell like: poopy. Scratching her head, Ellie looked around for any sign of where she might be. She scratched and scratched as if digging a hole through her skull would help her figure out the situation better, it did not. It got to a point where she couldn't take her hand away from her head, but that had more to do with the massive knot that formed trapping a ring in the mess of hair. Just another problem to throw on the pile.

So, lost, confused, smelly, and with one hand tied up, Ellie just began to wander the dank tunnel. She wandered long and far, all the while doing her best little teapot impression, shame there was nobody to see, but that was beside the point. The channel seemingly had no end. Either way she turned she faced darkness all around, and the further she went, the more intense the darkness became until it felt as though it were enveloping her. Undaunted by her stubbornness, however, Ellie trekked on only stopping to try and loosen her hand, which wasn't coming out. She continued on until she was met by a familiar scent.

The odour slowly pushed away the musty smell of waste; it was the smell of hope. She had smelt it before, recently, and it made her feel safe and comfortable, despite her being in less than ideal conditions...standing in poop water. She made like Sam and followed her nose through the rest of the tunnel, and it wasn't long until she saw something for a change. Something other than darkness. Something other than grey brick and brown water. She saw the light at the end of the tunnel, literally. Her pace quickened. Her feet splashed and her one-armed began to pump. The other nearly pulled her hair out. She stuck to one arm thrusting as she broke into a sprint towards the light.

Suddenly, though, she stopped. A wave of caution pillowed over her body and she thought to herself there's only ever two lights at the end of any tunnel, and neither are good. She began to think about it more, and the more precarious it began to feel. The long dark tunnel. Not remembering anything after smelling the most wonderful thing she'd ever smelt, from then waking up to nothing but a feeling of uncomfortable dread. It all pointed to one thing. The light at the end of the tunnel wasn't a train.

It was death.

It made sense. People described being in total darkness, only to be drawn towards the light while in a state of near death. Everybody said the same thing when they came back from the brink, though, they left out the sewer bit. Ellie could have really done with that information. It matters little really, she didn't own any rain boots. She wasn't sure, as she stood looking her potential maker in the eye if she were quite ready for the other side. She knew she wasn't finished with life, there

was so much to be done. She wanted to find a career, buy a house, get married and have a horde of kids. Not just a couple, not even a brood, but a horde. Like, 35 kids.
But most importantly she wanted to have all that with Chip. Without him it all felt empty and pointless. She didn't know if he were even alive. Who knows what that British dick did to him, or worse yet, those two barbarians that were with him. Maybe he waited for her in the light beyond, maybe her house and perfect life waited there in the afterlife. Maybe she had paid her dues and was reaping just what she sowed during life. Maybe it was meant to be. Maybe... Maybe she didn't have a choice.
As she looked behind her into the deep dark abyss and she knew. There was nothing left for her back there, just dark and empty wandering forever. There was but one path left for her, and that was straight ahead into the future, her future. She swallowed hard and squinted with determination. With one hand balled into a fist and the other firmly stuck to her melon, she marched on. The light intensified as she neared it, and just as she broke the plane, it expanded in the brightest flash she'd ever seen. Suddenly all the dark behind her scuttled off into some other recess of the world revealing a very memorable setting to her. Eyes wide, she vanished into the light.
"Like, hi," A rather stoned voice rang out in her ear.
"Hi?" She said blindly to nobody.
"I totally dig your free spirit."
"Uh, thanks?" Ellie said, but truth be told she had no idea about, well, anything.
"Your, like, choice of clothing, man. Dig it." A hippie came into view. It took a moment for her eyes to adjust, she wished they hadn't.
Oh, by the way, Ellie had somehow shed her clothing. She stood in the middle of what looked like Central Park naked.

"Eek!" She let out trying to cover herself up. She had forgotten about her entangled hand and let out several groaning noises in the process.
"Here," said the hippie handing her a brown and orange poncho. Upon closer inspection Ellie came to the conclusion that the orange wasn't meant to be part of the poncho, rather it was added. Cheesy dust?
"Thanks," she said.
"What were you doing in the sewer?" Asked the hippie. She *knew* it was the sewer, and she couldn't help but think was super gross. What, she is a girl after all.
"I was on a scavenger hunt," she said with the utmost sarcasm.
"Oh, that's cool, man. What was in the sewer that you needed...man?" Sadly, he didn't appreciate the sarcasm.
"It was more a to-do-list. I had to strip naked and wander through a sewer until I found daylight. I think I nailed it."
"Ahhhh, man. Totally," he said smirking. Also, if he called Ellie *man* one more time, she might very well claw his eyeballs out. Just a thought.
"Yeah. Anyway, can you point me in the direction of...somewhere that's not here?" She hoped he would get the vague question.
"If you go that way you'll hit 5th and Main. That way you'll end up at Joe's Diner...Mmmm," He drifted. It's to be expected with years and years of recreational drug use. Ellie could use some at this moment.
"Hello?" Ellie snapped in the hippies face. A goofy smile immediately appeared on his face.
"Hey, nice poncho. I had one like it once, but I lost it."
Ellie rolled her eyes and thanked the hippie. She at least knew where 5th and Main was, so that's the direction she headed. But what she didn't know was that as she walked, butterflies literally flew from her butt. Also, it was definitely cheesy dust. Double super gross.

Emerging from a runoff pipe in the middle of a park in front of a stoned tree hugger was one thing, but walking through the busy downtown core in nothing but a poncho tends to garner some attention, especially when there are butterflies escaping from every opening. She became aware of them not long after leaving the park. At first, she just assumed that they were in season or something. That's a thing, she thought, surely, butterfly season, right? But soon after that she peered down her poncho and saw a giant mass of them. No matter what she did they wouldn't stop, so she just accepted her fate and gave up.

Also, she couldn't help but notice the wide birth that she created with her increasingly aggressive butterflies. Some flew away to find their own ways. In fact, one particularly determined butterfly emerged into the world with a tonne of potential and free will. He thought the world his oyster and flew freely into the smoggy city skies with all the hope of starting a family, getting a meaningful job, and generally finding out who he was a butterfly. Was he just another pretty face, or would he accomplish more than any other insect of his kind, perhaps even save the world?

It was at that thought that he figured out what a bus was, and just how hard the windshield was. Ellie meandered on through the city streets until she could find a way to get a hold of Chip. For some reason, she thought he would know what to do.

Surprisingly enough, it was rather difficult to have somebody lend you their cell phone when you're naked, wearing a cheese dust covered poncho with butterflies escaping from every crevasse. Everybody's heard of the crazy cat lady, but that was a whole new level. It was actually quite an awkward meeting when Ellie ran said cat lady. The stare down was biblical, but that's a story for another time.

Just as she was about to give up a kindly stranger offered up his phone, well, if by grabbing his collar and threatening to eat his heart is kindly, then that's exactly the proper word. She dialled his number, but it went straight to voicemail. Instantly she assumed the worst, after all why wouldn't she. She tried Mort as well, but her luck wasn't improving. What's a girl to do when her boyfriend only has one friend, and neither one of them picks up their phone? Cry, that's about all there is to do. Now, Ellie had never been a crier, but if there was ever a time, it was now. She found an alley to crouch into so nobody would see her whimper, because *that* would be too embarrassing. Her wall of butterflies followed her into the alley as well, she sighed and pulled the poncho up over her head and began to sob into it, leaving orange stains on her face. She gagged and pulled the poncho back down. Crying was slightly foreign to her, and she knew that she was an ugly and uncomfortable crier, the kind of crier that if other people are around they make faces at one another as if to ask, *is she having a stroke?* However, despite her lack of experience and knowledge with crying, she was fairly certain that it was odd to have tiny little purple flower grow from the tears that hit the ground. It was a strange day.

# CHAPTER 5

Back at Bill's little shop of horrors, appropriately named, *Bill's Little Shoppe of Horrors* (Adding the extra P and E make it classy), Chip and Mortimer tell Bill of their experience in the Library of Everything Unknown, but Chip left out the part about the voice in his head. Mort, however, couldn't contain himself when it came to the disturbing librarian. He hyperventilated in between words and choked on his own spit not once, but twice. Chip was not amused, and oddly enough neither was Bill, who stood at the counter looking very unimpressed and impatient.

"So, did you get the info?" Bill said to Chip looking past a hysterical Mort.

"Why don't you just read his mind?!" Mort interrupted before bursting into another fit of laughter.

"What's wrong with him?" Bill asked.

"Past his nap time."

"Ah. So yes, info?"

"Yeah, got it here." Chip tossed the bag holding the golden light. Bill caught it.

"Excellent. Let's get started," Bill said signalling for Chip to follow.

The two walked around the counter into a small room hidden behind a curtain that Chip originally thought was a sex dungeon, or perhaps a small factory of imps making sandwiches. Turns out, he was half right about the sandwiches.

"I used to have a small army of imps back here making sandwiches, but I caught them skimming off the top if ya know what I mean. Little bastards, can't trust any of them!" Bill shouted as if there were somebody - or something else in the room with them. Chip took a step back.

"Now I just use it for incantations and stuff. Usually I summon sandwiches and other luncheon goodies," Bill looked back with a near crazed look in his eye. The Djinn liked his cold cuts.

"I see," said Chip, "and what about the bag with the light?"

"Ah, yes. We need an empty vessel for it to inhabit. It could be anything that can hold that sort of information. Sometimes a book or two will do, it depends on how vast the unknowledge is," Bill explained.

"Unknowledge?" Chip was sure that word was made up. It was.

"Yes, it's not known to any regular folks, only to the practitioners of the magical and mystical. Therefore it's dubbed unknowledge."

"You made that up didn't you."

"...Yes. But it sounds cool, right?"

"Yes, yes it does. Can we get started?" Chip asked eagerly.

"Of course, Lad. Let's do this. Grab me those three books over there," Bill said pointing to a rather old and dusty shelf. Chip picked up the only three books on the shelf. They were big, old, brown, and strange to the touch. They almost felt like his grandmother's arm when she would sit out in the sun for too long. The thought caused him to shiver.

"Put them on the table in a circle, make sure the corners are touching." Chip did just that.

"Excellent. Ok, now this is gonna be bright, like looking into the sun, so I suggest looking at your feet, or something."

"Alright," Chip said looking at his shoes. He liked his shoes, he couldn't help but think that they were very underappreciated, mostly because they were durable and comfortable, not to mention stylish.

"Ahh, that's a sight I wish I could never stop seeing," Bill said.

"Yeah, they are nice shoes, aren't they?" Chip replied.

"What? No, the light of unknowledge scribing itself to the pages of these human skin books," Bill stated. Chip's eyes widened.

"I missed it?!"

"Aye, lad, you did. I told you not to look."

"But you just said it was beautiful!"

"Yes, it is."

"So why couldn't I look?"

"Because I'm a prick?" Bill said with a smirk. Chips eye twitched. Bill picked up one of the books and held it close to his chest and nodded towards the other two for Chip to pick up, which he did.

"What's that one?" Chip asked in reference to the closely cuddled book in the arms of the ancient Djinn.

"Nothing. None of your concern," He replied. Seemingly disregarding any previous care for the book in Bill's arms, Chip realized something far more important.

"Human skin books?" Bill smirked and walked back into the main room. Chip looked down at the books in his arms. A hair stared back at him. He threw up in his mouth a little bit but followed nonetheless. He couldn't help but feel tiny little sandwich making eyes peer at him in the dimly lit space behind him.

Standing at the counter beside a now sleeping Mort was a young man with black hair, eyeliner, black lipstick and exceptionally pale skin. Chip turned his head like a dog hearing a human speak to him in baby talk. Dogs hate that, by the way. They aren't human babies, they're grown-ass dogs for Heaven's sake.

"Didn't you say vampires aren't real?" Chip mumbled to Bill.

"He's not a vampire, lad. He's a far worse creature," Bill uttered back.

"Hi there son, how can I help you?" Bill said with a smile approaching the counter.

"Yeah, can I pay for this here?" The worse-than-a-vampire asked.
"Certainly. Cash or credit?"
"Credit," he said producing a platinum card. Vampires be loaded.
"Wonderful," Bill said, charging the card, handing him the goods and closely watching him as he walked on out of the store.
"If that wasn't a vampire, and it was worse than a vampire, what was it?" Chip asked rather convolutedly.
"That... That son, was a goth." The fear in Bill's eyes was real. The two men shared a shiver at the mention of the beast.
"Anyway, lad you've got some reading to do," Chip nodded.
"Take this moron with you, will you?" Bill pointed to Mort who was curled up on the floor with a shrunken head. Chip sighed and hoisted Mort up under the arm. As he was leaving the store, Chip had a thought.
"Why didn't you just read our minds?" Chip asked innocently enough. Bill looked down and away in shame and then walked off to his former sandwich factory, presumably to summon another sandwich. Something wasn't right with Bill, and Chip grew three sizes in worry that moment. In the back room, however, Bill didn't feel beleaguered once he looked down at the title of his new book. He had asked Mort for it specifically.
*How To Summon The Perfect Sandwich: A Guide To Culinary Bliss*
Outside Chip carried his best friend in the whole world down the street, in the middle of the day, on a busy boulevard. Looks were exchanged with strangers, which Chip couldn't decide if that made the situation better or worse. Perhaps the shrunken head played a role in said stares. Regardless, they needed to get back to the apartment to rest, read, and probably eat some snacks. In fact, snacks were the most important. Chip's appetite had been off the chart since he resurrected the homeless guy, and with Bill going on about sandwiches, he

really needed to eat. He considered cannibalizing Mort, after all, he could just bring him back to life. A zombie Mort might be an improvement, really.

Thankfully the apartment wasn't too far from Bill's shop(pe) and Chip was able to drag Mort through the door with less of a struggle than first anticipated. Though, once through over the threshold Chip just dropped Mort on the floor with wet thud and stepped over his body to get to the kitchen. He didn't care what he was going to eat, just that he was going to. He opened the fridge and grabbed the oddest assortment of things. Grapes and turkey breast, a little hot sauce and a jar of pickles. He thought of taking the mayo, but that's just gross. He slammed the fridge shut and looked for some bread, but apparently Mort had used the last few slices to build mini tombstones for his tortilla chip army.

Nevermind, eh? A pair of frozen waffles would suffice.

Bill shivered in his sandwich emporium.

Food had never tasted so good before as some hot sauce ran down Chips chin. He closed his eyes and groaned in ecstasy. He couldn't be 100% sure... No, actually he could be. It was better than sex, and Chip *really* enjoyed sex. With every bite his stomach growled and rumbled in pleasure; every crunch music to is ears. As delicious as his makeshift sandwich was, he wished he had at least cooked the waffles, but there was no time.

"Whattya eating?" Mort whispered in his ear.

"Whoa! What!?" Chip shouted, "Where the... how did you get there, how long have you been there?"

"Couple minutes."

"You creepy sonofa..."

"Hey, is that a hot turkey, pickle, grape, and waffle special? I haven't had one of those in years! Is there any left in the kitchen?"

"Yes... What?"

"Awesome!" Mort said jumping to his feet.

"Oh, I can't believe I get to do this. Do you have any idea how badly I've wanted to do this around you?" Upon hearing Mort utter those words, Chip shimmied to the other end of the couch. Slowly.
"A waffle sandwich?" Chip murmured hopefully, helplessly.
"No, dumbass. This," Mort said closing his eyes. It was difficult to tell exactly what he was doing at first, but Chip could see his lips moving ever so slightly as if he were in some sort of trance. He never uttered a word out loud, but he was definitely talking to someone, or something, and a few seconds after he started, Chip heard some rustling slightly behind him. Too afraid to look, but also too afraid not to, Chip slowly turned his head, and what he saw he would be telling to therapists for years. Ironically enough those same therapists would laugh him out of the building, leading to more therapy, and more laughter. It was truly a vicious circle
From behind the couch, where Mort had made a graveyard of broken potato chips, came a being about three feet tall and wafer thin, made up of said chips. Fragments, misfits, and even different brands melded together into one lanky human-esque fetish of snack foods. It walked past Chip's gapping jaw, but stopped to look at him. The being turned what could only be his head, and then it closed Chip's mouth with its hand. That did little to help the situation. All Chip could do was watch as the being walked into the kitchen and opened the fridge.
By the time Chip looked back at Mort, he had a very accomplished look on his face. He was very satisfied with his creation. No, not a creation, an abomination; one cannot simply fuse together a *Dorito* and a *Tostito*, it's just not natural. Still, Mort didn't seem to care, after all, he'd always been for equality, especially among snack foods.
"What the Hell is that?" Chip asked. A reasonable question, really.
"Hmm? Oh, that? That's a fetish."
"Explain. Please. Now."

"Oh, well, a fetish is a thing that I kind of force to life. See, where as you can take spirits of living beings and place them in their bodies, I can draw from an ancient pool of spirits and have the possess an inanimate object for a short time. Pretty cool, eh?"
"That's why you kept the pile of chips." A minor moment of eureka passed over Chip as he figured it out.
"No. That were good soldiers! I figured they deserved a second chance, however brief it may be." Poetry.
"Mort, they were never alive."
"You're a monster." It was at that moment that the fetish returned with a plate containing a hot turkey, grape, and pickle waffle sandwich.
"Ooh!" Mort squealed.
"Look, man, enough messing around, we have some work to do, okay? The light came out of the bag -"
"Awhh yahy. Ooh aw da right?" Mort said with a full mouth.
"What?" Chip said, Mort swallowed.
"You saw the light? It's pretty, eh?"
"Yeah... gorgeous," Blasted Bill.
"Well, what do we have then?" Chip got up, gingerly avoided the idling chip monster and picked up the books he dropped beside the previously sleeping Mort.
"We've got *So You're Going To Raise The Dead, A Necromancer's Guide.* And *How To Kill A Demon, More Specifically Mephistopheles*. Mephistopheles?" Chip asked.
"Mephisto," Mort answered
"Shoulda known that," Chip remarked.
"Yup."
"I guess I'll get to Necromancer training. You wanna start on the demon killing thing?"
"Sure."
"Can you..." Chip started eyeballing the fetish, "Can you get rid of that thing? It's freaking me out."

"K." Mort waved his hand and the chip construct collapsed instantly.
What else would this strange new world hold, Chip wondered. He decided it would be best if he thought about such things alone in his room, with a pillow planted over his face and the covers of his bed thrown atop that. Usually, that'd be fairly normal, but Chip was curled up in the corner of his room. He thought that everything would be ok and that he had been cool with this new lifestyle of his, but the second he cracked open the instruction manual on how to be a necromancer, he had a small break down.
Okay, not so small. It went something like this.
Chip walked into his room and closed his door nice and tight, he didn't need any distractions. He tossed the book on his bed and then followed suit. He was excited, if not a tad bit anxious, but excited nonetheless. He slowly peeled the book open, and when he did a great bright and beautiful golden light sprung from the pages. At first he marvelled at it, thinking it must have been similar to how it looked when Bill looked into the bag. However, that soon passed and gave way to slimy, wriggling, and vile green pages. They undulated as if they were alive, crawling with maggots of something just as foul beneath the surface. It was about that time when Chip realized there was nothing underneath the pages, it was the pages themselves that were alive.
Instantly, he closed the book, grabbed the pillow and blanket and headed for the corner. He'd been there about 13 minutes. 13 minutes that were made worse by the slightly golden glow that the book put off while closed, thus making the room a dimly golden hue, which was unsettling to say the least. Part of being a necromancer is dealing with icky things, but why did the book have to be alive? It was just wrong. Unnatural even.
Once the 14th minute rolled around, Chip had found a small amount of courage and removed the pillow from his face. Next

to be removed were his socks, but after that the blanket came down and any protection he had vanished. Courage.

The book sat atop his bed, just as he left it, and as he approached Chip could swear that he heard the pages wiggling underneath the cover. This was confirmed when he saw a stray hair sticking out of the human skin binding shimmy in the wind.

It was another 16 minutes before Chip emerged from his pillowy blanket fort a second time, this time with all the courage and bravery of Lancelot of Camelot. He would conquer the book, he was determined to, after all, his damsel was in distress, which was no good for anybody. The only way to save her would be to learn to harness the powers of death and use it to his advantage. At least, that's what he assumed. The whole thing was still a little bit fuzzy, but he was pretty sure that was the gist of it. It was time to do some learning. Some book learning.

One thing Chip failed to notice the first time opening the book, which he became aware the second time, was that there were no words on the book. He looked frontways and backways, upside down and right side up, flat, from above, hell, he even shook the book up and down thinking maybe the words would simply fall out...or something. But after searching every conceivable angle, Chip gave up. He tossed the book on his bed causing it to fall open to a random page, and out of a minor fit of frustration, he punched the page. His hand was absorbed by it.

That was interesting.

Again, Chip poked the page only for his finger to fall through into some unknown wormy abyss. Curious, he flipped it to the first page and tried the procedure again. With an outreached hand, Chip lowered his palm to the first page, and this time his hand didn't sink straight in, rather the page seemed to envelop it. His original assumption that the book was a living being turned out to be true, somewhat. The pages were filled with something that resembled life anyway, and Chip began to feel something strange within him.

Slowly a pale green glow began to emanate from beneath his palm, it increased in brightness the longer he held it there. He didn't feel it at first, but the longer his hand was there the smaller the book got. The pages seemed to sink into one another, no, not sinking, absorbing. When Chip touched the pages out of order, they freaking out a little bit and tried to take him inside of it, but when he went the proper route, the book acted accordingly by shooting its rays of knowledge into Chip's very being.

Not all books of unknowledge work this way, however. Alternatively in the other room, Mort had to actually read the whole thing, and there weren't a lot of pictures, and the print was terribly small, almost on the side of torture. While Chip only had to touch a weird squirming living book, Mort had to read. It was Hell on Earth.

When the last few pages of *So You're Going To Raise The Dead, A Necromancer's Guide* absorbed into Chip's hand, it exploded with a glorious green light that filled the room completely and even stained it a strange off green, a green that was previously unknown to the human pallet. Let's call it glowing worm green. Once again though, Chip missed the brilliance of the light, but this was to due to his eyes being rolled into the back of his head. It was a small side effect from sucking up so much information in such a small time. He's quite lucky that his head didn't simply explode, as apparently, that was pretty common. Nevertheless, when Chip's eyes assumed their regular positioning facing forward, they too had a new hue of green to them. Glowing worm green.

The door to Chip's room opened with a might flourish, causing Mort to look up in a bit of shock. Gusts of wind and a very disturbing odour erupted from behind Chip like a wonderful and glorious fart. Though, it was merely residual information explosion, nothing important, not like a giant fart would have

been. Nevertheless, Chip emerged from his room looking slightly different than he had when he first went in.
"Chip?" Mort asked with a hint of fear in his voice.
"Mort," Chip said confidently.
"What's up...?" Mort asked hesitantly.
"I know..," Chip said very out of context.
"...Ok, I'll bite. What do you know?
"Everything."
"How long have you been holding that one in for?"
"About 5 minutes. Pretty good, eh?"
"Not bad."
Chip meandered over to the couch and sat beside his roommate.
"Any luck with Mephisto?" Chip asked.
"No, well, I mean, I've gotten through page one," Mort responded.
"Yeah? That's not bad."
"No, I mean, I looked at the number one on the bottom of the page," Mort confessed
"Oh."
"How about you, any luck with the Necro stuff yet? Taking a break?" Mort asked.
"Nope. I'm done," Chip said leaning back in a cool guy pose.
"What?" Mort asked, "No, wait... you had an absorby?!" He said frantically.
"Yup," Chip said pretending to know what he meant.
"Aww! Lucky!" Mort said turning back to his book pouting. "Stupid book," he said slamming the tome shut.

# CHAPTER 6

The rise of a brand new Necromancer has caused quite a stir in certain parts of the unknown world. Mermaids were bubbling to one another - such gossips they are - Atlantians were in a bit of an uproar over it, thankfully though there was little they could do about it due to the fact they were trapped in an interdimensional wormhole somewhere in the Mariana Trench and have been since about 2500 BC. However, some more relevant people's interest have been piqued by this revelation, potentially dangerous people.

Marco Wax happens to be one of those people, and currently he's on the move to find Chip, unbeknownst to him of course. Even if Chip had any idea that a member of the Order of the Ancients was after him, there would be little he could do regardless. A Necromancer was a big deal to these people, and Wax would stop at nothing to potentially end Chip. So Marco knocked on Chip's front door.

It was Mort who answered, still frustrated by not being able to simply sop up the information on how to kill Mephisto.

"What?" He said in a tone that said, leave me alone, I'm rather frustrated that I have to read a fairly long book. Shame Marco didn't care and held a blade to his throat. Mort swallowed hard. Suddenly reading seemed somehow trivial.

"Who is it, Mort?" Cried Chip from the kitchen. His appetite still unfulfilled.

"Oh, nobody..," Mort said with a whimper to his voice. Marco Wax ushered him quietly into the apartment and softly closed the door behind him.

"Was it some religious nut?" Chip shouted, "Are they go..." Chip walked into the room to see Mort in a rather precarious situation; a knife to his throat held by a pale man in a leather jacket and hoodie that covered the upper portion of his face. At first glance, he looked pretty cool, minus the whole hostage thing.

"Who are you?" Chip said holding another concoction of a random assortment of foodstuff.

"Ah, the necromancer," Wax said. "Only one who's hunger for death and decay would require such a meal," he finished, referring to the tuna, applesauce, garlic clove, and pizza sandwich. It's better than you'd think.

"Okay. You know who I am, clearly... Stalker. Who are you?" Chip asked again

"My name is of little importance, but if you must call me something before I send you to the depth of Hell to which you belong, it's Marco Wax," The hooded figure said.

"Okay. first off, this isn't 1625, or something. Proper English was killed years ago, man." Mort couldn't help but think that statement was a little off the mark, considering his predicament.

"Secondly, let him go. He's useless," Chip said both insulting and helping his friend. Mort took offence to it and huffed.

"I'd rather not," Wax said.

"Well, I mean, wait... Why do you want to kill me?" Chip asked. A much more appropriate question.

"There hasn't been a necromancer in the world for an age now, and they leave nothing but horror and destruction in their wake. I must end you, and your unnatural abilities before they come to fruition." He was rather poetic and made being murdered sound kind of nice. Nevertheless, Marco raised his dagger in a throwing motion and aimed right at Chip's heart.

"Whoa! Hold a sec. Can I ask you something before you kill me?" Chip said, halting Marco in a statuesque pose.

"Very well," Marco said quickly bringing the knife back to Mort's throat in one swift motion.

"What's the strangest thing you've ever seen?"

"I beg your pardon? Strangest thing I've seen?"
"Yeah, you seem like a guy who's seen things. I mean I saw a crazy troll-like lady early, totally creeped me out, but I'm sure you can top that." Chip was, of course, referring to the totally human librarian.
"A troll-like lady?" Marco said in confusion. "A necromancer's strangest encounter was a troll-like lady? What is this nonsense?"
"Hey, I'm new at this. C'mon, enlighten me."
"Fine, I once tore the heart from a Nightmare beast. It was formed in the mind of a psychic child possessed by a rather unruly Djinn. He was attempting to harness the boys power and unleashed a creature so foul in the child's psyche that it would break his mettle before too long. I was called into dispatch the beast and the Djinn within. I cut the black pulsating heart from the beast while projecting my own being into his twisted and corrupted mind," Wax finished, sounding just tad bit proud of himself, even if that is forbidden within his Order.
"Wow, that's... That's actually cooler than I thought," Chip said in awe, "How long ago was that? Like, a month ago or something? 'Cause that's when things started going weird with me. The smell started then, but I don't think anybody noticed..."
"It was a little over 10 years ago when I was seven years of age," Wax said nonchalantly.
"Oh," Chip said.
"Cool," Mort said.
"Enough of this! You must be brought to an end now!" Wax said.
"Wait!" Chip yelled again, halting his demise for a brief few minutes.
"What now?"
"I think I can top your nightmare demon story thing."
"How could you possibly?"

"Ever see a tortilla chip monster...thing?" Chip asked.
"What?" Marco said. What Marco was unaware of was that Mort had been exceptionally quiet throughout him being held hostage. If Wax had known Mort he would have found that strange, as Mort usually never shuts up. However since he didn't know any better, Mort was able to whisper the same incantation that brought his fallen soldiers back to life, thus creating the chip fetish once again. Currently, the fetish was just about to stab Marco in the leg with a tiny toothpick.
"Ouch!" Marc yelped out of character releasing Mort from his grasp, who stumbled across the furniture and took cover behind the couch.
A frustrated Wax kicked the fetish into oblivion sending bits of chip all throughout the room. It was a massacre. A small portion landed at Mort's feet, it writhed in pain for a brief second before returning back to its inanimate state.
"You monster!" Mort yelled.
"You witch!" Marc shouted back. Mort gasped at the insult. That hit him deep.
Marco pulled the toothpick from his leg and realigned his sights onto Chip, who for no good reason stood in the same spot the entire time.
"This ends now!" Marco shouted hurling the knife at Chip's head, while pulling to small crossbows from under his leather jacket. Chip managed to duck under the blade, but it was the incoming crossbow bolts that worried him the most. He hit the deck and laid flat on his belly successfully dodging the pointy projectiles.
"Mort, Mort!" Chip whisper-yelled. He looked over at Chip sullenly, teary-eyed holding a piece of his fetish in his hands. Chip rolled his eyes. He was on his own. Drawing from what he'd just learned, Chip rose to his feet and scanned the room for any signs of Wax. He couldn't see anything, nothing out of the ordinary, the assassin was quick as a fox. Nevertheless, Chip charged up his power and sent two beams of green

energy from his hands. Apparently, there's more to being a necromancer than simply raising the dead, which if he's honest, seemed a bit useless. It turns out Chip can harness the power of death itself, which everybody knows, is the most powerful and oldest of all energies.
The beams hit a bookshelf filled with everything but books causing it to explode into a million splinters. A rustling from behind a chair became audible, and Wax poked his head up firing two bolts headed directly for Chip's eyes. There was no way he could react in time. He closed his eyes and waited for the inevitable final blow. And he waited. And he waited some more, but the bolts either missed their marks, or Chip was invulnerable. It wasn't the former, and the latter was just plain ridiculous. When Chip opened his eyes, he was amazed, and scared out of his mind. The two bolts hovered just centimetres from his eyeballs. So close in fact that when he blinked, he shaved his eyelashes.
"What the..." He uttered.
"What new brand of sorcery is this?" Marco said.
"You fool!" A voice erupted from behind Chip, a familiar voice, a warm voice, a sandwich loving voice. Solidifying from thin air, Bill appeared and swatted the bolts out of the air.
"Do you have any idea what you're doing?" Bill shouted at Marco, growing in size as he did so. He's definitely going to need a sandwich after this.
"I'm purging the world from this evil!" Marco said lunging forward with two hidden knives up his sleeve. Bill vanished into thin air again, but as he did so, Marco froze. He just hung in there air like a photograph of somebody hilariously falling over a coffee table.
"Evil? You have no idea what evil is, nor does your pathetic little coven," Bill's disembodied voice said. Chip looked around but saw nothing. Mort also relinquished his hiding

place from behind the sofa to check out what was going on. Chip knew Bill had power, but this was on a whole other level. Wax hung in the air unable to move anything but his eyes. He didn't react to the insult.

"You and your cult have no idea who the real enemy is, and I can assure you he is not among us in this room," Bill said appearing between Wax and Chip. He looked Wax square in the eye and then released him. Marco crashed to the ground, but not before he fell through the coffee table.

"Are you going to behave, young man?" Bill said patronizingly. Marco scowled, but nodded.

"Okay, good then. We need to have a chat, the four of us. But first, sandwiches."

"I've got a tuna, applesauce, garlic clove, and pizza sandwich over there," Chip said pointing to the plate, which somehow was untouched by the ruckus.

Bill smiled, "That's perfect lad."

Chip wasn't overly accustomed to having a trained assassin from a special order designed to kill evil creatures, and himself, tied to a dining room chair in his apartment. This was, however, more common place for Bill and Mort. Marco Wax sat staring begrudgingly at the trio as they sat at the kitchen counter eating various degrees of disgusting sandwiches. Often times Chip would be too nervous to eat, especially in the given circumstance, but he couldn't resist. Wax, on the other hand, hadn't touched his Peanut butter, onion, tomato, and eggplant sandwich, which hurt Bill's feelings. He made it especially for him after Marco revealed that he was a vegetarian - perhaps the strangest being in all the unknown universe.

"So you want to kill the only necromancer in existence, eh?" Bill said quite clearly despite having a full mouth.

"It is my duty, handed down to me from the elders of my order," Wax answered.

"I see. And that's because... He's going to bring on the end of the world?" Bill questioned again, this time with an empty mouth.
"It is mere history. It's happened before, therefore it will happen again. My order killed the last necromancer. It's an honourable rite of passage, and to be chosen to complete the task puts faith in my potential for greatness," Wax bragged in a subtle way. The boy had an ego, that was for certain.
"Mmhmm. Let me ask you something, lad," Bill implored
"Why stop now?" Marco said with a hint of snark. Bill scowled.
"Have you heard of the demon Mephistopheles?"
"Heh, a child's fairytale," Wax scoffed.
"A fairytale?" Bill remarked with a raised eyebrow.
"Yes, a fairytale. Something that doesn't exist. A legend, a myth? Surely you're familiar with such terms."
"Bite your tongue, boy," Bill scolded. Wax didn't flinch.
"Let me tell you something about fairytales," Bill began, "The things of myth and legend that you speak off, they all have their beginnings in truth, surely *you* know that," Bill shot back. Wax rolled his eyes.
"Look at your life, son. Fairytales, they're real. You're living one," Bill finished as the fridge was opened by half of tortilla fetish.
"What of this Mephistopheles anyway? How if that name relevant?" Wax questioned.
"You see that horribly evil necromancer eating a pizza with jellybeans on it?" Bill said pointing to Chip. Wax nodded.
"Well, that demon that doesn't exist kidnapped his girlfriend late yesterday, the very same day he discovers what he can do. You think that's any sort of coincidence?" Bill said polishing off his sandwich.
Wax's eyes darted side to side as if searching inside his own mind for answers, answers which were not coming to him. The only thing he found were doubts of his mission, but the

evidence was circumstantial at best, and he dealt in what The Order told him. The three before him were misfits and miscreants, they held no real power. Hell, the witch doctor can summon snack foods to life and the necromancer can barely suppress his hunger. The Djinn, however, was strong, but misguided and jaded. He needed more information before he could simply abandon his duties.

"Oh screw it. Misfit this!" Bill said reading Marco's thoughts. He lunged forward and slammed his palm against the assassins forehead. There was a brilliant flash of blue light, blinding even, and then nothing. Bill stood leaning against Wax's chair, and Wax sat there wide eyed, like he'd just seen his parents having a roll around the sack.

"What the crap was that?" Chip muttered to everybody in the room. Mort shrugged and bit his sandwich. Marco's eyes came to life and met with Chip's.

"I... I can't be certain," Wax said ominously.

"Certain about what?" Chip questioned.

"I believe... I think he just transferred his collective knowledge to me," Wax said in a state of shock.

"What, why? Why didn't he do that to us?" Chip said to Mortimer, who shrugged again.

"He's given me everything. Do you know what that means?" Chip shook his head no.

"I know all his secrets, information that even our elders don't know. Information that nobody knows. This Bill character is old. Very old," Wax said slipping into a zombie like state again.

Chip snapped to get his attention, "Yeah, he's old. But what does it all mean?"

"It means, Necromancer, that I believe you. He'd vanquished this Mephisto demon before. I must take this information to the order. They'll know what to do." Chip and Mort looked at each other then back at Wax.

"Eh, we can't let you do that, right Bill?" Unnoticed by all during the dialogue, Bill had collapsed to the couch in the living room.
"Bill?" Chip said with a concern to his voice, "what's wrong with him?"
"Nothin'. He just ate a heaping serving of some sandwich that I couldn't even tell the ingredients of, He's just got the Iti-."
"Don't say it," Chip interrupted.
"Say what?"
"You know what."
"Why?"
"Cause it's offensive."
"To who?"
"I dunno, people of a certain...You know what, nevermind."
"No, no, go on, your majesty."
"Gentlemen!" Wax interjected, "I believe we have a more serious issue at hand than that of political correctness." He nodded towards an unconscious Bill on the sofa.
"Crap," Mort and Chip said in unison. The two rushed to Bill's side, and what they saw was not good. Bill's face was pale, paler than usual and his beard seemed to have more salt than pepper in it too. Blue veins slowly surfaced on his face and his eyes were perpetually open, staring off into nothingness. Nothing about his current state came off as good. Not a thing.
"Bill!" Chip said smacking his face slightly.
"Nothing. What do we do, Mort?" Chip never thought he'd be asking Mortimer Blake for medical advice. He once dramatically broke all the aquariums at a pet store because he thought the fish were drowning. That's what Chip was dealing with.
"I have an idea," he said disappearing to the back of the apartment.
"It drained him," Wax's voice rang out.
"What?" Chip said not taking his eyes off of Bill.

"The transference, it drained him of his power, and apparently his life force," Marco answered.
"No, that can't be. He's immortal, or something, right?"
"Not immortal. I recanted my tale of killing a Djinn. They don't live forever, they just live a very, very long time. His power had been weakening for some time now."
"And how do you know?!" Chip shot back. He'd only known who Bill was for something like 26 hours, and before that he was just the creepy random store owner who was always eating. But now, everything was different, and he felt a connection to the old creep. He didn't want to lose him.
"He gave me everything, necromancer. But I fear I gave him something back," Marco said looking into Chips sad, sad eyes.
"You did this!?" Chip said standing up. His eyes weren't sad anymore, rather they began to glow that Glowing Worm Green. Anger, anger is also another word for what his eyes showed.
"No. Not intentionally anyway," Wax said, still undaunted and maintaining eye contact with the pissed off necromancer. "I think it may have been a side effect. He transferred everything to me, but I bounce information back to him. The link must have been a two-way street. I saw his mind when he found it."
"Found what?" Chip said coming back to a level of normalcy that the situation allowed.
"The Djinn I killed all those years ago..." Wax started.
"I've got it, guys!" Mort said bursting into the room holding a box. "This will do the trick!" He opened the box to reveal a stash of Playboys.

# CHAPTER 7

Sadly, the playboy's did nothing to break Bill out of his coma. Mort was certain it would work, and was devastated when it didn't. The emotional rollercoaster that is Mortimer Blake may never be understood by another living soul. Though, there is a dead soul who understands. Martin McLeod of England, a simple farmer who lived from 1432 to 1501. During his life he suffered from many a panic attacks, followed by glorious fits of joy. He would cry perpetually for days, but not always of sadness. He would begin sad, but then laugh at how sad he was and would then cry tears of humour. Those tears would be followed by salty droplets of awe and wonderment at how happy and joyful he was. This was a cycle that he went through his entire life until one particularly sad day when he jumped from a cliff near Portsmouth.

Still, they had Bill to worry about. His guidance, wisdom, and culinary ability was the only thing holding Chip and Mort together, and without him, they were lost. Completely so. These guys are so lost that if they were little red riding hood, the big bad wolf wouldn't be able to find them. Has the concept of lost been pounded in enough?

"Chip?" Mort wallowed.

"Yeah?" Chip answered just as solemnly.

"We're lost, aren't we?"

"Yeah."

The two curled up on the loveseat together across from Bill. It was a sad sight, like seeing a tiger caged, or a pro boxer not able to stand, and it was heart wrenching, though, not so much for Marco, who still sat tied to a chair.

"I must report this to my elder" His voice rang out. Mort and Chip didn't bat an eye.
"At once..." Marco continued, "...Please?" He said begrudgingly.
"Hmm?" Chip finally announced, acknowledging Wax's existence for a brief moment.
"I have to report this," Wax repeated.
"What? No," Chip answered.
"And why not?" Wax asked.
"Because... Stuff...and things."
"Stuff and things? Really?"
"Yeah..." It was at that moment that Chip had a brilliant idea, an epiphany if you will. Suddenly he felt like Newton discovering the principle of gravity, or Fleming upon finding the mold that would lead to penicillin, or Colonel Sanders when he mixed together those wonderful 11 herbs and spices and came up with *KFC*. That recipe is so confidential that not even *the* library knows what it is. It's even baffled the divine for decades.
"Wait. You have everything Bill had. You're our new Bill!" Chip shouted. Mort perked up.
"What? Preposterous. Don't liken me to that *Djinn*," Wax spewed.
"No, no he's right," Mort chimed in standing up, "I mean you'll never be as cool or as bearded, but yeah. You know everything he does."
"I do not. We shared a few experiences, nothing more," Wax said playing coy.
"Who was the inventor of sliced bread?" Chip shouted.
"Otto Frederick Rohwedder," Marco answered instantly, "I mean... who doesn't know that?" He tried to save, swallowing hard.
"Ha, only Bill would know who invented sliced bread. Face it, you're our new Bill," Chip declared.

"There's nothing you can do to keep me here," Wax proclaimed.
"Oh, isn't there?" Chip said smugly. "There is, isn't there?" He turned whispering to Mort. Mort rummaged around the recesses of his brain for a few seconds and came across some fairly disturbing things, but among those things was an answer.
"Wait, I've got it!" Mort celebrated. He walked over to the box of Playboys and dumped them out, catching the last object in the box. He then walked over to Wax and plucked a hair from his head. He then took said hair and jammed in into the thing that fell from the box.
"No, we can't keep you here," Mort started, "But if you leave, you won't have a mouth to speak with," he said holding up a brand new voodoo doll up to his face. Apparently even Mort had a dark side, who knew?
"Very well," Wax said reluctantly, "where do we begin?" And with that Mort and Chip did their best to tell their story. Using a series of overdramatic behaviour, Mort described how Chip reacted upon finding out that he was a necromancer. Chip then told his tale of Mephisto and his knucklehead henchmen and how they kidnapped Ellie. Wax sat still and took in every last word. For fear of his head exploding from all the information, Mort checked in with Wax frequently. Too frequently in fact. Frequently enough that Wax managed to shoot Mort in the neck with a tranquilizer he had stashed in a hidden blow-dart gun tucked into his pants. That was by far the niftiest thing Chip had seen, and in an unprecedented expression of personality, Marco and Chip high-fived.
"So what might that be then?" Marco asked referring to the human skin bound book nestled on the table next to the couch between a copy of *Harry Potter* and *Twilight.*
"Oh, that. That's everything we need in order to kill the demon," Chip said nonchalantly.
"If you possess such power, why have you not harnessed it?"

"Have you seen how thick that is? It would take hours, no, days to read it. We only just got it."
"Ah!" Wax gasped. "Would you perhaps be keen to me reading it then?" Chip eyeballed him for a second.
"Sure. But you're not going anywhere with it. In fact, I think you're gonna be our new roommate until we can figure you what to do next. And no talking with your cult thing." That last detail was more important than Chip could comprehend.
"But I must communicate with them! They'll question my whereabouts, send another assassin should I not report back."
"Hmm." Chip thought, "I dunno. We'll just have some radio silence for the time being. But get crackin' on that book. We don't have a lot of time. I really, really want to find Ellie. I have to," He added.
"She means a lot to you?" Wax questioned.
"Uhh, yeah. She's my girlfriend," Chip snarked.
"I've never loved," Marco started, big surprise Chip thought, "But I understand its importance and nobility." That was bordering on sweet, which made Chip felt strangely awkward.
"Yeah, thanks?" Chip questioned awkwardly.
Clearing his throat, Marco turned to head down the hall, "Very well, I will let you know what I find out. Until then, I bid you farewell," He added.
"Marco?"
"Yes?"
"You talk weird."
"Aye, I know."
It was not part of the order's code or manifest that they taught in Olde English, or forced their members to speak as such, rather it was Marco Wax's choice. He'd always spoken like he was in a Shakespearean play, he thought it made him seem somehow more intimidating or intelligent, or both. Anyway, even his elder's thought it was strange. It was part of the reason they sent him on this mission. Frankly, he annoyed them and made some of them feel uncomfortable.

Life goes on, as they say. Chip had no idea what that was meant to mean or how it applied to him in this particular instance, nevertheless, it was the first saying that came to mind as he stood in his living room with an unconscious Bill and a drooling passed out Mort who indecently still had the blow dart sticking from his neck. Chip plucked it out and Mort's body flinched, almost as if he liked it. Chip shuttered. He sat on the couch and began to think about everything. His whole mission had originated because he wanted to save Ellie, but he'd barely thought of her in the past few hours. He hadn't had the time, really. But now he wondered if she was alright, if she was hurt, hell if she was even alive. Naturally, these thoughts made him sad.

Sadness wasn't a very good thing to be at the current, in fact, it was probably the least useful thing to be. He needed to change his mindset, for Ellie's sake. And so, just as he thought it, he did. He was a necromancer for Christ's sake, and on top of that he just gained all the knowledge he'd ever need to be a good one. He thought of all the powers he might possibly possess. He already knew of the green magic beam things, but what else? A wave of excitement invaded his body like an Egyptian scarab burrowing itself into his flesh.

What, they weren't just fancy pieces of jewellery. That was just a front - a Trojan horse before the Trojans. All those Greeks did was take credit when in reality it was the Egyptians who disguised the beetles as gems via magic and sent them to their foes to be feasted on. If truth be told, it was funny as hell.

The local cemetery wasn't a place that too many people hung out, especially in the middle of the day. It was dead (Pardon the pun), and it made for the perfect opportunity to test some things out, like raising the dead. It seemed like it'd be necromancer 101, but he'd only done it once, very poorly might he add. He chose a plot way in the back, away from anybody that might stumble through the graveyard hoping to talk to a long lost loved one. Talking to a tombstone was perfectly normal and acceptable by societies standards, talking to the reanimated corpse of a loved one who had been dead for years, wasn't.

Chip made sure to find a grave that would have no visitors. Victor Lampard, died 1932. Surely he had no living relatives swinging by for a surprise visit. It was time to see what he could do. Standing above the grave, Chip closed his eyes and concentrated. When he raised the hobo, it came almost naturally, but it was probably beginners luck and that sort of success wouldn't happen again. He may have gotten all the knowledge of being a master of the undead imbued within him, but he'd be damned if he knew how it worked. The green bolts out of his hand just sort of happened when he needed it to, and maybe that's how it worked. Maybe if he were in distress he'd be able to call upon the dead to aid him, or something. He didn't know. Maybe Mr. Lampard didn't have a body, maybe he was lost at sea, or sat on by an elephant and there was no body to bury, so there was no body to resurrect. You'd think there'd be a body at a cemetery to practice on. Chip plopped to the ground.

"Pardon me. I think I'm lost," said a voice from behind him.

The dead can talk. Who knew?

Meanwhile, back at the apartment, Marco Wax held a conference with the elders of his order in Mort's bedroom. It was all very clandestine, that is, until Mort awoke from his tranq induced slumber and barged into the room. His original intention wasn't to crash the party, so to speak, but rather find his warm and cozy bed. Instead, he did crash the conference, and boy what a scene he made.

The door swung open knocking Wax in the back, sending him stumbling, causing the astral projection to flutter slightly in the air. When the picture came back, the grandmaster of the order stood upside down and backwards. He very much resembled a Mr. Potato head assembled by a toddler. Of course, he had no

idea and incessantly asked what was going on. Mort, still oblivious to the situation tripped over Marco's leg and crashed into his bed. The effects of the dart clearly hadn't worn off completely, therefore it took him a second further to figure out what was going on.
"Hmm... Who's this?" He mumbled
"Uhh, nothing, nobody," Wax clamoured.
"Ah... Who's the art project?" He said referring to the Grandmaster.
"What? There's nothing," Wax said blatantly lying, frantically trying to end the call.
"What do you mean nothing? What's going on?" The projection cried in offence.
Snapping into the realization of what was going on, Mort shot up. He fumbled around his pocket for a second and produced the doll. He waved it directly at Wax, as if to say *Turn that thing off or you won't have a mouth, and maybe other things might go missing too*. Wax instantly felt nauseous.
"What's going on, Marco?" The make-shift man said.
"The fire has caught the star," Marco repeated in monotone, and instantly the figure vanished from the air. Code words and such, they go hand in hand with a secret ancient organization.
"Mind telling me what that was, Marco?" Mort said rather seriously.
"I knew I was forgetting something," He replied nodding to the voodoo doll.
"Yup. You're stupid. Now, what was that, and where's Chip? Did you kill him?! Where's his body? You ate him, you animal!" Mort asked then answered. He squeaked in worry and Wax turned his head.
"No, he's gone out," Wax said.
"Oh," said Mort, "Wait, then you betrayed his trust! I would have preferred you ate him. He's a sensitive boy - he may not recover from this," he said in genuine worry, which Wax had a very difficult time believing. He wasn't used to many people

with emotional and mental swings like Mort was prone to. It was bothersome.
"Yes, and in my defence, they contacted me. I don't have the ability to make that astral call. I lack the power. I merely send out a mental signal and they respond," Wax admitted, and it was the truth. He had entered the bedroom with every intention of studying the book, but once he was alone, the message came through. They weren't on call long before Mort burst in.
"Well, what did you tell him then?" Mort asked.
"Nothing."
"You're lying."
"I'm forbidden to lie."
"Forbidden forshmidden. You told him everything, didn't you? I'm going to have to kill you now, aren't I? Man, it's been like two weeks since I killed a guy. It was going so good," said Mort. Wax's head turned on its side. *He* killed somebody, Marco thought.
"That won't be necessary," Wax started, "besides, to my knowledge of voodoo, a vessel cannot kill, only harm."
"Yeah, sure. But if I break your legs I can just stab you in the throat," Mort said with a smile.
"Point taken," Wax replied.
"So, I'll ask you again. What did you tell him."
"I swear to you, witch doctor, nothing. You interrupted us before I could report anything. I don't believe I would have regardless," Wax confided.
"You wouldn't rat out a couple of guys you just met to your ancient order thing? Isn't that guy like your father?" Mort questioned.
"He is... more like my grandfather. But yes, I feel I owe a debt to the Djinn you call Bill." Wax felt as though he sat in a confessional, with the strangest priest in existence.
"A debt?"
"Mortimer, I killed Bill's brother."
Mort gasped over dramatically.

# CHAPTER 8

A strange day barely began to scratch the surface of describing Ellie's day, and it's only gotten stranger. Ever since finding out that butterflies were produced by her butt and flowers came from her tears, she'd been afraid to use any other bodily functions. She hadn't coughed or sneezed for fear that pollen might shoot from her face-holes and turn the side of a building into a tree, or something just as nonsensical. It was pretty bad, made worse by the fact that she really, really had to pee. But she wouldn't, she couldn't, and not just because of what might happen, but being naked in a public bathroom seemed a good way to get arrested. Just look at George Michael.

Nevertheless, Ellie managed to wander almost throughout the entire city, often having loose change tossed at her in varying amounts. Not to be rude, she picked it all up and thanked the generous people, even if they were sorely mistaken about her predicament. How are they to know that she'd just escaped from a demon and not actually homeless? As a result of her loose change gathering, she jingled as she walked, which was sort of relaxing in a sense. She still had to pee though, thankfully she was within sight of her apartment.

She thought of heading to Chip's place, but dismissed it. Chances are Mort was there, and given her current wardrobe situation, it would have been weird. And what if they weren't there? Hell, what if that demon bastard got to them? Wait, what if that smarmy arse is waiting in her apartment right now. It's probably best she doesn't go back there just yet.

But she could really use something else to wear - the cheese powder stains were starting to make her feel ill. She never could stand the smell of cheese. No cheese in particular,

though, some were most definitely worse; Brie comes to mind, naturally, there's Limburger, which was ironically enough the name of an uncle of hers who use to smell quite badly. Even more ironic, he fancied an assortment of cheeses to be a part of his daily diet. Come to think of it, that might be where her minor phobia of cheese and cheese related things came from.
Ellie decided it was probably best to avoid all familiar habitats, for now. Turning on her heels to head away from her apartment, she bumped into a fairly attractive woman, to whom she apologized for the collision. However, the stunning creature merely stood there watching her from beneath gigantic sunglasses and did not react. Ellie found this to be rather rude, and perhaps even made a face that exhibited her thoughts. In an attempt to shuffle on past the woman, Ellie was met by her moves being mimicked. Something was amiss. Upper-class women don't play games like this, she thought, they'd snarl or snicker, or scowl, or some other *s* word that demonstrates displeasure. Instead, this woman appeared to be acting very child-like, and there's a very good reason for that.
Forest nymphs, like most creatures, had to adapt to the ever-changing world around them. They slowly migrated from trees and flowers to blending into cityscapes. Of course, not all of them have evolved, just the ones close to cities or whose homes have been encroached upon by urban developments. They weren't bitter however, they were of a cheery disposition no matter what the situation which was fantastic at parties, but bothersome at and awkward, and sometimes downright insulting at funerals.
If it wasn't clear, the woman standing in Ellie's path happened to be one of those nymphs, now called a city nymph. They weren't very clever with their names, but everybody has their strengths. The creature lowered her sunglasses to reveal a pair of enormous black eyes, much like you'd find on a praying mantis. They swirled with strands of green and were truly mesmerizing. Well, they were for a moment before reality

kicked into Ellie's brain and she let out a shriek of disgust and fear. The nymph reacted as well, rearing back from the noise, which seemed to physically hurt her, which in turn made Ellie feel sad for no apparent reason.

"I'm sorry," Ellie said, not being sure why she apologize for being afraid of something frightening.

"It's okay," The nymph started, "I - We - don't like when you're in pain," She finished adding slightly to Ellie's fear.

"We?" She questioned.

"Yes."

"Who is we?"

"The forest realm."

"Right," said Ellie, not knowing what else to say.

"You believe me?" The nymph asked.

"Sure, why not? It's been one of those days, ya know?" The nymph nodded in understanding.

"You can't be here, it's not safe," The gorgeous creature said leaning in close. Ellie nodded.

"Where can I go?" Ellie asked. She literally had nowhere else to go. Her apartment was probably, at the very least, being watched. She didn't know if Chip was home, let alone alive, and again or the very least, being watched. She could either tell this nymph to go bugger off and wander around until she starved, got arrested, or exploded from having to pee. Or, she could follow this woman-thing and see where that lead.

She chose the latter. The woman extended her arm, much like a prom date would and Ellie latched on expecting to be wisped away, or something just as magical. None of that happened, the two merely walked strangely down the street arm in arm. Is it weird to think that this was the weirdest to happen to her today, because that's exactly what she thought. Despite all the looks and the dirty glances, she needed to find safety, and a place to stay, potentially shower, get fresh clothes, all the things a girl absolutely needs after a day like hers.

Oooh, a bubble bath, some candles, and a bottle of wine would do the trick.
Although she felt safer with the nymph who eventually introduced herself as Sterling, she couldn't help but feel in some kind of danger. It wasn't an imminent sort of danger, but a danger in the sense that something bad was going to happen very shortly. Ellie glanced over her shoulder and thought at the very least she was being watched.
She was, in fact, being watched.

Sterling led her through the city's core, much the way she had already gone. She could tell by the occasional stray purple butterfly fluttering about the smoggy air. Sadly, they didn't live long in this sort of environment. They either choked on the pollution, got hit by something, or eaten by something else, and for this Ellie felt quite awful. She was responsible for them after all, she gave them life and did nothing while they just got obliterated, some of them even looked like they had purpose. At any rate, she stopped producing them from her butt, which was a positive.
Ellie didn't often get attached to things, not like other girls. Sure she had a minor fit of excitement when she saw a puppy, but who didn't? They say even Vlad the Impaler had a soft spot for puppies, they were the only creatures he wouldn’t stick a pole through.
Despite Ellie's usual indifference, she felt strangely attached to natural life; the butterflies, the nymph, hell, the bloody pigeons, and even the trees. The trees for Christ's sake. It was made even worse when the couple walked into a large stone building on 37th street. The outside of the building looked like nothing special, just another structure amongst other structures. However, it did have one defining feature that was only noticeable once inside: a glass roof. Oh, and the vast amounts of mystical creatures running around the place. That was sort of unique as well.

Among said creatures were nymphs, like Sterling, fairies, seemingly sentient plant life, and things that Ellie could not, perhaps even would not be able to conceive mentally. Regardless of what everything around her was, she could feel all their life forces flowing throughout the room. It was all very overwhelming. She had to take a knee. Sterling didn't even recognize that her new friend had stopped walking, and continued on introducing her to the other things in the room, which earned her several curious glances. Around the 5th look, she realized that Ellie had no longer been with her and went back to fetch her from the ground.
"C'mon, mum. What are you doing?"Said Sterling as she lifted Ellie to her feet.
"I'm sorry, I just got a little light headed," Ellie replied, still dizzy from everything.
"It's ok. It happens. It's a lot to take in," Sterling mentioned.
"Yeah, and I don't even know what *it* is," Confessed Ellie.
"You don't?"
"Nope. What is all this, Sterling?"
"This is headquarters. Your new home, mum."
"Home?" Ellie asked, "mum?" She finished.
"Oh, yes. You come along one every few hundred years. You always look the same, but you never remember. I guess the ceremony takes a lot out of you," Sterling said, confusing Ellie much more than she already was. Her head began to hurt.
"Ok, first off. What? Second off, what the hell? Thirdly, my head hurts, and lastly what the crap is that?" Ellie said in reference to a large swirling purple mass that was practically the most beautiful thing she'd ever seen.
"Oh, that. Well, Mum, that's a portal to the glade. It's a slice of paradise tucked away in the middle of Central Park. Nobody can enter except for creatures like us," Sterling said with a smile. "It's where we're headed next," she said grabbing Ellie under the arm.

“Interesting. And about this ceremony… How do you know so much?” Ellie asked.
" I was there the last time, as just a little sprite. It was beautiful. Every 200 years you come back, sometimes you get a little lost, but we help you find your way. You're here to cleanse and renew."
"Cleanse and renew what?"
"Everything. Nature, time, everything that makes our funny little world spin."
"Huh?" Ellie questioned, "Why me... and still, what?"
"Mum, the ceremony will cleanse the world of a natural decay. Without it, everything would simply die off. All the plants would wither and die, or so the story goes. You're our saviour."
"Right. Why do you keep calling me mum?" Ellie thought it was a legit question.
"Because, you are mum - Mother Nature." Ellie thought her head might explode.

# CHAPTER 9

The cemetery: it's meant to be a place of reflection, mourning, and dancing on the graves of your enemy - or mother depending on your upbringing. What it's not meant for, and even though it's been tried countless times, is raising the dead. Usually that would be the ideal place, however corpses often come out like Victor Lampard: Old, withery, decomposed, the normal things one would expect. When looking to raise the dead, it's best left to sneaking into morgues after hours, or killing the person you plan to reanimate. Nevertheless, a cemetery is where Chip went, and the walking corpse of a 150-year-old is what he got. To be fair, he didn't exactly expect it to work. But here he is.

"So, Victor was it?" Chip asked in an attempt to make small talk.

"Yes," The corpse answered.

"Right. And how did you just sneak up on me like that?" Chip asked, referring to magically appearing corpse.

"I don't know. I've never been resurrected before, I thought you could tell me."

"Nope. No idea. I'm new to this too," Chip said.

"I see," said Victor, "A conundrum then."

"Seems that way. And even worse, I really don't know what to do with you now that you're here. I haven't really thought this through," Chip said as he slouched against Lampard's tombstone.

"I don't know either. I was kind of hoping you would send me back. I didn't like living the first time," Victor said standing over top of Chip.

Great, a suicidal corpse, Chip thought. He smiled at Victor and shrugged. He didn't know how to send him back. Maybe it was on some sort of timer or something and the body would just eventually crumble and the spirit would head back to wherever spirits hung out.
Just then, an idea hit Chip. "I banish you!" Chip shouted springing to his feet. It really wasn't a good idea.
"Anything?" Chip added.
"No," said Victor.
"I can't just leave you here and go home, can I?" Chip asked half to himself.
"You can do whatever, I think. Somehow, I think I'm bound to you and your orders," Victor chimed in.
"What? I thought you didn't know anything about anything." Chip raised an eyebrow.
"It's more a feeling than anything. I feel connected to you, I'd imagine that's how a baby feels about its mother. I didn't have a mother who loved me. This is a nice feeling," Victor confessed.
"I see. Well, I don't think I'm ready to be a parent," Chip said, "Sorry," He added.
"Neither was my mother. You know, I had a lousy childhood. My mum would send me around the neighbourhood asking the men if they'd like to ride the merry-go-round for a dollar, and -"
"Whoa! I didn't ask for your life story, man. Some people," Chip interrupted, but before he could turn around, Victor's spirit just simply vanished. There was seemingly no reason for it, but it left behind a stinking rotting corpse. Chip threw up in his mouth. One thing was for certain, dead things smell, but strangely dead things with a soul, or a spirit don't. It was interesting. Now, if only Chip could figure out how to control the whole summoning and banishing thing, he'd be golden.
Feeling satisfied with getting one corpse back to the land of the living after just one day of practice (if it can even be called

that), Chip decided to head back home. He wasn't overly sure how wise it was of him to leave Marco alone in the apartment with Mort unconscious. Sometimes he felt he was overly trusting; the time he lent his credit card to a complete stranger comes to mind. He did however present Chip with a very compelling argument consisting of facts, valid points, and a varying degree of diagrams. Unfortunately, the man wasn't dying from an extremely rare disease that requires him to spend vast amounts of money on senseless things.

After that, Chip felt as though he was spending far too much time with Mort. Nevertheless, he felt confident that Marco wouldn't try anything funny, he knew what Chip was potentially capable of... one day. That thought rapidly left his mind though when he walked through the door to find Marco tied to the same chair he was before, with a small ficus smacking him repeatedly in the face. Suffice it to say, Wax didn't look overly amused.

"Right. And what's going on?" Said Chip as he slowly closed the front door behind him.

Mort, standing behind the kitchen counter shrouded in shadows, poked his head at Chip with a flashlight. "I've animated that ficus to smack him in the face for all eternity," he said with a strange malice.

"Why...?" Chip asked while eyeballing the situation.

"Because, Chip..." Mort started all ominous like, "he killed Bill's brother, and probably put him in that coma on purpose!" He shouted leaping from the shadows pointing the light right in Wax's face.

"is that true?" Chip asked Marco. He pushed Mort out of the way.

"Yes and no," he said.

"C'mon, I trusted you. Talk to me," Chip pleaded.

"Well, Yes. I did kill his brother. But the coma wasn't me. He brought that upon himself. As I said prior, he's old. His power is fading."

"Wait, you actually killed his brother? Does Bill know that?" Chip said stroking the comatose Bill's hair.
"I fear he does. It may have been his breaking point. For that, I am truly sorry," Marco said sounding somewhat convincing.
"Sorry? Why do you care?" Chip asked.
"I have a connection with him now, Chip... He and I are one, in some way. I can understand his loss to a degree, and I feel guilty, which is an emotion I am all but forbidden to feel," Confessed Wax. Guilt he can ignore, but pride, he flaunts in a strange and subtle sort of way.
"Go on," Mort chimed in, "tell him what you were doing when I walked in on you. Go on, man up!" He finished.
"What happened?" Chip asked. Marco looked up with some disappointment on his face.
"You said you wouldn't mention that, Mortimer," Marco shot back to Mort.
"Yeah, well..," said Mort, swiftly proceeded by the always sophisticated tongue out fart noise. Oddly enough, it was repeated by Marco. That shut Mort up and sent Chip stumbling backwards as well.
"Err, my apologies," Wax said, "yes, one of my elder's, a grandmaster called via astral projection shortly after you left," He admitted rather nonchalantly, maybe even too nonchalantly.
"What did you tell him?" Chip panicked, he'd been doing that more and more lately, but not as much as he expected to be fair. Considering the circumstance, he'd remained rather calm, excluding the first time he met Bill, of course. That was awkward. But since then he'd been a house of sticks and loosely bundled twine. Bricks were still too sturdy to define his psyche.
"Nothing. Mortimer barged in scrambling the call before we could even greet one another. He must know something is amiss though. He will try to contact me again, of that I am sure," he said all pretentious like.

"You have to talk to him," Chip said, which was responded with a sharp "What" from both Mort and Marco. They eyeballed each other rather unkindly.
"Yeah. You have to call him back with your asteroid project and tell him you've killed me," Chip said feeling quite proud of his genius.
"That will never work," Wax said sternly, almost too sternly.
"And why not?" Asked Chip.
"He'll know I'm lying. He's very old and very wise, he's picked out a lie from a monk sworn to honesty. I would be no match for his guile."
"Nah, do it anyway." And with the compelling argument, Marco decided he was in no position to launch a dispute. He far preferred how things were done back at The Order. If a complaint was launched, it would have to go through three different scribes, each referencing and cross referencing ancient rules and laws before determining whether or not the request was breaking any of the said laws or rules. After that it went to the lowest ranking elder to determine if the complaint was worthy. He would then pass it off to the next ranking member to see if could be resolved with him. Should the complaint not be resolved, it would reach this highest ranking member who would often mistake the papyrus for a napkin and throw it in the bin after dabbing mustard from the corner of his mouth. It was a system that these primitive and seemingly feral beings could not grasp.
And so Marco sent the beacon out, and shortly after a floating blue figure materialized into thin air. Mort and Chip ducked behind the couch out of view with Mort making a remark about Mr. Potato Head which confused Chip. The conversation between Marco and his elder lasted just over five minutes, which to both Chip and Mort, seemed grossly underwhelming. Nevertheless, the two popped up from behind the couch.

"So?" Chip asked, "is it done? Do they think I'm dead?" Surprisingly, Chip remembered nothing after seeing the blue figure.
"More importantly, why don't I remember if I know if they think I'm dead?" Chip spat out.
"Well, you don't remember because the elder wished you not to. Which of course means that he knows you're alive, that I'm cooperating with you, and he's sent a team of highly trained assassins to kill you and exile me to 50 years of torture before eventually killing me," Marco said with a smile. Nobody in the room knew he was smiling, including Marco. He'd never been so afraid in his entire life, including the time he met an incredibly bothered gargoyle brought to life by an ancient magic sent to kill him. Usually that would be no problem, except he had just been out of the shower and totally nude.
"How'd he know?" Said Chip in utter disbelief.
"I told you that he was wise, correct?"
"Yes."
"He didn't need his wisdom. We left the gigantic bearded Djinn lying unconscious on the couch," Marco finished.
"I see," started Chip, "so, we're screwed?"
"Not entirely. I think the three of us could make a fairly indomitable team." A twinkle sparked in his Marco Wax's eye as he said that.
"Abominable?! As in snowman?" Mort shouted out, though he really didn't need to. He was only inches from the conversation.
"What? No," Marco scoffed, "We'll need to work on him," he said softly to Chip, who nodded in agreement.
"And you too, Necromancer. We'll need to harness your power if we want to survive the near future," he said resting a hand on Chip's shoulder.
"Where do we start?" Asked an eager Chip.
"What do you know?" queried a curious Wax.
"Nothing," said a smiling Chip.

"Wonderful," Marcos said disheartened.

Training was never a word that struck the fancy of Chip or Mortimer. It often meant learning and work, two words that both of them avoided. It was the main factor in both of them being underachievers in real life, before all this supernatural nonsense that barged into their lives like a bull at a red scarf. Naturally, Mort had an easier time with the transition to their current predicament, after all, he had been at the voodoo game for some time, approximately five to seven years. He couldn't remember exactly. Actually his earliest memory of being able to control the spirits was when he walked into the wrong storefront thinking it was a chicken shop. They had chickens, but they weren't to eat. His life was never really the same after interrupting that Haitian sacrificial ceremony.
But as many things in Mort's life, he embraced it for what it was and lived with it, that was until he met Bill, and well, that's a story for another time. Needless to say, Mort had a firm grasp on the situation, and so before too long it was he and Marco teaming up to train Chip.
The training in question was nothing out of the ordinary, more or less the basics on day one. How to properly harness the ability to raise the dead and have them do your bidding. Using the power of souls to project powerful beams of energy from one's hands - he sort had that covered, though he didn't know how he had. That bit of training nearly destroyed the apartment but it was salvageable. Mort had done worse when he attempted to make cheese fondue. The feisty ficus took a hit, too, which caused a spot of joy to swell up in Marco.
Although Chip had a bit of a grasp, he struggled with a lot of the why, which ultimately hindered his progress on the how. When Marco asked him to bring a dead rat in the alley below to life, Chip asked why, when Marco didn't give a satisfactory answer, Chip got stage fright and the rat remained dead. The saddest part of the situation was that Chip wasn't even asking

the right why's. Honestly, who cares about why Wax wanted the rat alive, the better question would have been, "Why can I do this, it makes no sense in our tangible world, and this whole thing is entirely absurd." Marco was thankful he hadn't gotten around to asking that question. He wouldn't like the answer.

"Wait a second," Chip said while staring at the dead rat. "Why am I able to do this? How does it make sense?" Right on cue.

Marco sighed, "You're not going to like the answer, Chip," he said.

"Hit me with it," He answered sternly.

"You are death," Wax stated, very matter of fact as well.

"Hmm? 'Scuse me?"

"According to the prophecy Death himself picks a vessel to imbue with his power. Nobody knows the reason for it, and why it seems so random with no set time frame. Some say it has to do with the Earths renewal, but others say even that is a myth. It's all very mysterious, but the general consensus is that the only being as old as time has his hand in it," Chip just nodded along blindly. He understood approximately 1% of that answer. However, with his mind wandering he noticed something scratching at his leg. He looked down and yelped like a school girl seeing a spider in her shoe.

Looking up at him with misting green eyes was the rat, and about a dozen cockroaches, accompanied by a cat with a tire mark over its stomach, and a bird with one wing that only flew in circles just above Mort's head.

"Heh, look at that," Marco said.

"I'm watching it," Mort said, eyeballing the bird just above his head.

"Whoa," Chip uttered as he scanned his small army of dead things that just looked at him, albeit with a degree of attentiveness.

"Hey, guys..." Mort started, "Can dead things - " The bird pooped on his head, "poop."

If one thing was learned it was that dead things can indeed poop.
Although the past day and a bit have been very strange, bordering on the bizarre, having been filled with mysticism, voodoo, magic, and an assortment of other inexplicable events, it was nothing compared to what Chip, Marco, and Mort found once they returned to the apartment. The three walked through the door very chummy, despite trying to kill one another mere hours previous, but what they saw both spooked and surprised the trio. A man. But something about him seemed out of place, and it wasn't just because he was in the locked apartment. It also wasn't the fact that he stood over Bills body, just watching him with a crane-like neck, though, if truth be told, that didn't help the matter.
There was just something odd about him. There was no other way to put it. Odder still was that a trained assassin, a voodoo witch doctor, and a necromancer stood quietly for fear of disturbing him. Chip cleared his throat which caused the stork necked man to tilt his head slightly. He whispered something under his breath.
"Watch out," The man said to nobody.
"What?" Chip spoke out.
"The ficus, it’s going to hit your friend in the groin," The half burnt ficus hit Mort in the groin. He fell; Marco laughed.
"How did you... Wait, you sound familiar..,” Chip said inching forward.
"It's good to see that you didn't give up." The stranger said spinning.
"My name's Ick. It's nice to meet you, Chip,” he said extending his hand.
"Ok." Was all Chip could muster. Nothing should be able to surprise Chip at this point - after all, he'd seen many a thing, and will undoubtedly see many, many more. To Hell with it, he thought and extended his hand, this caused Ick to reel back as if Chip tried to hand him a piece of poo... or something.

"No, that's not what I had hoped that you'd do. No no no no, not at all. Not good." Ick turned away and rubbed his pointy chin.
"Um. Ok." Chip - a man of many words.
"No, this scenario plays out in an infinite amount of ways, Chip. And only the bad ones have you shaking my hand with no reservations about it," Ick said turning with a worrying look on his face.
"But, that's the polite thing to do... isn't it?" Chip asked questioning his entire upbringing, which oddly enough, didn't take that much time.
"Yes yes, polite. But you're missing the point, Chip. I have seen - I can see everything, and that right there," Ick pointed to Chips still outstretched hand, "that is all kinds of bad." Ick's voice went high. Higher than usual. A dog down the street began to bark incessantly. The two events may or may not be connected.
"So you're a what? Another Djinn?" Chip asked.
"No - oh God no. I'm not one of those swine."
Chip cleared his throat and nodded towards an unconscious Bill.
"Oh, yes, you're attached to that one, aren't you. My apologies. I'm sure he's alright."
"You don't know?" Chip raised an eyebrow.
"No. Djinn are unpredictable and when they enter the situation, things become...tricky."
"So... Maybe my handshake isn't that bad?"
"No, it's bad."
"Oh."
"Careful, Mr. Wax," Ick said out of nowhere.
"Huh?" Marco said from across the room.
"You're next." The ficus, like a homing missile, locked onto Marco's junk and smacked it with the mightiest force it could muster. Wax fell to the ground.
"Why does nobody listen to me?" Ick said to himself.

"Well, up until like yesterday I would have called you a crazy Mofo. But now, well, whatever." Chip answered, despite the question being, well, rhetorical.
"Hmm, yes, I suppose. Regardless, Chip. We have to talk. Alone," Ick said eyeballing the two men on the ground in the fetal position.
"Ok," Chip said. "Where should we - Oh." Before Chip could finish, he was whisked away to the roof of his apartment. "Of course. Why not," he said nonchalantly.
"Alright, Chip - you need to listen to me and listen close. The handshake means we need to make this incredibly quick. So, no, don't tie your shoes. And the text you'll get in about 10 seconds is just spam from your provider. Take what they're offering though, you'll need the long distance. Anyway. It's about your girlfriend, and Mephisto, and everything that's going on.
You've probably realized by now that I'm not like anything you've ever met. I'm the last of my kind, I'm a traveller between planes, and I can see all that is and all that ever will be. I had hoped we'd be long and fast friends, but sadly, that's not meant to be. Your handshake has doomed that." Chip looked at him intently, he doesn't think he'll ever shake another hand ever again. His cell phone buzzed - and he did notice his shoe untied.
"Stay focused. Chip, you have to help Ellie perform the ceremony. You can't back down, and you must be prepared. Never before has a necromancer and the Mother been as you are. It's a sign, and if I've seen the correct future then this is important for all of mankind. You and her will be the saviours of planet Earth. Mephisto will be put in his place for all eternity, and all you need to do is-" Suddenly, out of nowhere a temporal warp appeared behind Ick. That was odd in and of itself, but the large Cthulu-like monster with massive tentacles and more than a dozen eyes that grabbed Ick around the

stomach, pulling him through the vortex and into its mouth...
Well, that was really strange.
Chip tied his shoe and read his text. The unlimited long distance for an extra seven bucks a month was a really good deal. Calmly, he walked over to the stairwell and made his way down to his apartment. He walked through the door and saw Marco and Mortimer sitting on the couch with bags of frozen peas on their crotches. The ficus had been secured with several meters of duct tape - it writhed beneath. Chip could swear he heard it sigh.
"What happened? Where'd you go?" Mort asked.
Chip didn't answer. He just walked over to the chair adjacent the two swollen members and sat down. Mort and Marco exchanged looks and shrugged.
The scream comes in various forms. There's the shocked little yelp, and then there's a whimper. After that it goes up a degree to a pained yelled, or a jovial shout. After that comes terror. Most researchers had thought terror, or alternatively horror, produced the loudest and most blood-curdling screams known to man. However, the shriek let out by Chip dwarfed all other screams. Mort and Marco covered their ears, but when that wasn't enough they began to hold each other and rock quickly back and forth.
The scream lasted far too long. In fact, by all accounts Chip should have dropped dead by exploding lungs. His yell defied all laws of physics and nature. Six minutes and 40 seconds exactly is how long the scream lasted. And when he stopped, he looked over at Marco and Mort, who were still holding one another, but now starring back at Chip with a look on their face that could only be described as *impaid*: Impressed and afraid.
"Hey, where's Bill?" Chip asked as if nothing happened. The two blinked.
"On the floor behind the couch."
"Oh," Chip said, being satisfied with that answer.
"So... Chip old buddy..." Mort started, "what happened?"

"Hmm?" Chip replied.
"You know, with the skinny guy, kinda looked like a crane."
"Oh, Ick?"
"Yes."
"A vortex demon killed him on the roof. I think it ate him," Chip said sitting back flicking on the TV.

# CHAPTER 10

Mephisto paced anxiously in his chambers. From one wall to the next he walked an invisible line waiting for the call. It was silly, he was a demon, and not just any demon, but a former general in Satan's own army. They were so close that Mephisto used to call him Stan, or Luc (Short for Lucifer, clearly). But all that changed when Mephisto decided to take matters into his own hands in 2001 when he possessed George W. Bush and had his legion of demon soldiers possess the rest of the federal government to ensure his title as President of the United States. Strange, he still almost lost - people really didn't like Bush. Nevertheless, Mephisto had grown bored waiting for things to happen on Earth. The war between heaven and Hell was taking far too long, so he thought he'd jumpstart things.

As with most bloodthirsty animals, they simply cannot be domesticated, and trusting one was just about the dumbest thing one could do. Despite this, the King of Hell himself had a special place in his heart for Mephisto and made him his right-hand man. Satan saw something in him that reminded him of himself. That was a lot of pronouns. Nevertheless, Satan seemed to love the young, feisty demon. Which, turned out to be not so great, and looking back at it, Lucifer really didn't know why he liked somebody that reminded him of himself. Satan defected from Heaven and started his own domain - he really should have seen the same thing happening with Mephisto.

So Mephisto was banished from Hell. But unlike when angels are cast out of Heaven, demons tend to stay in contact, and Mephisto still has some access to the depth of the inferno, but not much. That's what made him a perfect choice for the Order of the Ancients. They didn't want to entirely deal with Hell, that was a little too scary. But a castaway demon with just a bit of access: Perfect.

On his 324th lap of the room, the call Mephisto had been waiting for came through. The blue light swirled and filled the previously dark orange room causing Mephisto to squint ever so slightly. He faced the fires of Hell, a little blue light shouldn't bother him; he'd been away from said fires for far too long.

"Master?" He hated calling anybody Master, but it was a stipulation of their stupid summoning. He still doesn't know why he agreed to it.

"Status update?" The hooded figure shrouded in blue answered.

"Umm. Everything is fine and dandy, sir." Mephisto lied. What? He's a demon.

"Why do you lie, Mephisto?" The figure asked.

"Well, I am a demon - but lie to you, noooooo never!" He said high pitched and sarcastically. He instantly regretted it as he was brought to his knee by an excruciating pain ripping its way through his body.

"Do you like the pain, demon?"

"No. Quite the opposite really." He still had his wit.

"Then I ask you again, why do you lie? Do you think we are stupid? Do you think we aren't following your progress?" The figure said angrily before releasing Mephisto from whatever spell was causing the pain.

"I'm sorry," Mephisto said reluctantly. "Things got a little out of control. She broke out, somehow."

"You assured us she was unaware of who she was and the power she possessed." The figure growled.

"Yeah, well... She was bound to discover it at some point. It just so happened that she found her power while being held in

my custody," Mephisto said with a shrug, lighting up a cigarette.
"Our patience are wearing thin, you foolish creature. Get her back and finish the job." The figure said with authority and ending the call abruptly.
The cigarette in Mephisto's lips promptly burned up as his entire body began to glow a bright red. He was pissed. Foolish creature? He'd show them one day - he'd show them all his true power. But first, he had to find mother nature and wipe her from the face of the Earth. He has the book, he has the information, he knows what to do. Going about it though, now that is a totally different story. Where is he going to find a butterfly with the ambition of a God, and what was that nonsense about true loves embrace being torn to shreds like a pulled pork sandwich? Okay, maybe he didn't know what to do after all. But he was going to figure it out.

Meanwhile, have you heard that books are hard? Well, not so much books, some books have pictures. It's the books with words that are the challenge, especially *Mother Nature and how to Destroy her.* At least that's what's going on in the mind of Bort. Who's Bort? A legitimate question. Bort happens to be the other half of Jort. Right, who might Jort be? Bort and Jort are the other halves of each other. That should clear up a thing or two.
Oh, it doesn't? Well then. Bort and Jort (no relation to Mort(imer))are the loyal-ish minions of Mephisto, affectionately referred to as the idiot brothers and are of some sort of Neanderthal descent. Bort, the older of the two by approximately two seconds, has happened his way upon Mephisto's glorious book. The book that holds all the clues to him taking over the world. The book was totally worthless in the hands of such a buffoon, especially due to the size of the wordage used, as aforementioned. Nevertheless, since Bort is currently holding the book, Jort naturally wants it from him.

Unbeknownst to poor Bort, Jort had noticed the second he had picked it up, and began to devise a plan in his own mind on how to get it from him. The plan did indeed go through several stages of evolution ranging from just grabbing it, to stabbing him in the back of the neck with anything sharp. However, the plan on which Jort landed was a simple, yet devious one.

Bort was happily thumbing away at the ancient unintelligible text, when in the background Jort happened to be gathering the materials he needs to snatch the book from Bort's grasp. The materials in question consist of the following: rope, a live chicken, two dice, a box that weighs approximately the same as the book he wants, and a lighter. Somehow, in that broken, demented, and incredibly slow brain, all of those objects fit together to construct a trap so devious that the Devil himself would be proud... and ultimately confused. It was time for him to set it in motion. He wanted that book. And he didn't even know why.

Slightly further down the villainous compound that looks suspiciously like a suburban bungalow in a room three doors on the right sat Mephisto, still seething about the conversation he had. To top it off, he had just run out of cigarettes. He was really regretting smoking 17 at a time. What? It's not like he's going to get cancer - he's a bloody demon. In fact, he really only smokes them for image reasons. Smoking is cool, and mysterious, and synonymous with being a total badass. At least in his mind it was. Though, he was really craving one - or twenty. But he absolutely wasn't addicted.

Nevertheless, as he sat alone contemplating his next move and organizing his demonic thoughts, he heard a bang, and what he swore was a cluck, followed by a blood-curdling scream. Truly, it sounded like being in the pits of Hell's torture cells. However, he wasn't in Hell's paradise rooms, as he called them. He was at 32 Meadowbrooke lane, in the master bedroom of a bungalow which doubled as a villainous compound. Mephisto immediately sprung to his feet and darted out of the double bay doors, which he thought was a nice touch, and continued into the living room, and what he saw was both beautiful and horrible.

Hanging by his feet from the ceiling was Bort. Hanging from his waist was Jort. Below them ran a half featherless chicken pecking away at a couple of dice. All that was left that needed to be discovered was the lighter and the decoy book, both of which lay on the coffee table below Bort and Jort. Mephisto stood in utter shock as the two dangled above his precious blueprints for world domination. In an almost slow motion effect, Meph jumped forward to save the book. Just as he reached the point below the brothers, the rope from the ceiling snapped sending close to 1000 pounds plummeting to the Earth. Mephisto, spiralling through the air grabbed the book and landed on the couch just a fraction of a second before the brothers crashed through the coffee table, and then through the hardwood floor into the basement of the house.

Mephisto sighed and clutched the book dearly to his chest. Down the hole lay the brothers atop one another in a tangled mess of hair and debris, and amongst them lay the lighter. Slow to move, Bort and Jort roll apart and onto their backs. Mephisto, at this point, was watching the two closely, when he noticed something being pulled from under Bort's tattered tunic - a book. Mephisto's eyes open wide, too wide in fact that one nearly popped from his head - human bodies, pfft, nothing more than weak meat sacks. He then turned his attention to the book in his cradle. It was not *Mother Nature and how to Destroy Her,* but rather *Martha Stewart's Cook Book* but without a slip cover.

Little known fact about Martha Stewart and her books - they're all bound in human skin. The details have always been a little unclear as to why, however it is suspected that it has something to do with Old God worship - which would explain a lot of things.

The human skin bound book in Mephisto's grasp, which of course wasn't the right human skin bound book, was cause for concern as the next thing that Bort did was reach for the lighter on the floor next to him. He flicked it a few times before the flame shot to life. He smiled and looked over at Jort, who was slowly coming back to reality - well, his reality anyway - and hovered the book over the open flame. The thought running through Bort's mind at that moment was this: If I can't have it, Jort REALLY can't have it.

He didn't even think about it being his master's when the flame met the fleshy tome, which when it did sent it alight in a matter of seconds. It burned green and erupted in a purple, foul-smelling cloud. It took a matter of seconds for the book to turn to nothing, which scared the living crap out of Bort and Jort. It also caused Mephisto's eye to finally fly out of his eye hole. Not caring about the eye, Mephisto turned a deep shade of red and jumped into the crater which was so shrouded in smoke that visibility was at zero. He came to a neat and tidy landing on the concrete floor. He scanned the area for signs of anything. First, he spotted the brothers cowering in a corner. They knew they were screwed.

Mephisto set his sights on the boys and made a B-line for them. He was going to end them. Tear Bort's limbs from his body and beat Jort with them. He was furious, and just as he raised his fiery fist in the air to swing, he felt something beneath his feet. It was a clinking sound, like that of a dagger or a sword. He paused for a moment and looked through the smog floating around his feet. He saw the slight glimmer of something under his foot. In one smooth motion, he flicked the object into the air and snatched it. It was indeed a dagger, quite intricately designed in fact. The blade had a design of which was unidentifiable to Mephisto, and within the designs were symbols that appeared to be an ancient language, again it was something Mephisto could not decipher. The hilt was golden, with specks of emerald strewn about it. It looked rather Earthy.

He twirled the dagger in his fingers, inspecting every inch of it, and the brothers took this moment to shimmy away. The bottom of the hilt featured a small latch, which Meph flicked open. When he did so, a trap door flung open and spat out a small scroll. Curious, Mephisto opened the incredibly old scroll, expecting to find some foreign or forgotten language, but in plain English, a simple statement read:

*In the case that you can't find the butterfly, or you're just too stupid to figure out the book, just stick her with this.*

# CHAPTER 11

If truth be told, and it often is, Ellie was dead terrified of everything that had happened in the past couple of days. Being kidnapped by a demon will do that. Even meeting some kind of woodland nymph can be scary, even if she was elegant and beautiful, though her eyes were still a bit strange. However things were definitely getting better, being Mother Earth does have its perks, like having every living thing - both known and unknown to man - waiting on her hand and foot. As well, she'd discovered that she could pretty much grow anything she wanted just by thinking about it. Grapes, apples, avocados...corn, whatever her heart desired would spring from the ground and then be harvested by the closest being.

She once even had a rabbit gnaw down an entire stalk of corn, then shuck it, and pluck off each individual kernel, place it in a bowl and nudge it over to her. It was adorable, if not time consuming. Despite her not really wanting the corn any longer, Ellie still ate it. That little bugger worked so hard, it just wouldn't have been fair.

Despite all of the good, there still was a smidge of the bad. She couldn't stop having things fly from her butt. The butterflies, man did they tickle, the flies, well, they just didn't sound right, but it was the fireflies were the worst. Talk about burning and discomfort. Anyway, she couldn't stop worrying what the other creatures were thinking when a butterfly magically appeared out of nowhere. Nobody said anything, but she could tell that there were murmurs floating around the Glade of her bowel misadventures.

The Glade itself was beautiful. Despite the weather outside, it was always warm and sunny within. The trees that made up the border of the area were full and various in their genus. There were huge maple trees, cushioned between even bigger evergreens and spruces. Beyond those, there were long hanging weeping willows, with branches so low it was as if they were trying to snatch something off the ground. They acted as curtains to the outside world. They were so thick and plentiful that nobody could move them through physical force - only the force of Ellie's will could spread the wisps. It was a perfect fortress from which she and her new followers could be safe as they prepared for the renewal ceremony.

"Mum." Sterling the nymph whispered quietly to Ellie. Ellie shook awake from a small nap. What? it was hard not to sleep in the sun in the middle of paradise. The two met eyes, and Sterling immediately wiped some crusty sleep gunk from Ellie's eye. That was gross.

"Yes, Sterling?" Ellie asked.

"We have a problem," Sterling answered. Ellie stared at her expecting more, but Sterling just stared back, but with a goofy grin. Everything was always okay with Sterling. Even the time she and the fire spirit had a bit too much cane sugar to eat (which is equivalent to tequila to these Earthy spirits), and he accidentally set her hair on fire. It was funny as Hell.

"Yes...Go on?" Ellie prompted her.

"The Butcher's on the loose."

"Excuse me?" Ellie said with a bright-eyed dumbfounded look on her face.

"Yes, The Butcher. He's most likely been sent from Hell, or Alaska, to cause havoc, destroy the good in the world, and probably get your attention." Sterling explained, still smiling. "It's your duty to stop her, Mum. Well, I guess it's more a responsibility you could ignore. Though, I don't know who else out there can stop him. In fact, I'm not sure there is anybody else. He's kind of invisible to the common folk out there. He'll just blend into the regular world, ripping and

tearing apart the souls of nymphs, faeries, spirits...But I suppo-" Ellie cut her rambling short.
"Okay, I get it. But how am I supposed to...kill?" Ellie paused and looked at Sterling to see if *kill* was the right word. Sterling nodded, "how am I supposed to kill something called The Butcher?"
"Hmm, I guess if I knew that, Mum, I could do it myself. Sadly, I don't know." Sterling's smile faded for a brief second, but then it sprung back on.
"Is there anybody who knows? Anything that knows?" Ellie asked.
"Well, there is one being that would know. Well, he knows everything, but rumour has it he's not available at the moment."
"Isn't that just great..," Ellie said rolling her eyes and slumping into her adirondack chair.
"Where is he?" Ellie added.
"Where is who?" Sterling asked.
"The Butcher." Ellie completed.
"Oh. Central Park."
"...We're in Central Park."
"Yup."
"Right."
"Okay."
"Let's go...?"
"Sure thing, Mum."
And with that slightly awkward exchange, Sterling wisped Ellie to her feet with her long, slender, magical hands. Of course, Ellie was completely and utterly unprepared for what she was getting into. It seemed like yesterday that she was mad at Chip for something stupid, and now she's Mother Earth. The thought of Chip almost stopped her in her tracks. How she missed him, and she was kind of angry at herself for not thinking of him really since she'd entered paradise. Last she saw him, he was trapped in some weird time bubble thing. She

didn't quite understand it, and if truth be told, she wasn't even sure if he was alive. Apparently, there were bigger things at stake - like a Butcher running around Central Park. Joy.

"So, let me get this straight... It just came out of a hole and ate him?" Mort asked Chip for the 4 billionth time.
"Yes," Chip said calmly for the 4 billion and one times.
"That is SO COOL!" Mort exclaimed. "Well, I mean not for the skinny seer dude... But still, makes for a badass story. Think he saw it coming?"
"Yes," Chip answered again.
"Phew. Shit's been cray, lately eh, Chip? Hey, where's Wax?" Mort asked, looking over his shoulder into the empty apartment.
"Dunno," Chip said. His vocabulary has been limited to a few syllables since the whole eating of Ick thing. It was like that time he found out that he was a necromancer and could control the dead, and shoot beams of green things from his hands. Oh, wait, that was like...yesterday.
"You've gone boring...er, Chip. I mean, you used to be fun...ish. And now you're like...not. Damnit, I lost the metaphor."
"Yes," Chip responded.
"Ahhhhhhhh!!" Mort screamed in Chips face, half out of frustration, and half trying to get a reaction from his best friend. He was unsuccessful, although Chip did flick a crumb of something off his shoulder that came from Mort's mouth.
Mort was just about to wind up for another round of screaming, and he was really gonna let him have it, like Jaws eating a T-Rex style of scream. But just has he inhaled, Marco came smashing through the front door, causing it to obliterate the ficus. Mort frowned and let out a little whimper, but then turned his attention to Wax, who was out of breath and clearly distraught.

"Uhh...You have to poop, Waxy?" Mort asked.
"What? No, shut up. Us assassins use the facilities once every three months. We can't afford to be left vulnerable like that." Wax paused to catch his breath. "We have bigger problems on our hands at the moment."
"Bigger than pooping only once every three months?" Mort asked.
"...Yes. Central Park - there's a creature known as The Butcher on the loose. He's no doubt one of Mephisto's soldiers."
"The Butcher?" Mort asked.
"Yes, his only goal is to find, torture, and kill spirits of goodness. He devours their souls. We have to stop him, for I fear there is nobody else that can," Wax said.
"Alrighty! Ya hear that Chipster? We're going on an adventure!"
"Joy," Chip said, sticking to his monosyllabic answers.
"Oh come on, not even Bilbo gets you excited? You've changed, man," Mort said turning his attention back to Wax. "Are we going like...right now?"
"Momentarily," Wax said meandering down the hallway.
"Where are you going?" Mort asked, standing in the middle of the living room, looking like a total buffoon for no reason other than that's how he always looks.
"It's been three months," Wax said looking straight ahead walking away from Mort.
"Oh," Mort said. "I think we're gonna have to move, Chip."
"Yes."Chip said looking over his shoulder down the hallway at the awful noises coming from their bathroom.
"Whattya say we let him catch up? I don't wanna be here when that door opens," Mort said tugging on a semi-lifeless Chip's arm. Chip nodded and stood from the couch.
The two left the apartment, leaving Marco to expel whatever demon was lurking in his bowels. Bowels which haven't been emptied in approximately 90 days - try to think about that for a second, and the pain and anguish that poor soul was

experiencing. Women giving birth to octuplets *might* understand the torment Wax had to go through every three months. It was so intense, the feeling of pain, mixed with that sweet relief; most beings couldn't comprehend it. The act of excretion... or pooping... for a member of The Order was a sacred and spiritual act which tested the limit of the member each and every time.

Wax's brow was drenched in sweat. His arms held so tense against the tiled wall that it began to crack and weep beneath his palms. Bits of porcelain tumbled and fell to the vinyl flooring with sharp and piercing tones, at least to Marco's ears it was. During that sacred time, all of his senses become heightened due to a presence that could be lurking around any corner waiting to pounce. Though, the noises and smell are usually enough to keep most creatures away. Most creatures: there is at least one known exception. The Babylonia Mongoose, who is immune to most everything in the universe, and multiverse, is known to be attracted to the act being performed by Marco Wax.

This was discovered in 1234 BC, when a member of the order had hit his 90 days in the field during a siege within Babylon. He was forced to take refuge in a nearby cave when he was attacked, mauled, and subsequently eaten by the Mongoose. Despite the member's best efforts, he perished before he could finish. A disgrace in the eyes of the Order. However, the Mongoose has not been seen since, much to the joy of Marco. 20 minutes in, he flushed for the first time. That was stage one of five. He might be a while, which wasn't a good thing, as Chip and Mort have very little idea what they're getting into with The Butcher.

"C'mon man," Mort said to Chip, nudging his shoulder as they walk down the street. The sidewalks are buzzing with all sorts. Businessmen too preoccupied with their phones to watch where they're going, bumping into everybody and giving the other a dirty look, as if to say "How dare you walk into me when I'm not watching where I'm going. I'm in a suit, therefore I'm important." It's always a laugh when two suits brush up against each other. There's always a slight pause, and a size up, as if each is trying to figure out who was the more important prick.

Besides the Wall street elite, there's the average Joe, a few skateboarders and cyclists, hot dog vendors, and of course, the supernatural, which are either invisible or hidden in plain sight. Mort can spot them no problem, Chip, well he's still working on that skill. Of course, they all know that Chip's a necromancer, which causes many to be cautious, and others to be angry. However, they will never attack - after all, having power over death is kind of a big deal.

"Cheer up. It's a good day to die out here," Mort said, trying to get Chip's attention through his fear of dying, which is a bit ironic when you think about it.

"Look, we're gonna put your new skills into action. Central park is ripe with dead things. God knows how many bodies are down there from various mob hits, gang murders, or just crazy wives killing and dumping their hubbies. You'll have no problem raising an army to take out that Butcher punk. You won't even have to get your hands dirty," Mort said trying to boost Chip's confidence.

"Yeah," Chip said. Hey, it was better than the usual *yes*.

It was about that moment when a small faerie flew square into Chip's forehead, knocking both of them to the ground, which to the average onlooker looked incredibly strange, as they just saw a man fly back like he took a punch from Mike Tyson. Even the suits took a second look, but more likely to internally criticize his casual jeans and t-shirt combo. Mort shook his head and mutter some profane exclamation under his breath before saying, "Are you okay?!" Chip nodded and said, "Yes." as usual. Mort looked at him with a bit of a surprise on his face, "Yeah...You...that's who I meant," he said before turning

back to the little faerie, who looked a lot like Tinkerbell, but far sexier, if that's even possible.
"Yes, yes I'm alri...Is that a necromancer?!" She said scurrying backwards in a panic, clearly fearful of the dejected Chip, who was just taken out by something no bigger than a dragonfly.
"Hey hey hey," Mort said quickly. "it's okay, he's a good guy, I promise. He's just a little flustered. He just saw a guy get eaten by some time monster popping out of a space vortex thingy."
"Oh, poor guy. I remember when I saw that for the first time. Really makes you think what else is lurking out there..." The faerie said, standing up and dusting herself off.
"Yeah, really...wait, what? That's terrifying!" Mort said, kind of bewildered. "I've never thought about it like that before. What else *is* out there?!" Mort started pacing on the sidewalk.
"Great, I happen to fly into a mute, and a paranoid nut job. Just my luck. If The Butcher wasn't enough." The faerie said, starting to walk away.
"Wait," Mort stopped, "The Butcher? You've seen him?"
"Yeah," said the faerie, stopping in her tracks.
"That's who were on our way to stop," Mort said.
"You two?" She said eyeballing the two of them. And then she burst out into uncontrollable laughter.
Mort stood there and watched, Chip sat on the ground still and watched. The laughter seemed to go on for too long, it was becoming faker and faker by the minute. Actually, it was just awkward with Mort looking around and tapping his foot. Chip even pursed his lips and shifted his eyes around.
"Oh, you're serious. Alright, I guess somebody's gotta try. At least he's a necromancer, and you're...whatever you are." The faerie said, wiping tears from her face.
"I'm a witch doctor. Ya know, voodoo... a voodoologist," Mort added, though the faerie didn't really care.

"Great," she said, oozing with sarcasm. "Come on then, I'll bring to him. But you'll have to carry me. Mopey McMopester over here broke my wing."
"Fair enough," Mort said picking the little pixie up in his palm. He sat her on his shoulder and said, "I'm Mortimer - Mort for short. Heh, that rhymed." The faerie rolled her eyes, "And Mopey is Chip."
"Chip and Mort? sweet Mother Earth, we're doomed. Anyway, I'm Ezmeralda , or Zed for short. Heh, that didn't rhyme. Idiot," Zed said holding on to Mort's shirt.
"Geeze, such attitude," Mort said.
"Yeah," Chip said, with a slight smirk.

# CHAPTER 12

The giant hole in the ground gave Meph an idea. As he stood below, looking up, it reminded him of one of the deepest, darkest pits of Hell; the part where not even demons linger for fear of what may happen. Truthfully, nothing was safe in the kitchen. After all, Hell's Kitchen got its name from somewhere, and Meph likes to attribute that to himself. He and The Butcher had a great relationship. Mephisto would lure unwitting souls into the pit for The Butcher to feast upon. It was glorious and gruesome, and short of Satan himself, Meph was the only one who could fight back should Butch (That's what Meph called him) decide he wanted his soul. They'd had it out a few times, but ultimately, Mephisto was too powerful, despite the sheer amount of lives The Butcher had within him. Another reason why Meph was so enthralled with Butch was due to his origins, or lack thereof. Some say he was there, mulling about in the pits of the underworld for centuries before the first of the fallen took up shop. It wasn't until almost 500 years after Satan began his reign that he even discovered Butch, and he thought the grotesque creature was nothing short of beautiful, however, that relationship ended, and he was once again forgotten about. Stan had the attention span of a gnat, to be honest, so once he got bored, he just left Butch up to his own devices, and let him play in the pit, which ultimately transformed into the kitchen.

When Meph found his way down there, even he felt a chill in the heat of Hell. Chains and hooks hung from the ceilings and walls. Flesh and sinew dangled from nearly every elevated bit of paraphernalia within the kitchen, and the smell, oh boy, the smell was that of tens of thousands of rotting corpses. The thought often made Meph hungry. But alas, the beast known as the Butcher was forgotten by Meph after he was expelled from the underworld. That was until he looked up from that hole in the floor to the bungalow above. He lit up a cigarette that he found in the basement. He knew he had a spare pack down there. He took a nice, long drag, blew the smoke straight up, and in the blink of an eye, was standing in the middle of Hell once again. It was just as he'd left it. Hot and smelly.

The flames grew around him, and the temperature was hot enough to turn lava into nothing more than a puddle of warm liquid. Expulsion meant very little to Meph, after all, there's no keeping the general of Hell out for long. He knew every inch of that place, secret hidey-holes that Stan forgot about centuries ago, and he used that to his advantage. He moved around disguised as nothing more than a lowly filth demon to throw off any scent or trace of him being there. He lurked and slithered around with the crowds of demons, every so often breaking off into a side path or an offshoot, making his way deeper and deeper into the depth of Hell until he eventually made his way to the Kitchen.

He moseyed on through the door and shed his masquerade, for which he was quite grateful. In the distance, he could see the giant beast of a demon, or whatever he truly was, hacking away at an unsuspecting soul. Ripping and tearing it limb from limb sending soul juice all over the place. Meph walked up behind him calmly, with his hands in his pocket.

"Aww, mate, that's the good stuff, right there," he said wiping some arrant spray from his shoulder. The Butcher stopped his hacking, leaving the disembodied being on his cutting board, squirming, still alive, and turned to face Meph.

"And here I thought you'd forgotten about me," Butch said.

"Aye, I did, if truth be told. But hey, let's forget that. I'm here now." The Butcher eyed him as he said that.

"Last I heard you were exiled," Butch said in a deep and echoing voice.

"Yeah, well, let's forget that for a second, too."
"I've heard the rumours. You've got some cohunes, and even bigger ones than I thought what with you coming back here," he said, slamming his enormous cleaver down on the writhing soul on the table, blinking it out of existence, and absorbing into his own body.
"Mmm, tasty. That one was a murderer up there. Killed a bunch of kids. I swear I can taste the lives he took too."
"That's great, big guy," Meph said, swallowing hard, turning up his nose at The Butcher choice in diet. Meph could never stomach souls. They always tasted off to him, but hey, to each their own, especially when that "own" is a 10ft Hell beast.
"Look, Butch. I'm not here to just say hi. I've got something for you, if you're interested."
"Go on," Butch said leaning back on his table.
"How would you like to head up to the surface?"
The Butcher grinned.

# CHAPTER 13

*Oh, The Humanity!* would be the perfect phrase to use at the sight of Central Park as Ellie and Sterling broke through the threshold of Paradise and into the Butcher's playground. All around them lay bodies of their fallen kin. Actually, fallen doesn't do the scene justice. A more apt description would be something along the lines of mauled, or perhaps decimated. Maybe no utterance of superlative and adjectives would be applicable.

There were limbs and gore hanging from trees, with a variety of goo's and globs of unidentifiable liquids pooling in the grass. Souls were being ripped from creatures before they even had the chance to take in what was happening. Some were brave and stood up to The Butcher, however, it was in vain, as even the strongest and boldest Earthen warriors were too meek to stand face to face with The Butcher and live to tell the tale. The size of a planet, he was to many of these nymphs and faeries, and it seemed as though he had a gravitation pull about him. Many of the beings that called the trees of Central Park home would find themselves in the path of destruction, and they were soon part of the horror taking place. All Ellie could do was stand and watch as her people died around her, albeit they'd only been her people for a very short while, and she didn't even know what a lot of them were, let alone know them personally. Still, it was a very upsetting scene. That was about the time she noticed the sky above began to turn black as night. The sun made every attempt to break through the ever swelling clouds, but alas, the sun could shine no more. The wind picked up with a ferocity never before seen in New York, and as Ellie stood at the tree line, watching the gargantuan, blood stained, reptilian skinned, wide mouth, and toothy-grinned demon tear innocent beings to pieces, she became overwhelmed with rage. A rage that was being translated into the current weather system - what with being Mother Earth and all, that was bound to happen.

However, despite the terrifying weather above, the demon known as The Butcher was unfazed. He continued to demolish everything in his way, that was until a bolt of lightning struck the ground just a few feet from him. That caught his attention.

Extreme conditions were nothing new to The Butcher, you know, with being in the deepest darkest pits of Hell, but lightning was new to him, and quite frankly, it excited him. He could feel it's energy in the mark it left, and for a few moments, it drew his attention from all the tasty souls waiting to be reaped. He wanted more of it, and just as he wished it, Ellie granted it - unbeknownst to her.

Another bolt hit the ground at The Butcher's feet, sending him airborne. Ellie had thought she nailed him head on with it, but little did she know, that when the smoke cleared, the only thing that emerged were glowing yellow eyes, energized by the power of the elements. The Butcher ignored all those around him and stopped swatting faeries as they flew too close. He stomped, making craters in the ground with every step, towards the lightning's power source.

As the wind increased, so did the obvious bubble of air growing around Ellie, which was protecting her from the surrounding elements. It was a target, and The Butcher was the arrow headed straight for her. He marched now, quicker, with more purpose than before, for her soul must be the most delectable of them all, and he was a demon with an insatiable appetite. The weather turned harsher the closer he strode, and the rain began to cut sideways, and hail the size of golf balls poured down, pelting The Butcher, but he was undeterred and unmoved by any of it. Ellie swallowed hard.

She didn't know what to do, plain and simple. She stood there, angry and afraid as this enormous being closed in on her. She trembled, but was determined not to show any signs of fear just in case he could smell it... or something. As The Butcher neared closer, she could see just how toothy his smile was. He had more teeth than anything, including a shark, would ever need, and they glowed as yellow as his eyes. He was excited, there was no doubt, and the more eager he became, the quicker he moved. The distance that he covered in the brief time since he noticed her was extraordinary. He strides were enormous, but his movements were deceiving. Before long, he stood just in front of poor Ellie, grinning and licking his lips.

"And what do we have here?" He said as a tennis ball sized chunk of hail shattered on the side of his face. He didn't flinch. Ellie didn't react. She didn't blink, she just stared into his mesmerizing eyes. She noticed something almost swimming behind them.

"What, cat's got your tongue, princess?" He said leaning in closer to her bubble. He reached out to grab her, but the bubble did its job and halted his progress. Curious, he thought, but also infuriating. He wanted her bad, like a fat kid wanted cupcakes. Regardless of the colossal cliché, it was true, and when he couldn't get her as easily as he wanted, a look of bewilderment crossed his face. With a twitch of his illuminated eye, his expression changed from curious, to furious.

He struck down fast and hard with his cleaver. The impact sent a shockwave from Ellie's bubble that spread for a dozen yards causing branches to snap from trees and grass to fly up in the air, only to be carried away by the powerful winds.

He struck again. And again, but to no avail. Ellie smirked, which probably wasn't the best thing she could have done. The Butcher took his cleaver in both hands and swung has hard as he could, and in one mighty motion came down on the very top of the force field. A thunderous bang erupted from the

impact, so loud in fact that it was nearly deafening to everything around. The creatures that lingered in the aftermath covered their ears and hit the ground, writhing from the noise.
When the smoke cleared, a tiny crack appeared the point of impact. It was nothing more than the smallest of pebble chips on a car windshield, but it was enough. The Butcher's smile stretched from ear to ear.
It was only a matter of time before he broke through her shield, and the mighty Butcher knew it, too. Licking his chops, he swung once again, this time with as much force as the other swings combined. The deafening crash rang out again, and the crack grew, like the web of a spider, slowly creepy and sprawling. Again he wound up, but just at his highest peak, about to slam the bubble, he was halted. He tried and tried, by his arms were suspended in mid-air by some unseen force. Frustration boiled within him like a tea kettle. Steam may have come out of his ears, it was hard to tell with all of the wind and such, but let's go with it.
It didn't take long for The Butcher to spot the issue, a little woodland nymph stood beside Ellie's force field. She had her hand outreached, and was using everything in her mystical being to halt The Butcher's final swing. She winced and contorted her face, clearly in pain, but this little nymph was determined to save her mother - even if it killed her.
She approached the grotesque, gore covered demon, which seemed to increase the strength of her hold. So much force was she exerting that her silky smooth skin began to crack and crumble. Blood, or something like it began to ooze from those fresh wounds. Soon after her ears and eyes began to leak the same fluid. But it was worth it. The Butcher began to take small steps backwards, which clearly pissed him right off. He fought against this strange little girl's power, but he seemed powerless to resist. He ducked his head, narrowed his glowing eyes, and dropped his shoulder in one last ditch effort to fight this nymph.

Resolute, the nymph was not going to lose this battle. She gathered every ounce of bravery, and power, and ultimately love, that she could muster and in one heavy breath, she forced everything she had at the demon. The force hit with such power that it sent the abomination soaring through the sky for hundreds of feet. He landed on the other side of the battlefield with incredible force, enough to crater the ground and send everything - living and dead - nearby airborne itself. She'd won.

The nymph turned to face Ellie, and despite the clear anguish and pain she was in, she was still able to squeeze out a smile before falling to her knees. Her big black eyes turned pale and glossy, with her blood streaming like tears from them. Ellie looked at her saviour, her friend on the ground in front of her. She could fight back the tears no longer, and began to weep softly for the sacrifice the nymph just made.

The winds died down, and Ellie's magic bubble dissipated just in time for her to catch the poor nymph in her arms. Still smiling, the carefree creature looked up at her and said,

"Everything for you, mum."

"But...But..." However, before Ellie could finish, an enormous blood stained cleaver fell from the sky obliterating the poor nymph from existence, narrowly missing Ellie herself.

"Sterling, No!" Ellie shouted grasping at thin air. As she stood up to see The Butcher making his way back to her, more determined than ever, she could see some of her own hair drifting in the wind. That bastard not only killed the sweetest thing since unicorns, but he made her layers uneven.

Two hours and forty-seven minutes of pure, unadulterated torture. That's another reason why The Order has the 90 days as a discipline. If a member can endure that expulsion of waste for that long, there would be no torture known to man, Heaven, or Hell, that will break a recruit. Hell, even surviving the aftermath is something to behold. The odour produced can literally peel paint off walls and kill trees. Rest in peace, ficus, rest in peace. Mort will be heartbroken, and Chip will be devastated by the state of the bathroom.

Marco attempted to flush, but it only caused the pipes in the apartment below to burst, and then back up which caused it to spray out of Chio's toilet bowl. It brought a whole new meaning to chocolate rain. He thought that might happen, which was why he took a towel out of the bathroom, closed the door and laid it down across the threshold. That should keep *most* of it in there. Besides, he didn't have time to dwell on the matters of plumbing and bathroom etiquette, he was already late for what is sure to be an epic battle.

The Butcher was nothing more than myth and lore within youth ranks of The Order, ghost stories if you will. He never put much thought into it, as some kids went as far as to say he was God in disguise, which would explain why nobody has ever seen him, or God. Surely it was a foolish notion, but the fact that The Butcher exists is a testament to the truth behind myth and legend. Nevertheless, Wax shot from the apartment, slamming the door behind him, leaving behind nothing but a wilted and dried up ficus plant, and a still unconscious Bill. Something to consider: can unconscious beings smell?

Chip, Mort, and Zed raced through the busy streets of New York, bumping shoulder with both common folk, and a surprising amount supernatural critters. Something big must be happening, the three of them thought. Zed had seen a bit of the devastation before she hauled ass out of the park, but surely it's gotten worse. The sky began to blacken, and the wind was nearly blowing her off of Mort's shoulder. She knew that could only mean one thing: Mother Earth is on the scene, and that worried the little faerie.

Mort couldn't help but notice the ever changing weather as well, of course though, that just blew the smell of street meat deeper into his nose. He began to salivate, which with the gale

force winds sent bits of drool over Zed. She was not pleased, and also a little concerned for her new ride. Nevertheless, Mort trudged on, resisting with all of his will power the delectable aroma of the delicious hot dogs.
Actually, he couldn't resist, and soon found himself stopped digging through his wallet for a couple of bucks in front of a rather rotund Italian hot dog vendor. It took Zed a second to realize they'd stopped moving - the wind had picked up so much that she couldn't tell which way was which. However, once she did realize they stopped, she grabbed Mort's ear, pinched his neck, and did everything she could to scold him.
Now, this made for an interesting sight to Pasquale, the hot dog guy. Naturally, he couldn't see the tiny faerie beating up the full grown man. No, all he saw was a guy swatting and swearing to himself crying in pain until Mort turned and left. Frankly, Pasquale didn't care how crazy the guy was, he was just sad that he'd missed another sale. Pasquale became too sad, perhaps the saddest hot dog vendor to have ever existed. Mort hoped he'd be alright.
Chip, on the other hand, hadn't noticed his entourage was no longer with him. He just wanted to get to Central Park, kill this Butcher guy, and be on his way. Strange thoughts, if truth be told, for a guy like Chip. Usually, he'd pee himself and run in the other direction. Don't mistake this attitude for confidence, no, it's more like apathy. He just didn't care anymore. The way he thought about it, his life was no longer his to live, and he figured with an infinite amount of timelines and universes, he'd be alive somewhere else, probably playing Nintendo and drinking a beer, not on his way to fight some Hellspawn.
So oblivious was Chip that he barely noticed the change in weather. When they made their way out of the apartment, the sun was shining and the weather was warm, however it took a near brick sized piece of hail to hit him in the neck - the neck of all places - for him to realize the change. It was also at that point that he realized he had made his way to the gates of

Central Park. He also came to the conclusion that he was alone, and his forehead suddenly hurt. What the Hell happened?
Slowly he slipped from his the daze he was in from seeing Ick eaten by that... time thingy. But still, even with the terrifying realizations he's just had, he didn't feel afraid - maybe the apathy is still kicking around, or maybe he'd finally grown a pair. Could this be the point in his story where he realizes his true potential and rises to become the hero he's meant to be? A thunderous crash roared out from the heart of the park. Chip may or may not have peed a little. Hero might be a bit of a stretch...
He stood at the entrance to Central Park as Mort and Zed rushed up behind him. In a single, and maybe their only, cool guy moment, Mort and Chip met eyes and nodded before taking their first stride over the threshold, entering the battlefield. Zed rolled her eyes. Another deafening bang rolled across the sky. Chip threw himself at Mort, who strangely expected that and caught him. Heroes.

He couldn't believe that they left without him. The foolishness of that voodoo priest and fledgling necromancer; they clearly weren't aware of what they were getting into and how badly they'll need him. Just as Mort and Chip had done early, Marco was thrashing his way through the busy New York streets, knocking many important looking fellows to the ground. Marco cared not however, they were nothing but peons to him, and by the state of the weather, he knew the situation was worse than he'd first thought. This was no regular battle, there was more to it.
He tore through the streets at near super-human speeds, dodging the hail that rained down from the Heavens above. It was quite a sight to those who could see it. He was nothing more than a whisper in the wind, passing by people and creatures alike at a speed that was generally reserved for sci-fi

movies. Just like those movies, when he moved, it wasn't as though he was travelling at the speed of light, but rather the world around him seemed to slow down. He could see every rain drop hover in the air, every particle of dirt. Literally everything. Sometimes things he doesn't want to see. Like the old lady with the...Nevermind.
Stopping to get his bearings for a brief second, he spotted Chip and Mort in the distance from behind a street light. And in the same instance that he stopped, he bolted back into action, weaving and dodging people, the weather, and dust towards the elegant iron gates.

Chip and company meandered through the carnage left behind by The Butcher and his rampage. There were carcasses, and that mysterious goo everywhere. Both Chip and Mort cautiously stepped around pretty much everything that wasn't grass. Zed, once again, rolled her eyes. She couldn't believe that the only two entities in all of the multiverses brave enough to stand up to the Hellbeast were these two idiots. You get what you pay for, she thought. And since she didn't pay anything, she pretty much expected to end up dead. It wasn't ideal, but it is what it is.
It really didn't take long for Chip and Mort to run into The Butcher. After all, he's in the vicinity of 10 feet tall and about 1000 pounds. He's kind of hard to miss, especially when there were thunderous crashes of horror ringing out through the sky. They more or less followed their ears, and the path of wreckage to the cause of it all, and when they did, there wasn't a may or may not - they full on shit themselves. The sight of something from the deepest pits of Hell wasn't something a human should be seeing, magical and mystical powers or not. Only the truly decrepit and sinful souls should ever see anything remotely close to The Butcher, let alone The Butcher himself. So, suffice it to say, the scene to human eyes was

nothing short of pure terror. It was literally the thing of which nightmares are made.

Carrying the tradition of not knowing what to do, Chip and Mort just sat and watched as the beast loomed over a poor and seemingly helpless soul who, despite it all, was standing tall and brave. They both knew she would be a goner in second. However, Zed had other plans.

"Oh, sweet crap." The *sweet* little faerie shouted out, "That's mum!" She took off from Mort's shoulder, broken wing and all and made her way towards the obviously doomed girl.

"Mum?" Mort questioned. "Frankly, I don't see the relation." He finished looking at Chip, who took a page from Zed and rolled his eyes.

Unfortunately for Zed, her wings didn't have much power, and soon after takeoff, she crash landed a few feet from the boys. Mort felt bad, maybe it still had something to do with Pasquale, but seeing the tiny faerie face plant into a puddle of ooze didn't help. He jaunted over and picked her up, and wouldn't he know it, the poor thing was in tears.

"Awwwwwwwwwwwwwwwwwwww," Mort let out, looking back at Chip, "She's crying." He pouted, and his eyes welled up with tears.

Chip sighed and knelt down beside the two.

"What's the matter?" Chip asked, the first sentence he'd spoke in hours.

"Well, the little flying thing is crying," Mort said.

"Shut up," Chip said, "Go on, Zed." He added. Mort pouted more.

"She can't die, I can't let her - but I'm useless thanks to your stupid big forehead." Now, Chip knew she was upset, but he didn't think his forehead was overly big, or stupid.

"Why's that?" Chip asked.

"That's Mum. If she dies, everything dies. We can't let that happen!" Zed let out, and in an oddly powerful thrust, which drove an unsuspecting Mort into the ground, The faerie took to the air once again. Chip looked on in wonder as he watched her buzz through the air, right towards the humungous Butcher.

If David And Goliath were a thing of myth and legend, then the battle between the Butcher and Zed was beyond biblical. Zed, the faerie weighing in at approximately eight grams versus the behemoth Butcher weighing in at 1000 pounds. It's really hard to say who'd win. The odds in Vegas must be neck and neck...Or not. Probably not. Zed really didn't stand a chance. But that wasn't going to deter her, she has a purpose and a reason for her actions, something Chip and Mort were desperately lacking.

However, the sight of a mosquito flying headlong into spider's web to save something she truly loves was more than inspiring. A small spark ignited within Chip, and to himself, he said *screw it,* got to his feet and charged towards the demon. There'd been enough horror for one day, and if he can save this one helpless girl, it might just be worth it. Might, but probably not. There's been a lot of death.

Filling with a sense of purpose, Chip readied his hands, and almost instantly a green smoke began to billow around his palm. He lurched forward just as The Butcher grabbed his cleaver from the ground. The ball of... green? Sure, the ball of green ricocheted off the back of his skull, lurching his forward and knocking him off balance. He turned around with his glowing yellow eyes and grew furious. He let out a roar that was unmatched by anything else in nature and charged forward to meet Chip, ignoring the girl in the bubble.

Chip launched a half dozen more balls of energy at the charging Hellbeast, some landing and causing burns on his flesh, but most missed. He wasn't exactly the most athletic guy, and sports where he had to, ya know, throw weren't exactly his forte. As he and the Butcher got closer, he realized this fight wasn't going to go well in close quarters. He was more of a distance fighter. In about as fluid a motion as he

could muster, Chip pulled a complete 180 in the slick grass and began to run back the other way towards Mort, who was no longer in sight. Chip then panicked more than ever.
He looked over his shoulder. He wished he didn't look over his shoulder. He could feel the ground shaking; footsteps neared closer and closer, so looking back was pointless, and just caused more fear to swell within him. He blindly chucked back a couple of energy balls, but he was certain that they missed their barn-sized target. Sadly, they missed their barn-sized target. Chip then cursed his parents for not encouraging him to do sports as a kid. Remember folks, always blame your parents for everything.
Chip continued to run as fast as his little chicken legs would take him, which wasn't very fast as The Butcher gained three steps for every one of his. Looking back again, he could almost count The Butcher's teeth as he had them taut and barred. However looking back was an even worse idea than before; he took his eyes off of the proverbial road, stepped in some extra slick goo, and wiped out harder than what you see in those internet videos. You know the ones, they get like a billion hits. Anyway.
Chip ended up flat on his back like a drunken sorority girl on a Saturday night. His head and back began to throb, but that passed the second he saw The Butcher stand over him. He wasn't going to savour the kill like he was doing with Mother Earth - no, that ended poorly last time. The Butcher wasn't going to waste and time, and in one quick motion he took a final step and raised his cleaver. Chip closed his eyes. He missed Ellie and was heartbroken that he wasn't going to get to say goodbye, and that she might never know what happened to him, and that he died a hero. He then thought of how Mort was going to survive without him to guide him in life. He thought about the bravery of the little faerie, and he hoped Bill would pull through. He also sort of regretted cursing his

parents second ago. He then thought that he was able to have a lot of thoughts in the seconds before being dismembered.
Chip opened his eyes to see quite a sight. Apparently, when he closed his eyes and accepted his fate, that brave little faerie had buzzed by The Butcher's ear, distracting his just enough to throw off his swing, which meant his cleaver went sailing into the air. He swatted around his head like there was a bee doing bee things - annoying people. In that time Mort was able to summon a small army of fetishes made out of stick, grass, and cloth from his close. Which would explain why he was wearing nothing but a bundle of leaves around his waist.
The fetishes began to hack and slash at the ankles of The Butcher with tiny little sharpened sticks and thistles. Hey, Mort worked with what he had, which wasn't a whole lot. but it was enough to save Chip's life for the time being. Zed continued her aerial assault, and between the ground troops and the air force, The Butcher fell to one knee, not knowing who to attack first. He swung and flailed as if being eaten alive by an army of fire ants. All seemed to be going marginally well. Chip scurried to his feet and went into a trance. He began murmuring random words and phrases, which Mort saw from a distance and he instantly began to question Chip's sanity, which was a tad ironic.
And then things began to pop up from the ground, various creatures from goatmen to skeletons, from recently fallen nymphs, to half-decomposed corpses. They all began to come from the Earth. Mort quickly dismissed the thought of crazy and began getting excited. Nobody's ever seen an army of the dead before, and if truth be told, he was quite proud of his friend. He just hoped that he could control the army. If not, things could go south in a hurry.
Chip muttered and whispered until he could no longer. Apparently raising the dead is quite exhausting, but when he opened his eyes and saw the militia before him, closing in on The Butcher, he smiled, and quite frankly proud of himself.

Proud of himself for not only being able to raise the dead, but mainly because just a short while ago he may or may not have peed himself when he saw the dead hobo in that alleyway, and now, only a dribble or two came out. It was turning out to be a *good* day.

The army closed in on The Butcher, who continued to fight with Zed and Mort's own little army. The thing about fetishes; it doesn't matter how beat up or broken they become, they'll keep going. There was a small steak shaped stick about the size of a baseball bat attached to a hand that's attached to nothing still stabbing The Butcher on the top of his foot. However, with all of the trashing and flailing, many of the inanimate things were utterly obliterated, and though they still had life in them, they couldn't make their way back to their target. Slowly the army dwindled.

The dead approached the incapacitated beast from the deepest pits of Hell. They began to clamour over the fetishes and climb onto the back of The Butcher, scratching, biting, gnawing, pounding him. There were a lot of them, but they didn't seem to be doing much damage. Some left a few flesh wounds, but they seemed to be nothing more than an annoyance - a distraction at best. In fact, many of them were being broken apart just as easily Mort's creations. The numbers were there, but there was no organization, which was playing into the favour of The Butcher. He began to use the corpses against one another. Picking one up, and swinging it like a bat at the others, clearing out a line of a half dozen.

The thing about reanimated corpses, they aren't as determined as the fetishes. Once broken, the soul dissipates back into the Earth. Luckily, these souls already have a claim to the grave making The Butcher unable to collect them.

The battle persisted, but quicker than anybody would have liked the armies shrunk. Mort joined Chip's side and put his arm around him to help him up. As soon as Chip realized that

Mort was more or less naked, he shrugged him off. Mort shrugged himself and just watched the losing cause.
"What the Hell are we gonna do?" Chip asked. "Look at that thing. How can anybody possibly kill it?"
"I...Well, I don't know," Mort answered, clearly not the response Chip wanted.
Once again Chip found himself staring down the barrel of a gun. Except this gun was in the shape of The Butcher. It's funny, isn't it, what can happen when you're being marched upon by something that will literally tear your soul from your body? Chip and Mort merely held each other as they watched the last of their forces get battered away. Sure, some damage was done, but was it really enough? Despite the constant onslaught, The Butcher seemed unfazed, mildly annoyed at worst. And just as the last skeleton was obliterated, The Butcher stood, shaking off the dust of all those he'd just destroyed. Zed flew over and landed on Mort's shoulder.
"Well, fellas... We tried," she said, wiping a tear from her eye.
"At least we saved Mum," Zed said pointing out towards the girl in the field.
Chipped looked at the little faerie and smiled. Her optimism in the face of martyrdom was admirable. He then followed her finger to the girl. The girl whom he hadn't gotten a good look at prior. In almost a slow motion moment, he caught a glimpse of the one called Mum flick her hair and look over her shoulder as the remaining survivors ushered her away, back into the tree line.
"El...Ellie?" Chip said to himself, wide eyed and astounded. Could it actually have been her?
"Ellie!" He shouted as loudly as he could. His voice couldn't possibly carry the distance across the park, but he could swear she heard him as she looked back quickly once again.
"Holy crap, Mort!" He said shaking his buddy by the shoulders. "That was Ellie!"
"Huh, who?" Mort asked in a daze

"Mum... Mother Earth. The person Zed's been talking about."
"Nah, you're just hallucinating 'cause you're about to die. That's all. Nice final thought though," Mort said solemnly.
"No, Mort! It was her. I swear it! I have to get over there. I have to see her again," Chip said in a panic.
"Good luck," Mort said, pointing to the giant with a cleaver raised above his head. Chip swallowed hard, closed his eyes, and flinched as the cleaver came crashing down.
Except, again, the cleaver didn't actually hit its mark. Actually, it never did get to complete its swinging cycle. Chip was one lucky bastard.
When Chip opened his eyes, he saw nothing but The Butcher shadow boxing, or something like it. He was flailing like a lunatic chasing the invisible leprechaun on his shoulder, you know the one. He tells you to burn things. Many think that the leprechaun isn't actually there. Shrinks for years have been misdiagnosing people with schizophrenia and that split personality nonsense, but it's just a little jerk in a green suit being an asshole. He's one bored little fella.
Something told Chip that it wasn't a leprechaun that The Butcher was fighting though. There has to be something else at play, but what?
"Look!" Mort shouted out. "It's a bird, it's a plane, it's...Actually, I don't know. I've just always wanted to say that," he said smiling, "but it is *something*, right?"
"I think so," Chip said creeping closer to the fight with one invisible opponent. His eyes widened at his discovery.
"He's bleeding. Guys! He's getting cut by something." Chip exclaimed.
"Well, I'll be..," Zed said. "There's only one thing in the universe that I know of that can do that."
"What is it?" Chip and Mort said in unison. They looked at each other.
"Jinx!" They said together.

"Jinx... jinxjinxjinxjinxjinxjinx!" The said in complete harmony. "Damnit!" They both blurted out.
"...JINX!" They said together again.
"Boys!" Zed yelled, getting both of their attention. "Bigger fish, children." Chip looked down slightly ashamed. Mort looked at her puzzled.
"A fish is fighting The Butcher?" Mort said; Chip and Zed face-palmed simultaneously.
"How... Just how?" Zed said to Chip. He just shrugged.
"Anyway... The only thing in the universe that can do that is an assassin of The Order. But I thought they were a myth," Zed said.
"Nope, they defo aren't a myth," Mort said, "but they don't have any fish... Unless..." his eyes widened and he gasped, "They're fishmen! I knew it. See, I knew it, those lizardmen, those are just a decoy by the fishmen to keep their identities safe. Clever bastards." Chip and Zed just blinked. Chip shook the cobwebs loose and turned to Zed and said,
"That's Marco. He *is* an assassin of The Order. Funny story, he was sent to kill me, but couldn't bring himself to do it, and now we're kind buds." Zed's jaw hit the floor.
"You have a friend in The Order!? This is too much. First a necromancer, then The Butcher, now The Order. Chip, things are worse than I thought. None of these things have been heard of in centuries. Many didn't think any of them were real, but now look, there are three unbelievable things standing within feet of each other. That's like..." Zed paused to think of a really good metaphor, like a really, really good one. She didn't want to blow it.
"Like getting *three* Poptarts in a single package?!" Mort blurted out. He smiled, proud of himself for that one.
"Unbelievable. " Zed said.
"Actually, I thought that was pretty good," Chip said nodding at Mort.

"Oh, shut up. Enough jibber jabber, your *friend* is saving your life, and you're not even helping," Zed said.
"Right!" Chip said igniting his fists with green energy. Mort just stood there holding some sticks over his junk still. He looked at Zed and shrugged.
Flashes of green lights began to pelt The Butcher all over his body, and despite the force and ferocity of the energy blobs, they seemed to have no lasting effect on the creature. Sure he stumbled and swung his arms like a crazy drunk person, but he didn't appear to be hurt in the least, in fact, he looked to be smiling, laughing even. Despite this, Chip and Marco continued their onslaught with Wax doing his insane assassin things, and Chip blasting him with green stuff. Although it didn't seem to be doing any harm, The Butcher was being kept at bay for the time being. He wasn't killing anything, and he wasn't causing any further chaos, but how long the pair could keep it up was the real question. Marco, trained nearly from birth, could probably keep at it all day, whizzing and whirling around at the speed of light, but Chip was new to this, and it began to show.
The green balls of energy, which started off at about the size of a basketball, were slowly dwindling, and now sat in the palm of his hand like a baseball. He began to sweat and pant with every toss, as if the energy he was chucking was his own.
"This isn't working!" Mort yelled from behind his foliage codpiece.
"I...I know," Chip said falling to one knee. He attempted to gather the strength for another energy ball, but it was futile - he collapsed on all fours. Mort rushed over to him to help him up. When Chip caught his breath, he was eye level with something he never wanted to see. He saw something that both mortified him, and inspired him to move faster than he'd ever moved before. Mort's Junk. Dangling in the wind. Unpleasant.
Chip fell to his back and crawled away, a la Exorcist crab walk with a look of shock and horror on his face. He'd just fought a

demon, and some genitalia that just ruined his day. Talk about priorities. Regardless, as Mort covered back up, rolling his eyes, Marco Wax continued to swarm The Butcher, however the smile simply would not leave the beasts face. He was a real smug prick.

The Butcher with a smile; he truly enjoyed his work, and his time on the surface was spectacular as it just reiterated the fact that he was the most powerful creature in the plains of Heaven or Hell. He was absorbing everything around him, the atmosphere, the souls of his fresh kills, the experience, and he didn't think he'd ever try to leave, and frankly, nothing could make him. He grew in power, toying with the bug flying around his head. He thought that he was strong and fast, but in fact The Butcher was having fun with this - just another way for him to exert his power. However, the buzzing was becoming quite a nuisance.

"Well, at least Wax is holding his own, right?" Mort said, tying together another bushel of leaves.

"Yeah," Chip said panting.

In that exact breath, both Chip and Mort were bowled over by one Marco Wax. Apparently The Butcher had enough, and grew bored of the buzzing around his ears and promptly swatted the fly (Marco, duh.) away with enough force to send him spiralling through the air, and enough accuracy to take out his two allies.

If things looked dire before, they were about to get a whole lot worse. The three heroes lay on the wet grass in a total wreck. One of them naked, still. Marco had taken a hard, hard hit, which left him bleeding and unconscious atop both Chip and Mort. The two were shaken, but not seriously injured and managed to heave the broken Marco off of them. When they did that, they were met with the face of pure evil staring right down on them. Mort clawed at Marco to pull him back on, when that failed, he played dead. Chip cowered under the menacing gaze and the swimming yellow eyes.

For a fourth time that day, all seemed lost for the necromancer. As he did the first two times, he closed his eyes an just waited for the inevitable. Well, there was a bit of hope there that closing his eyes somehow saved his live prior, why not a fourth time, right? Hey, any logic is good logic when facing your own mortality.
As luck would have it, closing his eyes and whimpering seems to be Chip's lucky charm. For a third, yes, a third time the imminent cleaver strike did not arrive. Curious, he thought. Maybe The Butcher decided he wanted to see Chip's eyes as the blade sliced him in half. It could be anything, but what it actually was, well, Chip didn't see it coming. Not in the least.
When Chip peeked through his eyelids, he saw a figure. It was a familiar figure. It was an unkempt figure. It was a fat figure. Between Chip and The Butcher stood, with his back to Chip, none other than... Bill. But how? He was as good as dead, or so everybody thought. But in this topsy turvey world, who knew? Well, Ick knew, then again, he didn't even see that temporal monster coming to eat him. Or he did and was powerless to stop it. Or... bullocks to it, there's too much nonsense with time travel stuff.
Bill stood before Chip in all his brilliance, and even The Butcher seemed taken aback. There are two possible reasons for this, A: He's afraid of Bill. Or B, and the more likely one: He's beyond confused as to why there's an old bearded man standing in front of him, and what in the name of all that is the universe is he going to do about it.
As that thought passed through The Butchers mind, he found out. Emanating from Bill came a gigantic invisible blast that sent The Butcher into the atmosphere. Literally. Reports at NASA can confirm the anomaly, and a young scientist by the name of Frank Beans, a very unfortunate name, spotted the blip on a radar. Upon telling his colleagues he was not only laughed at, but ridiculed by them. As if having a name such as his wasn't bad enough, he now had to live with being the guy

who spotted the smallest UFO in history. He would go on to win a Nobel Prize.
Bill turned to Chip and smiled.
"Hey lad," he said.
"Bill!" Chip sprung to his feet to hug the galoot.
"There there." Was all Bill could muster. He was quite hungry, what with being asleep for as long as he was.
"How are you alive, and well...here?" Chip asked.
"Well, you see, it's quite complex..," Bill thought about it and stared off into the distance, most likely for dramatic purposes. "Somebody took a really massive and revolting shit in the apartment and woke my ass up."
"Oh," Chip said.
"I've heard that can happen." Marco chimed in from behind.
Bill narrowed his eye.
"Before you say anything, Djinn..." Just as Marco started, he leapt forward and pushed Bill to the ground. Chip, and even Mort stood at attention in shock of the random aggression, however he didn't follow it with another move. All he did was glance back and smile at his two new friends before the mammoth Butcher fell back to Earth, causing a car-sized crater where Wax once stood.
"NO!" Chip and Mort yelled in unison.
"That sonofabitch," Bill muttered to himself, "That's a nasty way to go..."
As the smoke cleared from the impact, Bill looked across the new pockmark in the Earth and yelled to the boys,
"Are you alright?!" of course, he knew they were. He still knew everything. But, he wanted to seem concerned.
"Yeah!" The two yelled back, "But...But Marco!"
Bill made a face he'd never made before, it almost came across as sadness. He quickly shook it and ran around the crater to Chip and Mort.
"Let's not make is sacrifice moot, lads. There's only one way to kill this arsehole. You've gotta take out his eye. Those

glowing yellow stains of floating piss - gotta pop 'em somehow," Bill said.

"Well...that...that seems a little too obvious doesn't it?" Chip said.

"Yeah, that's the beauty of it. It's almost too easy and predictable, nobody would think of it," Bill answered.

"Fair enough. So, just what... throw a green ball of goo at him?"

"Oh, no, that won't work. It can only be pierced by a human bone. A righteous human bone no less," Bill said a little too smugly.

"Where the Hell am I gonna get one of those?" Chip protested.

"Well, not Hell. That place is full of pricks."

"Where then?"

"You're the Necromancer, aren't ya? Summon something, rip its arm off and poke the beast in the eye," Bill advised.

"Yeah, about that, I'm pretty sure I've summoned everything within 2 miles of here already, and all it did was slow him down slightly. If at all. I think he was just playing with us actually..," Chip said drifting off at the thought of how powerful the demon truly was. It was rather intimidating.

"Think then, Lad!" Bill said with a wink and a motion toward the crater. Chip tilted his head and looked into the hole, which he wish he hadn't. When he gazed down into the abyss, the abyss looked right back at him, except this abyss, unlike the one from the movie, had glowing yellow eyes. The eyes in question began to move in a very specific direction - right at his face.

Bursting from the hole like a bat out of Hell... poor choice of words? A little too on the head? Anyway, The Butcher leapt from the grave like a salmon and landed on his feet just in front of the trio of heroes. Chip gulped, Mort peed a little, and Bill picked some fluff, or maybe a crumb from his beard. Faced with his doom again, starring at the Butcher with a smile, Chip had an idea that he will claim was his own, and had nothing to

with Bill pointing down at the crater with a smidge of urgency. He closed his eyes and muttered a few words, opened them and smiled right back at the Butcher.
"Why are *you* smiling?" The Butcher growled.
"You'll see," Chip said overly confident.
The Butcher took a step towards Chip, but in the blink of an eye, literally, The Butcher's eyes were plucked from his head and landed on the ground in front of the fledgling soul summoner.
"Or maybe you won't," Chip said as he squashed the eyes on the ground.
"Well...Shit," The Butcher said before exploding into a billion or more souls which polluted the air and skies above before being sucked back down through the Earth in a blue wave of energy.
"Whoa!" Mort exclaimed, "That's a great cool guy line! How long have you been holding that one in?"
Chip took a deep breath and tried his damnedest to remain calm and not freak out over the level of cool. He failed.
"Oh my God, I just thought of it as it was happening! It was totally cool, right?" Chip said turning to face Mort giddy as a school girl who just got asked out by the popular and cool guy in class.
"Ladies," Bill interrupted with a concerned voice. Mort and Chip turned to face him like scolded dogs. "Well done boys. And yes, the line was super cool," Bill finished with a smirk.
"But wait... How, what was that?" Mort asked. Chip smiled into the distance where he saw the corpse of Marco Wax watching.
"It was an old friend, buddy," Chip said quite ominously, actually. He smiled again, closed his eyes, took a deep breath, and when he opened them again, the corpse was nothing more than a pile of ground beef lying on the plains of the battlefield. Mort looked over and didn't see anything. Nothing. He figured Chip had finally snapped and lost his mind. It happens.

Of course, a battle as large as the one that just happened doesn't go unnoticed, especially by the cigarette smoking wannabe British demon. Just on the edge of a treeline, away from the battle stood the figure, mostly unseen, except for the time he drew a breath on the smoke that lit up like the creepy guy filming a homemade porn. He didn't care for the wellbeing of The Butcher, no, rather he was far more interested in where Ellie scampered off to, and wouldn't you know it, his plan worked a charm. He smiled that crooked evil smile and walked off towards the tree line opposite of him. Surely, he had that Earth-loving hippie now.

He wasn't concerned about how those three idiots in the distance killed The Butcher. He should have been concerned, but he wasn't. After all, they had only killed maybe the third most powerful demon in existence, but it wasn't a big deal. It's not like it was the second most powerful creature in the universe or anything. The second being Devil. The first being the God - that prick.

It was a bit ironic, actually. Meph rebelled against the Devil, much like how he rebelled against God. God threw him and all of his followers out of Heaven. At least, that's how most people know it when in reality it went something a little like this.

"Quit hitting thyself, quit hitting thyself!" Michael, the Archangel, champion of the Heavens proclaimed as he took Lucifer's hand against his own head. Lucifer, not nearly as strong as Michael, was powerless to resist the self-inflicted whopping he was taking. This, most certainly, annoyed the angel known as the Morning Star. He gritted his teeth against one another until the grinding was so loud that it was confused as thunder on the Earth below. Michael, prompted by the thunderous clashing of teeth, stopped his fun for a moment.

"Lucy, what's the matter? Aren't thy having fun?" Michael questioned earnestly, for he was having fun, and given his

sense of entitlement, thought that everybody involved in his game was having fun.
"NO!" Lucifer shouted out. "I'm not. And I'm telling dad that you keep calling me Lucy." Lucifer threatened.
"Oh, father? He won't care for your petty complaints. He's too busy." Michael said, still holding Lucifer's wrist - however with a less meaningful grasp. The thought of their father not being present and loving to him, and his brethren did make him sad, even if slightly.
"Busy? With what?" Asked a concerned Lucifer.
"With them," Michael said pointing down to Earth. Below the feet of the two angels were two...things. They looked a lot like the angels in Heaven, and even God himself. But they were somehow different. They had parts that the angels weren't used to, and one had different parts than the other. Confused and frightened, Lucifer reeled back and gasped. He broke free of Michaels grasp and held his hands over his mouth.
"What...what are those things? They're...they're..."
"Kind of beautiful." Michael finished.
"What? No, they're hideous, disgusting abominations!" Lucifer shouted. "What are they?"
Michael turned his head, never hearing such foul words before, "father calls them Humans."
"Oh, so dad came up with these things?"
"Yes. His latest creation. And I think they might be his best yet, despite him loving them more than us."
"HE LOVES THEM MORE THAN US!?" Lucifer shouted in disbelief.
"Yeah, but it's okay. We don't need his love as much as they do." Michael tried to explain.
"Maybe *you* don't. But I kinda like it. I'm gonna go get dad, he'll clear this up. I'm sure you're just mistaken, Michael. it's okay, it happens."
"No, actually it doesn't," Michael said arrogantly. Lucifer shot him a look. He was beginning to exhibit behaviours that were

very uncharacteristic of angels. Like, free thinking, and jealousy, and anger. In fact, Lucifer may have just brought these emotions into existence.

"Dad! Father! I wish to speak with you right now!" Lucifer shouted like a disgruntled child into the...well, the heavens.

After a moment of waiting, a voice responded with a sigh, "Yes, Morning Star?"

"What is going on down there? Why are these...things walking around?"

"I believe Michael explained it already, son. They're humans, and they need my love and attention, at least for a little while." God explained.

"What?!" Lucifer shouted out. "No, why do you need them? Aren't we enough for you? We love you unconditionally." Lucifer explained. Of course, God kind of already knew that.

"Yes, yes. Love. it's great. But what have I done to earn that love? You're programmed to love me, and you know no other way. The humans, well they have something I like to call free will. They have to believe in me, and love me because they want to, then they can join the ranks of Heaven one day."

Well, that did it. Lucifer's eye began to twitch and a feeling grew within his belly that he'd never felt before. How could God allow those disgusting things up into Heaven? He surely wouldn't.

"Heh, you're funny, dad," Lucifer replied.

"It's not a joke, son." Lucifer balled his fists.

"Then can you at least tell Michael to stop hitting me and calling my Lucy?"

It was at that moment where God snickered slightly under his breath for the first time.

"Oh, you angels - always goofing around. Have fun, Lucy." And with that, God's presence left. It was a palpable difference in Heaven from that moment on, as if God had stepped out to get smokes, and 6000 years later, he'd still not come home. Of course, Lucifer was not beyond pissed.

"DAD!" he shouted. "DAD!" Again, but there was no answer. Lucifer clenched his jaw so hard that his teeth cracked, and thunder rang out across all of the Earth below.
"FATHER!" He screamed out in a growl. A noise never before produced by an angel.
"God, your all loving father and creator isn't in at the moment. Please leave your message and I'll get back to you." Rang out over the entire heavens. Many angels ignored it, getting on with their daily angel duties. However, a select few had a sudden feeling of abandonment and fear. Other's had a seed of anger planted, and it was a feeling that they did not enjoy.
Lucifer changed in that moment. He felt as if all the shackles were off and a sensation of power surged through him.
Michael crept up from behind and whispered in Lucifer's ear, "...quit hitting yourself," he said grabbing Lucifer's fist.
But this time it was different. Lucifer was able to resist. In fact, in his anger induced state, Michael couldn't even make his arm budge. Lucifer slowly turned to face his brother with a look of pure hatred in his eyes. It was at that moment that Lucifer created the entity known as evil. God may have created the world, humans, and the universe, but it was Lucifer that created emotion, and parity amongst those who chose to think for themselves. Lucifer, at that moment, had as much claim to anything as God, even his precious humans.
When he met Michael's eyes, he saw nothing but blind stupidity, which enraged him more. He threw his arm up, breaking Michael's hold on him, and tossing him like a rag doll to the floor.
"You want to have fun, Michael?" Lucifer said with an ever-deepening voice which echoed and spread further and further across Heaven. He slowly walked over to the shell-shocked angel.
"Let's have some fun then," he said raising his foot and promptly stomping on Michaels' face.

From there the most epic of wars erupted. Angels battled for what seemed like centuries until Lucifer and his band of rebels took their ranks to the underworld and created Hell. Along with Hell came temptation, sin, and most importantly, hate. Before The Devil took the reins of Hell for himself, nobody felt the rush of hate, or the feeling of hating. He was even sneaky enough to get Eve to eat that little piece of fruit. Satan was a little more hands on back in the day.

As Meph recalled that story, he couldn't help but be pissed that the Devil didn't appreciate his attempt at a rebellion. What a hypocrite.

# CHAPTER 14

So much death; so much destruction. Ellie barely knew where she was when one of the woodland nymphs literally smacked her back into reality. It was quite a wallop, actually. Probably more than was needed, but nevertheless, it worked. She shook the cobwebs loose and looked around her. Before the battle, the garden was full and lively, now it just seemed so desolate and miserable, but more importantly, it felt empty. So many lives lost, many of which she didn't know, but it didn't matter, she could feel that their presence was no longer there. What was once a vibrant and jovial place was nothing more than the equivalent to a concentration camp after a war.

She looked in a panic for Sterling, not remembered what had happened to the poor nymph. She called out for her over and over, her cries soon turned into a shriek, and before long it transformed into a sob. She knew what had happened even if she did block it out. All the other creatures and beings looked to the ground in sadness, not quite knowing how to comfort her, and so they stood around and did nothing while their queen, their mother sat in sadness and anguish.

On hands and knees, Ellie peered up from under her brow, and as the sadness subsided, an anger filled within her. It was unlike anything she'd ever felt before. This wasn't like having the barista at Starbucks mess up her order, or getting in a fender bender, which was the only degree of anger she knew. This was pure, unadulterated anger. She began to writhe, which turned into a vibration throughout her whole body as she rose to her feet. The attention of all those around her was slowly being focused, and many of the smaller creatures began to back away, for they had never seen a thing like this before.

There have been many Mothers, more or less one ever couple hundred years since the beginning of time - whenever you consider that to be in this topsy-turvy world of mythology and religion, but none has ever faced the adversity that this one has. The ceremony went on without a hitch, and they Mum never had to worry. She relaxed and was treated like the royalty she is until her time came to reinvigorate the Earth, and with the ritual just a day away, nobody knew how her attitude and emotions would affect the cleansing and rebirth of all of nature. It was terrifying. But, as they say, the show must go on, and that responsibility was taken up by the smallest of beings in the grove. A little nymph named Zed.

It's funny where bravery can be found, and how it's often in the smallest of things. Like the trope goes, it's not about the size of the dog in the fight, but the size of the fight in the dog. Unless it's like a pit bull going up against a Chihuahua, then well. Good luck. And though Zed might be an 8th of the size of a Chihuahua, she's got the heart of a lion. Which was good, because she'll need it after flicking Ellie in the forehead.

"Alright, alright. We get it, you're super pissed," Zed said rolling her eyes, "but this isn't the time. You've got crap to do, and calming down is one of them. I don't know what happens if you perform the ritual in this bitchy state, but I'm not prepared to find out. Hell if I'm living in some thorny weeded wasteland 'cause you can't get over some death." Zed finished in one long-winded breath.

Ellie, at first, grew even angrier, and for a split second, Zed thought that she'd made a terrible mistake, and even swallowed hard. Something she never, ever does for no apparent reason. But like all storms, they pass, and a moment later Ellie's eyes lightened, and it was quite clear that she was coming down from her rage induced trance.

"You're right," Ellie said, which kind of shocked everybody. "This is a time for focus and crap. Not a time to get angry and vengeful...Even if t is a lot more fun." She finished.

The little faerie smirked, "That a girl. Besides, we're all lucky to be alive. I mean, if it weren't for your boyfriend coming -" Ellie held up her hand and interrupted Zed.
"My what?" She said raising her eyebrow
"Well, I guess he was your boyfriend. He got this lovey look in his face when he saw you, but it wasn't like a crush, it was like he knew you. So I put two and two together, and made the assumption, which I guess is totally wrong now." Zed explained.
"No, I mean. Maybe. Did he have a name?" Ellie asked intensely.
"Chad? Chirp?...Damnit, what was it?" Zed said looking around her own thoughts, hovering in the air with her hand on her chin.
"...Chip?" Ellie asked meekly.
"YES! That was it. I knew it was something stupid," Zed said. "Uhh, I mean, wonderful. Something wonderful."
"There's no way...but, how many other people are named Chip?" Ellie said searching her shoes for some kind of answer as people often do when they're thinking. Shoes, they have all the answers to life's tough questions, like when being questioned by your wife as to why you didn't come home last night. Look to your shoes.
"That's true. Well, was your boyfriend a necromancer by chance? And hang around a bumbling idiot who might have been brain-dead and has a bad case of dandruff?" Zed asked.
"Oh my fuck!" Ellie proclaimed, "that's him...but last time I checked he wasn't a necromancer...whatever that is."
"Hmm, well, he may not have been before you were taken. He seemed kinda new and sucky at it. No offence," Zed said, looking smug, "oh, and a necromancer raises and controls the dead."
"Hmm, makes sense, I think," Ellie said, "but...but how, and why?"

"Dunno, Ma, there's one every few hundred, or thousand years. I can't remember which, but it usually means something not so good. They have a lot of power, and I mean a lot. And you know what they say about power," Zed said.
"Absolute power corrupts absolutely?" Ellie said, sounding rather smart.
"Nope. Turns 'em into giant assholes."
"Right.... But I can't believe he's okay. And he saved us, didn't he? I swear there were corpses running around."
"I guess. But he didn't do a very good job, I mean, it should have been quicker...I mean. Ugh, fine, he didn't alright, I guess," Zed said rolling her eyes. For a supposed jovial creature, Zed's sort of a bitch.
"I have to go find him...little faerie. I'm sorry, I didn't get your name."
"Oh, yeah. Zed."
"Zed? That's not a name, it's a letter," Ellie said, Zed rolled her eyes again.
"Ugh, it's short for Ezmeralda."
"Oh, Okay. Well, Zed, I have to go find Chip. I have to see if he's okay."
"Oh, he's fine. Before I got in here, I saw him, that idiot, and some fat guy use a superhero corpse to kill The Butcher. 'Sall good," she said smiling.
"Wait, what?"
"Never mind, Earth Lady. We have more important things to do, like keep you safe. A Hellspawn like that doesn't escape the depths of Hell without some kind of help. I just have a funny feeling that it was just the start of something. That demon that kidnapped you before, he wants you, but we can't let him have you, now can we."
"Well, I guess not."
"And travelling into the big busy city probably isn't the best course of action then, is it?" Zed said, a little more patronizing

than Ellie would have liked, but not as much as Zed had intended.

"No," Ellie said, reluctantly, kicking the dirt.

"Good," Zed said smiling. She liked this whole bossing people around thing.

"But, where are we gonna go?" Ellie asked.

Zed hovered and thought for a second, the only audible noise was that of her little wings buzzing a million flaps a second.

"You know what... You might be on to something with the city. Screw keeping you safe," she said, which garnered an eyebrow raise from Ellie.

"Go on..," Ellie said quite inquisitively.

"Well, your boyfriend's a necromancer. He wants to protect you, and we need to get this little demon out of your hair. I say to Hell with running, let's go on the offensive and lay a little trap out. Let's give your BF all the ammo he needs then," Zed said with a smile.

"Calvary Cemetery!" The two said in unison, with about the same level of excitement too. But the excitement faded for Ellie after a second or two.

"Wait, how can be we sure that Chip will be there, or at least show up when we need him," Ellie asked disheartened.

"Mum..," Zed said uncharacteristically caring, "It's fate. We have to have faith that things will work out. They have to, after all."

"Bullshit." Ellie proclaimed. "If I'm leaving here, I want to be damn sure that we're gonna have all the reinforcements that we need."

"Fair enough," Zed said looking over her shoulder. "Fab...Fabian!" She cried out, "get over here!"

Ellie raised an eyebrow, "What the Hell are you doing?"

"Calling Fabian. Fabian! Where are - oh there you are." Looking up at the floating faerie stood a chubby, and somewhat retarded looking pigeon.

"Fabian, go find that necromancer and tell him to meet us at the Calvary Cemetery tonight. Tell him Zed wants him there." A look from Ellie shot daggers through the faerie.
"Oh, and Ellie, I guess, too." She added. The pigeon stood there for a second looking completely lost and dumbfounded.
"Fabian!" Zed snapped. Fabian fluttered back to reality, "Go," Zed said. With that trademark pigeon nod, the bird took flight. Slowly. And quite laboured too. Ellie worried not just for the message arrival, but also if that poor bird can even make it out of Central Park.
"Thank you!" Ellie cried out as the bird struggled to ascend.
"Is he gonna be alright?" Ellie asked.
"Yeah, he'll be fine. After all, I thought he would have been the first to bite it when The Butcher was...well, butchering. He's full of surprises, that one. " Zed paused, "Now we just need to hope this demon has a trace on you, so he ends up at the cemetery, too. Kind of the whole crux of this plan..."

Meanwhile, unbeknownst to Ellie, Zed, Chip, or anybody else really, the cigarette smoking outcast from Hell knew exactly where Mother Nature would be for the time being. Literally, nobody is safe, that is until the group safely gets to the cemetery, which isn't even all that safe, as their plan could backfire. The ceremony to save all of... well everything, must take place in paradise, it simply won't work outside of those walls, so not only does the plan have to work, it has to work fast. Luckily, Meph did indeed spot the dopey looking pigeon take flight over the tree line, which will hopefully, for the sake of the world, lead the demon general to his fate.
"Interesting," Meph said with a cigarette hanging from his mouth as Fabian flew over his head. Knowing that he can't just walk into the holy ground, Meph spun on his heels and sauntered in the direction of the pigeon. With a snap of his fingers, he turned himself into a bat. Yes, a cliché horror trope bat. It's all that he could do, bats are known to have ties with

the underworld. That whole thing about Dracula and bats was actually pretty accurate. In fact, it's a little-known aspect about bats, but they are actually birds. Well, sort of. About 11,000 years ago a bird and a rat became friends, it was an odd pairing, but they somehow bonded, despite, ya know, being completely different species. Think of it as the first real interracial relationship.

But, as it's well known, boys and girls can't ever really *just be friends*, can they? And so Reginald the dove and Regina the rat grew close, too close some may say, and it just so happened that one day they made sweet, sweet whoopee together. Now love is generally a wonderful thing, isn't it? Not in this case. The strange interspecies erotica pissed off the God above. Even though he'd been absent for an eon, he still kept an eye on things, and unfortunately his eye caught this unholy union. The foetus growing within Regina was cursed by the holy creator, and what she gave birth to was not a bird, and not a rat, but something hideous and grotesque; a bat.

Although God disapproved and thus created this horrid beast, he still loved it, for it was indeed a creation of his, and therefore he let it live. The Devil, on the other hand, was also watching this relationship between the bird and the rat unfold, however it was for more perverted reasons, really. The details of which really don't need to be disclosed. Nevertheless, he took the opportunity claim his stake in this bat creature, and deemed it a product of Hell.

Survival of a new species, especially a one of kind, like a bat, was not too promising. So the Devil began to breed the unlikely animals until he produced an army of bats, which then bred within themselves. You know how the story goes. However, since the Devil was the one who ensured survival, bats owe themselves to Hell, and their form is given to any high power demon at their command, hence the bat form Mephisto just took. Simple, right?

And so, from a distance, Meph followed the bird, which wasn't as conspicuous as he would have liked, but he was hoping that the people below just thought he'd have rabies, got confused, and started to fly during the day. Come to think of it, turning into a bat is really only useful like, half of the time. Nevertheless, he flapped on. He wasn't worried about the dopey bird spotting him, but he kept his distance regardless.

The city below was filled with busy and bustling people, still somewhat confused about the freak storm, hail, tornado, and... well everything that had just taken place. Some went about their day, the suits, mainly, who barely noticed the storm, but others were in tears, children crying, homeless dying, it was all music and art to Mephisto. He loved watching the humans suffer, so much so that he nearly crashed into a billboard, which was a bit ironic, since it read: **The Rapture is comeing! Praise the LORD and pray for salivation!** spelt just like that, with the date of the supposed rapture two weeks past. Brilliant.

Meph the bat followed Fabian the pigeon deeper and deeper into the city, and he couldn't be sure if the stupid bird was lost. That was when Fabian took a nose dive towards a small apartment building in the middle of a pretty average and nonspecific part of the city. Meph was disappointed, but he took roost a few buildings away and began to listen. That was one perk of being a bat - supersonic hearing.

The bird dove in and landed on fire exit stoop and pecked on the pain of glass. Nobody answered. Fabian did it again. Nobody answered. Meph could hear somebody inside, but they weren't answering. Fabian pecked again, and again, and againandagainagainandagainagainandagainagainandagain againandagainagainandagain, until finally the window slide up and a very familiar looking character stuck his head out and began shouting obscenities and trying to shoo the bird with a broom who kept dodging the bristles with ease and calm. Fabian was quite nimble despite his outwardly dopiness.

However, the guy holding the broom? Mortimer Blake.

"What's up with you!?" Mort shouted at the perched bird. "And how am I not hitting you? And how are you so calm? And why don't loafers have laces? Nothing makes sense! Why are there so many unanswered questions in life?!" He continued.
From behind him watched Chip with a sort of morbid curiosity. Who would win, the bird or the birdbrain? Chip had his money on the former, with an over/under on him falling out of the window to his death. Chip could always resurrect him anyway.
"Whattya doing?" Chip asked nonchalantly, eating an ice-cream cone.
"Trying to get this stupid annoying bird off the window. I can't hit him though," Mort said filled with frustration.
"I can see that. Why do you want him gone so badly? Ya know, just outta curiosity." Chip added, taking another lick of the ice-cream.
"He was banging on the window like an asshole! Wait, where did you get ice-cream?" Mort said dropping the broom.
"In the freezer?" Chip said suspiciously.
"Ooh!" Mort exclaimed walking away from the window. Chip shook his head and walked over the wall beside the open window and leaned against it as he watched Mort rifle through the freezer. There was no ice-cream. Chip had gone to the store after they got home from Central Park. He asked Mort if he'd wanted anything, but he was too preoccupied with the stench that was lingering from Marco's... time. Smells didn't seem to bother Chip anymore. Lucky guy.
Anyway, as he leaned and watched Mort go through every inch of the freezer in a panic, he inadvertently turned to face the peculiar pigeon, who was starring right back at him.
"...Sup?" Chip asked, feeling a little foolish for doing so.
The bird tilted its head and hopped into the apartment.
"That's interesting," Chip said pushing himself off the wall.
"Can I help you with something...Pidgy?" He made up a name for it. Yeah, it's not great, but he had to think fast, okay?

"It's Fabian, and yes." The bird replied. At first, Chip opened his eyes wide, rubbed them, and was about to scream when he realized, this might be the most sensical piece of nonsense he'd come across in the last couple of days. He relaxed.
"Go on..," he said cautiously and squinting. He didn't know why he was squinting, it just felt right.
Fabian looked to the sky and his neck began to elongate, ever so slightly. He took in a bunch of air, held it, looked at Chip with more intensity than a pigeon should be able to muster, opened his mouth, and...nothing came out.
"Well, that was anti-climatic," Chip said.
"Sorry. I think I ate some bad seed...or something." Fabian said hopping towards Chip, "Look, you've gotta go to Calvary cemetery, like right now. Since you have to use your legs like a sucker, it's gonna take you a while to get there." Fabian said with a bit more sass than Chip would have liked.
"And why would I do that?" Chip questioned.
"Look, when a talking pigeon flies into your house and tells you to do something, you've gotta do it. It just makes sense." His logic was infallible.
"You bring a good point. But I've been burned by doing something just 'cause somebody told me to. I'm gonna need more from you, Fabian. If that is your real name," Chip said, sounding more like Mort than he ever wanted to. He shuttered.
Fabian sighed, and let a slight coo, which was sort of adorable, but after the two realized the situation, it became a bit awkward. Silence commenced and uncomfortable glances ensued.
"Fine. Mother Earth and Zed are going there, they need you for protection from some guy called Mephisto." Fabian said.
Carrier pigeons are a special breed. They be a bit of an acquired taste, but they're handy. Just given a few brief words from the message giver, they learn of all the details involved, even if things change. It's a unique bond they have with the message giver, and it's much more convenient than any other

form of communication - except texting. That's pretty convenient.
"Mephisto?!" Chip shouted. "That prick is still at it? And he wants Ellie?"
"Mother Earth, or Mother Nature, or just plain mum." Fabian interrupted.
"Wh-What?" Chip said.
"That's her name. Not Ellie."
"Oh, shut up. One and the same."
"Nope."
"Oh, bugger off. I've got more important things to worry about, like a demon still going after my girlfriend."
"Fine." Fabian conceded. "It's still mum." He whispered.
"Mort, Bill! Get out here!" Chip shouted.
Bill came meandering in from down the hall and looked a bit surprised to see a pigeon standing on an end table. Mort came rushing in holding a toilet brush, a towel around his waist, and a shower cap. Even odder was that he wasn't at all wet. Bone dry. Bill and Chip just shook their heads.
"What the - Mort, you were in the freezer like 2 minutes ago... How?" Chip started.
Mort opened his mouth to speak, but Chip cut him off, "you know what? I don't wanna know."
"Good idea, lad. Anyway, what's this we have here?" Bill said.
"Oh, you don't know?" Mort asked sarcastically.
"Well, no. I've been a bit hazy since being knocked out. My seering skills haven't been all too great, lad," he said looking sad. Mort instantly felt bad.
"Well," Chip started, "this is Fabian, Ellie and Zed sent him. He wants us to go to the Calvary Cemetery to protect Ellie from Mephisto. So, let's go," he said, summing everything up nicely. If the necromancy thing doesn't work out, he'd make a great carrier pigeon.

"Ahh, a cemetery. Good idea, and the biggest one in New York, too. Clever," Bill said combing his beard with his finger. He was secretly hoping to find some stray food.

"Well..." Mort started. "Really, it's not that clever, is it? We really should have thought about that sooner, and the fact we didn't kind of makes us look like realllllllly big idiots," he said with a smile.

"Hey!" Chip exclaimed, "...You have a point." He confessed.

"Oi, I've been unconscious for a lot of this. I don't even know what day it is. Can't blame me for not thinkin' up somethin'," Bill said, looking sort of smug. "But, no excuses or anything." He added sheepishly.

"Mmhmm." Both Mort and Chip said in unison, which caused them both to rear back a bit in terror. They've been spending way too much time together, and Mort's apparently been spending too much time with Latisha.

"Wait," Mort said, "Why should we trust this overly agile bird? How do we know it's not a trap?" Mort finished flailing his toilet brush in the direction of Fabian, how just stood there looking at him very unimpressed.

"His name's Fabian, Mort," Chip said matter of factly.

"...And?" Mort said waiting for more of an explanation than that. Chip just looked around and shrugged.

"He said his name is Fabian, and now you trust him?" Mort asked suspiciously.

"Yeah," Chip said nonchalantly.

"What the crap, man?! How...why... In what universe do you jut trust a talking pigeon called Fabian?"

"I dunno. The same universe that allows magic, and reanimating the dead, and demons slaughtering creatures that shouldn't exist in Central Park."

"You!...You bring up good points," Mort said resting his hands on his hips. "I still don't trust him!" Mort said leaping forward with the toilet brush out like a sword aiming towards the heart of a mighty dragon; if Fabian were a mighty dragon and not a sassy pigeon. Mort sailed through the air as if he were lunging in slow motion. The bristles of the white toilet brush swayed back ever so slightly, his hair fluttered in the wind, and his towel drifted from his waist to the floor. The latter happened far too quickly and didn't quite match the slow mo epicness of the lunge.

The sound of slightly damp hardwood floor meeting the elastic like nature of Mort's skin was ear piercing. He had hoped to slide after reaching his destination, but instead he stopped dead with a painful squealing noise. Of course, he missed Fabian all together, who calmly lifted into the air to avoid the toilet brush. He promptly landed on Mort's shower cap covered head. He then proceeded to poop.

Mort, defeated and hurt - both emotionally and physically - looked up at Chip and said, "Fine. We'll trust the stupid bird." Before dropping his head to the floor.

Unbeknownst, it's the word of the day, to the trio in the apartment, the demon bat lurked just a few buildings down, with his sonar hearing transfixed on the window in which Fabian leapt. A cemetery, he thought to himself, was indeed quite clever, and just as Mort, he thought it took far too long for anybody to think of it. Sure the plan has potential. Lure him into a trap so that the necromancer can overwhelm him with corpses and tear him apart or something. Sadly, the details were a bit fuzzy, but he could only assume it was meant to be something destructive and not to his benefit. Nevertheless, he would have to go, after all, everybody he wants to kill is going to be in one spot, and a trap isn't a trap if he's prepared for it. Well, it is still, sort of, but not really. It's a trap to half of the constituents involved, but not all. Ugh, it's all very confusing at this point.

Regardless, Meph had a plan of his own, and a Necromancer can only reanimate corpses with a soul. Meph began to laugh, which only came out as adorable little chirps, and to human eyes made him look like a bat with rabies. That's why Meph really shouldn't have been too surprised when a giant net wrapped around him on his perch and yanked him inside the apartment he was of which he was hanging outside.

*Oh, bother* he thought to himself as he struggled instinctively to escape. Just to make it clear, that wasn’t the demon fighting a thin piece of nylon, it was the bat. Bats scare super easily and confuse even easier. Nobody said bats were perfect. Cute, adorable, charming, and beautiful sure... wait, nobody said that either.

# CHAPTER 15

"Explain it to me again." A hood shrouded figure said sitting upon a throne encompassed by other hooded men in smaller thrones asked.
"It's Marco, Master. He's dead." A smaller robed man answered. He clearly wasn't as important as the rest - he had no hood.
"How did this come to be!?" The important hooded man shouted, his voice echoing through the enormous hall in which he and his compatriots sat, hooded of course, covered in darkness, signifying their pure and utter evilness. The non-hooded man shuttered ever so slightly, which caught the attention of the big Kahuna.
"Young one," he said leaning towards the apprentice, "you needn't be afraid. I am not going to hurt you in the least," he said sitting back in his chair.
"Thank you, Master," The young man said.
"No, You simply won't feel a thing," The Master said before snapping his fingers. Upon said snapping of the fingers, the young robed fella simply burst into dust leaving behind just his silken dark purple robe. He was so magically ground up that there wasn't even a pile of dust remaining. He simply evaporated without a trace. He hadn't even earned his hood yet.
The master straightened himself and looked to the other men in the room. They weren't equals to him, nobody was. However they were of the Elders of the Order, and they held a degree of power in the organization, and they all had one thing in common - they were scared shitless of the Master.

"Now, is there anything else anybody would like to tell me?" He said looking around the room. He was met with silence.
"Good. Now we can proceed with our next course of action." The room remained silent.
"Master?" One of the hooded figures asked. The Master nodded. "What is our next course of action? Marco was never expected to fail in his mission. The Necromancer walks free, and the ceremony is but a day away. We can't wait another 250 years to set another plan in motion." He finished. The Master pondered for a moment in complete silence. A fly farted on the far side of the chamber, which echoed its little squeak like the smallest balloon in the world let out a smidge of air. It promptly poofed into dust.
"We need to move on to protocol 17." The Master proclaimed calmly. A murmur fell over the crowd as the hooded men spoke to one another in hushed tones.
"Is there a problem with that?" The Master asked. The murmurs fell silent once again.
"Excellent. We shall start the plan in motion then. Prepare my equipment. I've been trapped within these walls for far too long. It's time I stretched my legs." The Master said as he rose from his throne. As he stood, it seemed as though the rest of the room shrunk. His stature was immense. He stood well over 9 feet tall. His arms, thin and lanky were taller than most men, and his legs outstretched like tree trunks. It's no secret around the Order that he was once a feared and revered warrior who'd seen many battles - some would say he'd seen them all.
How he rose to power is a story all its own, and it's one that not many can agree upon, but one thing is known as gospel truth; he killed the previous Master, the only one to had ever reigned. If the stories that some of the elders told were true, than it wasn't even a fight.
A younger Sharok grew to be the largest and strongest warrior the Order had ever seen. He was as powerful physically as he was with magic, and that caused unrest amongst the ranks.

However, little more is known beyond that. It was told that he was summoned to the chambers of the elders to be disciplined, but even they under estimated his strength. The Master, thought to be the oldest and strongest of all the members of the Order, cast a spell on Sharok, but he simply absorbed the blast and harnessed its ancient power.

Legend has it that the last thing The Master saw was a crooked and menacing smile before he was given the same fate as the gassy fly - turned to dust with a snap of his fingers. From then on the name Sharok was never uttered again. He became the new Master.

There was a rustling and an air of unrest about the room as the council of elders shifted around uncomfortably. The entire community was abuzz, right from the Elders to the fledglings, but there was also a nervous energy swarming. It'd been almost a millennium since Sharok stepped foot outside the confines of the Order, and nobody knew what to expect. Something terrible had been set in motion, and it wasn't that the 90 day expunging for many was approaching, although, that was pretty awful.

"I do declare..." The Master started, "That from this day fore-" RINNNNNNNNNNG.

"What in the almighty - "

"Master, you old sonofabitch." Shot out in a British accent from a familiar blue being the middle of the room. Why are holograms almost exclusively blue, and why does nobody question it. Nevertheless Mephisto, with his impeccable timing decided to hologram in with a status update. Sharok stood, visibly angered, and stared at the floating message.

"Hmm, is this a bad time, big guy?" Meph said in a sarcastic tone.

"What is it, *demon?"* Sharok said with a particular distain on the demon part.

"Oh, nothing... Unless of course you count that I know where that pesky Mother Nature will be in, oh... I don't know. Now?" Sharok's interest piqued.
"Go on," he said.
"And why should I tell you? Maybe I just wanted to rub it in," he said taking a puff of a cigarette, and blowing the smoke like that cocky douche outside the bar. You know the one, the one who's alone but thinks he's the hottest shit? Everybody hates that guy. Mephisto is totally that guy.
"*Demon!*" Sharok said with even more hatred than before, "You're forget who released you from exile, and you're forgetting who can send you back. I assure you, you do not want to test me."
"Alright, alright," Meph said swallowing hard. "I was just teasin'. They're headed to the Calvary Cemetery. Home to about 3 million or so corpses."
"A cemetery. Interesting. And what of the Necromancer?" Sharok asked.
"Oh, now look who needs me," Mephisto said with a smirk, which quickly dissipated into a look of fear when he saw the look on Sharok's face. Body language - the great equalizer.
"*Demon!*" Sharok said with a low and deep growl.
"Fine," Meph said, "he's on his way there too."
"That's what I thought. A clever plan, no doubt." Sharok said rubbing his chin in thought.
"That's what I thought!" Meph exclaimed. Sharok ignored him.
"But corpses are useless without souls." Sharok half said to himself, and half to nobody. He's forgotten that Meph was still there.
"Ahh, Master, lad, we're finally on the same page," he said. Sharok perked up, remembering his unwanted visitor.
"Hmm? Oh, yes, you're still here. Take care of those souls, I'll handle the rest. And take that piece of string off of your shoulder. You look like an imbecile." Sharok said.

"Oh, ha, yeah.. Funny story, that. An exterminator caught me hanging around. The look on his face when I transfo -" Sharok terminated the call mid sentence. He too was a giant douche. Emphasis on giant.

"rmed... That giant douche," Mephisto said to himself after Sharok cut him off. "I really, really hate that guy." He spun on his heels and threw his cigarette down the giant hole caused by Bort and Jort.. The butt landed on a pile of other extinguished butts that had to have been 6 feet tall and 4 feet around. Roughly a million cigarettes. But he didn't have a problem. He wasn't addicted. He lit up another one.
"Bort! Jort! Get out here." Meph yelled releasing a bunch of smoke into the air. The two Neanderthal brothers came rushing into through a doorway too small for one of them, let alone two. They broke the frame like it was a cracker; they didn't even feel it. Mephisto shook his head and began to rub his forehead. There are far more important things to worry about. But still, c'mon, how dumb can they really be?
With a sigh, Mephisto began, "Boys, please. For just a single, solitary moment, can you grow a brain between the two of you? I mean, look at the door!" He said waving his hands around like a maniac. The boys looked at the door, then at each other, and instantly began to blame each other for the wreckage. It started with pointing, then to gentle pushing, then to a slap, and then all out brawling.
"Well, that escalated quickly," Mephisto said, throwing yet another cigarette butt into the pile below. He hovered over the enormous hole in the ground and landed beside the brothers, who were literally beating the crap out of each other. Yes, literally. Crap everywhere.
"Enough!" Meph shouted, suspending the two idiots in the air, in that same magic bubble that held Chip. The brothers looked

shell shocked. They had forgotten what Mephisto was actually capable of doing.
"We are about to enter a very critical time in this war we're in, boys," he said, lighting up yet another cigarette. "Our freedom from that prick, Satan, is at stake. If you want to stay surface side, then I suggest that you behave and listen to me. I swear by the nine Hells that the slightest disagreement between you two, and I will end you. Hell would be too good for you. Do not test me further," Mephisto said descending, and finally landing softy on his feet.
"Do we have an understanding?" He asked softly to the brothers. They nodded in agreement and the bubbles popped. The cam crashing to the ground on top of one another. Mephisto watched them closely to see if they'd bicker in the least. However, to his surprise, they helped each other to their feet. He smiled.
"Just like dogs. Gotta show 'em who's boss," he said tossing the latest cigarette into the pile.
"Prepare yourselves, we have a lot of...pre...paring to do. Damnit. Just stop being idiots. three-million souls aren't gonna banish themselves" He added.
Beneath the generic suburban address of 32 Meadowbrooke Lane sat a dark and dank lair dressed to the nines in skulls, upside down crosses, and an assortment of skins and sinew. It was quaint. Although most of everything that hung from the walls and ceiling was just for show, the lair itself has a purpose - it's a sanctuary for the purest of evil. Summoning and sacrifices were standard for a place such as the cellar, however Mephisto had a darker, and much more sinister procedure in mind. What could be more evil than summoning and sacrificing? Well, there is one thing, and really only one thing.
When a body dies and its soul either ascends or descends, ya know, depending on those little decisions the person made in life, like whether or not to throw that old lady into traffic or not. However, no matter the direction in which it goes, the soul

still lives on and the entity continues to thrive, or suffer for all of eternity. But again, the key is that the life form lives on and gets to, in its purest form, be. But what Mephisto had planned takes the soul in its purest and simplest form, and casts it into oblivion, essentially snuffing it out of existence. Poof. Gone. No more.

There are fates worse than Hell, and being extinguished from existence is it. A searing pain followed by nothing forever, and not even death himself can describe what lies in the nothingness. Nobody can say for certain what happens when a soul is erased, but it's generally agreed upon that it is the worst fate, and sadly, once chosen, it's a fate from which nobody can escape. And Mephisto wanted to condemn upwards of three-million souls.

Condemning souls isn't the easiest of tasks, even for one of the most powerful demons to have ever been demonized. It takes preparation and time, both things Mephisto didn't really have, which means the old summoning and sacrifice thing is going to have to come into play.

"Jort, Bort. Please come see me in the lair." Meph yelled out. The two boys come meandering in, single file of course.

"Good boys," Meph said walking over to the giant buffoons. He smiled and caressed their heads individually with care and a gentleness that even surprised him. He sighed, and looked into each of their eyes and saw... nothing. He saw nothing behind those eyes. But that made them adorable in a sad and pathetic sort of way. They were dumb, but it wasn't their fault. They were loyal to a fault as well. When Meph decided to rebel and revolt, they were the only two that followed. They had an admiration for him. Or, at least they thought he had some Mexican Chilli to eat, even if they still didn't actually eat. He didn't, which was disappointing, but they quickly got over it.

"Oh lads, you're good boys," he said stroked Bort behind the ear. He smiled. Meph ignore the huge snot glob dangling from his nose. He turned his attention to Jort, smiled, and mimicked the head stroke.

"It's a damn shame, I tell ya, that it had to come to this," Meph said. He turned to face a large red curtain that back dropped a pedestal with an empty basin sitting on the top. With one hand on Jort's head, the other grabbed the curtain. Meph balled his fist, grabbing hold of the fabric and looked at Jort in the eye and smiled sheepishly.

In one swift motion Mephisto, the former general of Hell's army, yanked the curtain to the floor revealing a swirling purple vortex that was suspended in mid air. It was completely silent, and it seemed to suck everything from the room, including the sound. As the curtain piled on the ground, Mephisto pulled a blade from his belt and just as quickly as he pulled the curtain, he unsheathed the knife and ripped it across Jort's throat. Blood spewed outwards and as if guided by an invisible drain filling the bowl atop the pedestal.

As the blood pooled in the pedestal's top, the vortex turned from purple to orange, then from orange to red. It picked up speed and began to swirl at a fierce pace, and suddenly, there was sound within the room, but it didn't come from the room itself, but rather the vortex was emitting screams of horror and pain. Pure and utter terror. It wasn't a doorway to Hell, not even close. It was a doorway to something far, far worse.

As Jort bled out, Mephisto saw something leave his being, something he didn't know was there. A soul. He'd hoped there would be one – it was sort of the crux of his plan. Nevertheless, it had to be done. It was all happening too quickly for Bort to really understand what was going on, but in the violence, Mephisto saw something vanish from him too, as if a piece of him died with his brother. He'd always figured there was a bond between the two dolts, but he couldn't have imagined it was that powerful.

This plan might just work after all.

The vortex swirled and whirled with a ferocity not before seen in this world. Meph dared not stare into it for too long in fear that something, anything would suck him into the abyss. It takes a lot to scare a demon, a vortex into the unknown is one, and garbage water is the other. Strange, isn't it? Regardless, Meph turned his attention to a growingly distraught Bort. It began to hit him that his brother had just been murdered, the building blocks of an intense rage started to form within him.

Now, Mephisto was pretty sure that his plan, as cruel as it was, would work. He was also pretty sure that one brother would simply forget about the other. But in the moment, there was one thing he was pretty unsure of; can Bort rip his head from his body? It sure as Hell looked like it.

Bort's eyes grew wide, and turned a shade of orange, almost matching that of the vortex. He turned his attention to his brother's slayer, an attention Meph, frankly, didn't think he'd had in him. He certainly hoped that it wouldn't be maintained - it was freaking him out. Despite Mephisto's hope for Bort's gaze to drop, and for something shiny to grab his focus, it only seemed to grow. Meph began to look around himself as if to say, *what? Me? No, no, you're quite mistaken, I didn't slit your brother's throat and throw his soul into a portal of condemnation.* It's a very specific look.

Meph quickly threw his hand to his side and pointed at a sword hanging from the wall, "Look!" He shouted abruptly, "shiny!" He finished. Bort didn't flinch.

"Eeb." Meph muttered. Bort charged at him like a bull at a matador. He stomped his feet and threw his head and should down and began his charge. Dust kicked up from his feet as he marched forward with only one thing in mind - revenge. Jort and Bort may not have been the smartest of creatures, but they were stronger than they rightfully should have been. Apparently while enraged, they were even stronger. The ground began to shake around Meph's feet at Bort charged

forward making him have to think quickly, which luckily enough was one of Mephisto's stronger traits.
Quickly, Meph floated over the charging Neanderthal, who crashed into the solid concrete wall which tore like a fist through paper. In the process, Meph smacked his head on the ceiling, which he told the realtor was too low for what he needed, but do they ever listen? Nope. They just want the bloody sale. She'll burn in Hell with all the other sales people out there, no doubt, except for maybe JoJo Bonaman.
The year was 1923, and JoJo was nothing more than a door to door salesman. He sold a variety of thing from vacuums, to radios; from watches to fancy writing pens. He did it all, and with a smile, and good old JoJo sold everything under cost, which means he actually lost money. Of course, this wasn't his intention as it was a constant clerical error, mixed with his near inability to read. Nevertheless, when he sold items, they sold like hotcakes (which was another thing that he sold), but the profit margin of the company went from black to red and was never able to recover.
JoJo currently sits in heaven, playing cards and billiards with his old highschool chums (the ones who made it anyway), and as of today, is the only salesperson to have ever made it past the pearly gates. You may be asking why? It really had little to do with his sales goals, but more for the fact that his ignorance led to the downfall of a company that was employing slave labour, the top suits were all racist, and one was even a pedophile. Once the company went under, thanks to JoJo, they all killed themselves thanks to a silly suicide pact clause that state specifically if the business ever went under due to botched numbers, they'd kill themselves. It was in all of their contracts. Really, really dumb if you think about it.
Nevertheless, JoJo was a hero and was welcomed into the eternal Graceland with open arms.
Mephisto continued floating above the pacing Bort, who leapt at him occasionally, like the raptors from *Jurassic Park*. As

the revenge fuelled beast below leapt, paced, and snarled, Meph had an idea. He needed all the help he could get, and Bort was the perfect specimen. Driven by that intense rage, surely his soul was just plain engorged with soul juice, ready to burst. He needed to get that power into the Vortex, which would without doubt, be more than enough to get what he needs from it, the power to manipulate three-million souls.

Once he had that, it would be easy to summon them (he's already in the chamber for it) and reopen the vortex. After that, all he'd have to do is release them into the nether. Easy peasey - if it weren't for Bort being difficult, but he's still an idiot, after all. It can't be *that* hard to lure him into a pit of death and beyond.

After looking around the room for something, anything, to use to force the giant into the swirling hole of doom, he decided the simplest course of action was probably the best. Though, he had to try one more thing before he gave into simplicity - it just wasn't his style. He mustered up all the energy he had left after the vortex summoning. He tried to form a bubble around Bort, but all that came out was nothing more than a soap sud; a teeny tiny bubble that floated through the air right in front of Bort, who stared at it for a brief moment and swung madly at it, as it were the sphere filled with air that did his brother in.

Plan B made Mephisto really uncomfortable.

The demon general floated to one end of the room, furthest away from the portal, which drew his suitor with him. In the blink of an eye, Meph disappeared and reappeared about a foot from the mouth of the vortex. He could feel the energy being sapped from his body being as close as he was. Bort was confused for a moment at the disappearing act, but he quickly found his target. Again, he dropped his head and shoulders and charged like a raging elephant at Mephisto, who at the moment had his eyes closed in concentration. He felt the ground around him vibrate with the impact of Bort's march, and when he felt

it was time, he gently, but quickly ascended to the ceiling - where he hit his head again.
Mephisto opened his eyes just in time to see Bort slam on the brakes, but it wasn't enough. He caught the lip of the vortex, which was very unforgiving, and sucked him in. Meph caught the look in his eyes as he went in, and it went from anger, to confusion, to fear in a matter of a second. Meph slowly descended and lit up a cigarette. He felt something he'd never felt before, in any existence, or lifetime. It was unpleasant. He felt... bad, or was it sad. Either way, he felt something after seeing his last loyal servant fall into oblivion. Business was business, after all, and sometimes cuts had to be made. Or soul sacrificing, that worked too.
However, the feeling didn't last long for as soon as his feet hit the ground, a beam of pure energy shot from the vortex and into Mephisto's chest. It burned and scorched his body, and he stiffened in pain - another newish experience for him. Sure the elders could inflict something akin to pain, but the beam was something entirely different. He gritted his teeth as he began to hover inches off the ground, which was not by his doing. The power within the beam was so concentrated that it was forcing him off the ground. It was more powerful than he could have ever imagined. No ordinary mortal, creature, or demon would be able to harness the pure power emanating through him.
Just as quickly as the beam lurched out at him, it stopped. It didn't suck itself back in like an arm, or slowly dissipate, rather it just halted completely, and the portal closed. Poof, just like when Sharok snapped his fingers. Meph fell to the ground, and sat on his hands and knees for a moment, catching his breath. He noticed his cigarette didn't go out. He picked it up and took a hit.
"Wow. it's time to fuck shit up," he said looking straight ahead, with glowing purple eyes filled with enough oomph to corral

say... three-million dead souls and send them into nothingness.

# CHAPTER 16

Built in 1847, or thereabouts, the Calvary Cemetery was first home to a number of unfortunate folks suffering from cholera, a truly unfortunate disease. From there, people just kept on dying, and the original New Yorkers had nowhere to put 'em. What do they do? Take a massive chunk of land and throw the rotting corpses in there. Over time it's become quite the attraction, and quite the storage facility for corpses. In and around three-million souls were laid to rest there, many of them Catholic, which pretty much guaranteed them a spot in Heaven, which will be a rude awakening for them if Mephisto can bring his disgusting plan to fruition.

The cemetery might be home to millions of the dead, but it's also been home to a number of supernatural creatures looking for solace in world over-run by closed minded mortals who would just run screaming at the sight of them. Sadly, not all creatures are as beautiful as faeries, or can cast a glamour spell to hide in plain sight as a human, or a squirrel. Yes, squirrels. Ever wonder why there are so many of them? Exactly. However, the peaceful, if not gothic, cemetery was now sanctuary to another guest. Mother Nature.

Tombstones litter the grounds in seemingly no particular order or pattern; some are near monoliths, while others are simple pieces of stone with nothing more than a date and name etched into its surface. In between the chaos of stone and mounds sat Ellie and her small entourage consisting of Zed, a rabbit named Frank, a hummingbird called Alice, and warrior centaur by the name of Bruno. The company did their best to hide from sight by finding a cropping of large monuments, and setting up a small camp.

Ellie sat with a shroud covering her face, and a thick wool blanket wrapped around her shoulders. She was nervous, shaking a touch, which made the weather around her turn to a bitter cold. The wind picked up with every anxious breath, which set a crisp chill down her parties spines. They could feel the tension in the air, and they all knew what was at stake. It was quiet as they all huddled around one another, with Bruno and Frank acting as lookouts, and Zed resting on Ellie's shoulder. Nobody spoke, and only the rapid fluttering of Alice's wings could be heard throughout the radius of their camp. Every gust of wind kicked up a fuss of leaves and dried bouquets, which sent a shot of attention through Bruno, who turned and pointed his spear in the direction of the rustling. Frank just ate the debris.

Ellie wish she had more followers at the moment, however she couldn't blame the rest for wanting to stay under the protection of Paradise, and she wasn't about to force anybody else to come. This mission was strictly voluntary, and she cherished the few that showed. But she was worried, not only for those left behind, but for the whereabouts of Chip.

"Are you sure Fabian got there alright?" Ellie asked of Zed.

"Sure he did," Zed said calmly, if not a little unconfident.

"How will he know where to find us? This place if massive." She asked with a hint of worry.

"Fabian knows. He'll be with them. Try to relax. I'm sure things will work out. We're surrounded by millions of corpses and skeletons. I'm sure your boy can get them up and going again. He'll be like a shot of Viagra in these limp wieners. " Zed said with a smirk, Ellie shot her a confused look then smiled.

"Viagra? I didn't think you woodland folk needed that."

"Oh we don't. I mean, at least I've never been with somebody who's needed it. But, can you blame 'em, look at this body," Zed said twirling off Ellie's shoulder and giving her a little spin around, followed up with a wink.

"Super sexy, Zed," Ellie said very solemnly, which in turned bummed out Zed. She floated back onto Ellie's shoulder.
"I was sure sex would spark the conversation. I mean Frank and Bruno are kinda hot. I wouldn't mind just tearin-" Zed stopped and bit her lip. Ellie looked shocked.
"Wh-what?" Ellie asked with eyes wide.
Zed cleared her throat. "Sorry, it's been a while, ya know? A faerie has needs, and I'm not picky, if you know what I mean," Zed said with another wink.
"You're a whore?" Ellie said half jokingly.
"Hey, hey...that's only...okay, yeah, kinda. I mean if we go by human standards. Faeries are notorious for their 'sexcapades.' It's in our nature, we can't help it. We're tiny, easily killed, we've gotta reproduce to avoid dying out. C'mon, mum, simple evolution." Zed explained.
"That actually makes sense," Ellie said.
"Of course it does, I just made it up, but it must be true." Ellie squinted in a weird sort of disgust and curiosity.
"Anyway..," Ellie said.
"Yeah, we need a topic change. I'm about to grab Alice and use her to fuck Frank."
"Whoa!" Ellie exclaimed, "a little bit TMI."
"Fair enough. Now I know where the line is," Zed said with a smile, "are you ready, by the way?"
"Ready for what?" Ellie replied.
"For any of this? Where you warned. I don't really know how this works. That was always Stirling's thing," Zed said looking down. Stirling was quite the popular girl. She knew everyone, did everything, and was always friendly. The two looked down in sadness remembering their fallen comrade.
"Well, honestly? No idea. I didn't know until that bastard kidnapped me however long ago that was," Ellie said looking to the overcast sky. "I've lost track of time, Zed. Everything's moved so fast, but my life seems at a standstill. How much do you know about the ceremony?" She asked.

"A little." Zed responded.
"It doesn't end well for me, does it?" Ellie asked with an awkward smile.
"In the past, Mother Nature just sort of disappears into a billion little golden flakes. It doesn't seem painful or anything, it seems quite peaceful. But yeah, I'm pretty sure that it's a one way trip. I'm sorry," Zed said lying down on Ellie's shoulder.
"Nah, don't be. I mean, sure I'll miss everybody, and I'll miss Chip, but I mean, if I don't do this, who knows what will happen, and I might not get to see him ever again anyway. So it's for the best," Ellie said, as a raindrop landed on her head.
"Cheer up and try to not think about it. We have to stay focused," Zed said hovering under Ellie's chin and lifting it.
"There, there." Zed added, wiping away a tear from Ellie's eye. She smiled softly.
"Thanks Zed. Hey, maybe you should take Alice and Frank back to the sanctuary. I don't want you guys to get hurt... or worse. I can't see any more friends die. Bruno and I will be fine, I'm sure," Ellie said. Zed zipped back a few inches from Ellie's face and looked her right in the eye.
"Frank, Alice, Bruno, get over here would ya?" She said not breaking eye contact with Ellie.
"What? What are you doing?" Ellie asked as the rest gathered round.
"Mother Nature here wants me to take you guys back home. She doesn't think we can handle it." Zed proclaimed
"Hey, that's not true at all... I don't want to see you guys hurt. And I said Bruno can stay," Ellie said, in a poor attempt to defend herself.
"Mmhmm. Guys, even if I dragged you out of here, would you stay gone?"
"Nope." Frank said.
"Notta chance." Alice said.
"It's my duty to protect, and I am honoured that you requested my presence." Bruno said.

"Okay there, B - at ease, or whatever," said Zed, "But see, Ellie. None of us are going anywhere."
Ellie flashed a sad smile, you know the one, when you ask somebody if they want to tag along somewhere, but it's really only out of guilt and you don't really want them to go, but they agree to come? It's awful. However, in this instance, it was really sweet of them. She just really prays that they don't get hurt - or dead. That would be bad.
"You guys are the best," Ellie said. They all looked at each other with admiration, and they each felt it was super appropriate to hug it out, and so they did. A bunny, a Nymph, a hummingbird, and a faerie. Suffice it to say - it was an awkward hug. Nobody really knew where to grab, and it more turned into a weird cuddling session.
"Alright," Ellie said as they all pulled away from one another, "Let's hunker down and wait for our cavalry. " The group nodded and went back to their prior patrols along the parameter of their little base camp.

Meanwhile, Chip and his companions made way for the enormous cemetery in Queens, and this time Mort wore clothes. The trek wasn't a long one, and it was sort of boring too, if truth be told. They didn't have to cross mountains, nor did they have to fight orcs and goblins. There were no wild beasts to slay, and nothing to really get in there way. Though, there was a close call with an angry cabbie, and the lights at Alan Street and 1st Avenue were treacherous. But that's just New York City living.
"I'm hungry," Mort said as they passed their 18th hotdog stand.
"Me too," said Bill in agreement.
"Seriously, guys? We're about to go save the world, and you just wanna eat?" Chip said halting in the middle of the sideway.
"What? Can't save the world on an empty stomach," Mort stated.

"You ate before we left!" Chip exclaimed.
"Yeah, but that was like...I dunno, half an hour ago. I'm a growing boy," Mort explained.
"You're like 25 years old!"
"Yeah, but it's a known fact that boys grow until their late 40's. I'm still a baby who needs his num nums," Mort said with a smile.
"Nu...Num Nums? Jesus Christ. Bill, would you talk some sense... What is that?" Chip said in reference to the turkey sandwich Bill was chomping down on.
"Hmm?" Bill said swallowing hard, "this? Oh, I knew I had it stashed in my beard somewhere. Couldn't find it earlier, but this whole conversation got those old cogs a turnin', and voila, sandwich." He finished explaining, and then took another bite. He had a literal shit eating grin on his face.
"Awwwwwwwwwww! Lucky!" Mort proclaimed staring right at the sandwich.
"Oh for the love of... Get a freaking hot dog," Chip said throwing his hands in the air.
"Yay!" Mort cheered like a six year old girl. "But I dunno if I feel like a hot dog."
Chip's gaze at that moment was beyond sending daggers into Mort. It was more like a nuclear launch, and all the missiles in the world were aimed directly at him.
"What do you want, then?" Chip snarled through gritted teeth.
Mort, feeling the pressure cowered like a scolded dog. "A hot dog, a hot dog will do," he said while scuttling over to the nearest stand.
"Aww! They don't have hot peppers." He yelled from a the short distance. Chip's eye twitched.
"Mort!" He snapped.
"Okay!" Mort yelled back in a panic. "I won't be happy about it though," he said to himself.
"It's like he's a child," Chip said to Bill, who finished the last bite of his sandwich.

"Hmm, laddy, you're both children. And you've both been thrown into something you have no business being in - but here you are, brave and strong. It's admirable, and you have to give it to the boy, he's coping well. You should have seen him when we first met. When he realized he could control things, he literally shit his pants and fainted. Talk about a child/parent relationship. I had to wipe his bloody arse," Bill said, which made Chip chuckle, it also put the situation into perspective.
"Heh, when was that? Like 20 years ago or something?" Chip asked.
"HA!" Bill bellowed, causing all those around him to give him a questioning glare. "No, like 6 years ago." He added.
"Oh," Chip said. It was all he could muster.
"But, I knew it was going to happen, so I was prepared. Same I knew that you'd eventually come across that corpse. And that you'd harness your powers," Bill said as he glanced over at Mort, who was still piling condiments onto his wiener. It looked less like a hot dog than it should and more like a spill in aisle six at Wal-Mart.
"So, if you can see everything to come, Bill... How's this going to end?" Chip asked morbidly.
"I dunno, lad. I can only see certain things. Stuff like the end of the world, ultimate fates, that sorta jazz. I have no idea. There are too many possible outcomes, and it hasn't been written yet. Life has some predefined paths. Sometimes they fork or wind, but they always lead to the same destination. Other times the path is being forged as it's walked. This is one of those situations," Bill explained.
"Whattya talking about?" Mort said walking up behind the pair with a mouth full of ketchup and relish.
"Nothing, Mort. Just about the end of the world," Chip said with a smirk.
"Oh, okay then," Mort said taking another bite.
The trio carried on their not so merry way towards what is sure to be something colossal in scale. What that was exactly, they

couldn't be certain. One thing was for sure, the fact the Fabian had been flying above them the whole time was making the lot of the nervous. Hey, a pigeon flying over your head for miles at a time would make you nervous too, though, they say it's good luck. Those people clearly have never been crapped on by a bird.

The city remained more or less the same as the passersby really had no idea of the potential consequences should Chip and friends screw everything up, which was entirely possible. In fact, it was more probable than possible. Chip was having some kind of luck, what with slaying the giant Butcher demon and not dying. He wondered how much longer his luck would last. After all, he's never been particularly lucky. He's never won the lottery, a raffle, or even a single roll of roulette. He's never beaten the house at a casino, and he'd never been the one millionth customer at a grocery store. Hell, even sure things, like when he was in the 8th grade and was the only person to put his name into a draw for a free backpack, he didn't even win. That one still perplexed him.

History has that nasty habit of repeating itself, but all he could do was hope that it wouldn't. The worry wore on his face despite his best efforts to contain it. Bill knew what he was thinking. Mort was oblivious, but he could tell something was off, which was even worse as the cemetery was in eyeshot, and the scene was being set by the ambient feeling of the slow sunset which painted the sky a multitude of colours. Orange and purple soared across the heavens, but there was a darkness lurking beyond the beauty. Heavyset clouds were rolling in across the horizon, and in no time they would surely cover the sky completely.

Chip looked at the ominous skyline and gulped.

"What's the matter, pal?" Mort said throwing his arm around Chip's shoulder.

"Hmm?" Chip responded snapping out of his gaze. "Nothin'. Just thinking, buddy." It was turning into a real emotional moment. Pet names were being used.
"You've always been a bad liar. Unlike me, who's been lying to you for months about this whole voodoo thing. Yeah, I know I'm the master," Mort gloated.
"Yeah, yeah. I dunno. I'm just thinking what if this doesn't work out? What if we fail? There's more than just our lives are at stake here. The whole fucking world will die...probably... if we fail. That part's still a bit blurry." Chip confessed.
"Hey, come on now. We're the best team since peanut butter and broccoli. We can't fail. Besides, what's the worst that could happen? Some trees die? Doesn't seem so bad. I'm really only here to help you get Ellie back."Mort said.
"Interesting," Chip said taking a moment to think, "I don't know, Mort. I feel like if there's a super powerful demon involved, the stakes are probably higher than just a few trees dying. It probably has to do with Hell on Earth, or something," Chip said.
"Well, you might have a point there." More agreed. "It doesn't matter though. If this guy shows up, you'll have all the ammo you'll need to create the largest army of the undead that the world has ever seen. I wouldn't worry," Mort explained.
"That's if he shows up." Chip muttered.
"He'll show. He seems to know everything."
"What if he knows it's a trap?"
"He doesn't."
"But you said he knows everything."
"Everything but that it's a trap."
"Right."
"Glad you agree," Mort ended.
"Ladies! Enough chit chat. We're almost there," Bill shouted out from up ahead of the two.
"How do you know where to go, Bill? The cemeteries huge!" Chip asked.

"Follow the bird," Bill said pointing up.
"Oh yeah, Fabian," Chip said.
"That bastard," Mort said looking up, breaking the cardinal rule when a bird is flying above you. Out of spite, Fabian let one go, which was like a homing missile towards Mort's face. He instantly regretted everything he'd ever done to that bird.
*The final march was on. The cemetery within eyeshot, a damsel in distress, a fellowship of heroes, and Mort, with bird shit on his face. It was damn near picture perfect. As with any good story that segues into its final act, the band of unlikely champions face insurmountable odds, against an enemy that simply shouldn't exist. Yet, they go in with blind faith and a bit of beginners luck, hoping for the best possible outcome. History will be written, but just because the heroes march courageously doesn't mean it's going to be a happy ending.*
"Mort!" Chip shrieked.
"Yeah?" He said snapping back to reality.
"Stop narrating this! It's creepy."
"Sorry."
*The heroic three, led by their fearless leader, Mortimer Blake, master of voodoo, controller of inanimate things, babe magnet, march forw-*
"MORT!"
"Sorry."

It wasn't just three odd, yet powerful human beings, or whatever Bill really was, and a very strange pigeon, making the pilgrimage to the cemetery. From the opposite end of the city walked a very powerful looking Mephisto. He surged with the energy provided to him by the vortex, and at times he struggled to keep himself on the ground - literally. With every step he felt as though he were weightless, as if walking on the moon. In stark contrast, he felt more powerful than he'd ever before. He felt both light and heavy with power. He walked past unwitting strangers on the street, who would occasionally

bump shoulders with him. It was the last thing they ever did. The energy that enveloped Mephisto simply could not be harnessed by a mortal, causing those who got too close to vanish, leaving nothing behind. No clothes, no possessions, nothing was left of the individual. They were absorbed into the Godlike entity that was Mephiso.
With every soul absorbed, he felt his power grow. He could almost see the energy flowing from his finger tips. In fact, it was. Despite his power, he wanted to maintain a level of conspicuousness. Unwanted attention from The Devil - or even worse, God, would be bad. Besides, he wanted the element of surprise. He was pretty certain that the group had no idea he knew of their plan of trapping him. Which in turn made his plan of trapping them that much better. He couldn't help but shake at the anticipation sending three million souls into the vast nothingness beyond that vortex. The power and the rush he'll get from absorbing them would be beyond anything he could fathom, and it excited him like a highschooler about to get laid.
"In other news, there have been a rash of strange occurrences in the city today. Freak weather, noises which sound like explosions, and an entire bus disappearing. More to come on these stories, and more at 11 o'clock." A TV news anchor reported on a screen in a store front.
"Things are about to get a whole lot weirder," Meph said to himself.
"What did you call me?" A woman stopped after hearing Mephisto mutter to himself.
"Hmm?" He said, confused.
"Did you call me a whore?!" She squawked in a thick New Yorker accent. "I think you called me a whore!" She yelled louder causing a scene.
"Uhh... No, I didn't. But if that's what you heard, then that's what you must be," he said in return, turning to walk away.

"Ohhhhhhhh, no you didn't!" The sassy black woman exclaimed, only the way a sassy black woman could. "Imma call the cops!" She threatened, which obviously didn't faze Mephisto.

"Police! Police!" The woman screamed at the top of her lung, "Rape! This man is trying to rape me!" She shouted louder and louder. Meph rolled his eyes, but noticed a small crowd was gathering around the scene. Mephisto tried to walk away. He tucked his hands into his pockets to hide the energy surging from his finger tips. Thankfully, he already wore mirrored sunglasses to hide the purple effervescent glow emanating from his eyeholes.

"Oh boy," he said to himself as he tried to walk away, but she kept going about rape this and rape that. He couldn't help but think this woman wanted nothing more in life than to be raped. Classic playing the victim.

"Where do you think you're going, pal?" A big burly fellow in a stained white wife-beater said stepping in front of him. Meph said nothing and turned around, trying to ignore the bouncer.

"Nuh-uh, buddy. You don't offend and rape a woman around here and just think you can walk away." The man said, clearly jumping to conclusion. Meph stopped in his tracks. He rolled his eye, sighed, and cracked his neck.

"Lad, if I raped her, she wouldn't be able to walk, let alone have the energy to go on like this. Just ask your sister," he said with a smirk; always the antagonist.

"What the fuck did you just say to me?" The barrel chested man asked, clearly offended. The woman who started the whole thing made some obnoxious noise and started to giggle waving her hand in the air.

"Oooooh, you gonna get yours now," she said in reference to Meph.

"Please, luv, wait in line," he said over his shoulder. "Look, mate, you're gonna just want to turn around and walk away

before you get yourself hurt," he said staring the big man in the eye, which of course he couldn't see due to the shades.
"Me? ME? Ha. You're funny, pal." The man said before rushing towards him.
"Sigh," Mephisto said, yes, the word sigh, not the gesture. "Fuck it. Nobody really liked this street anyway," he said.
Those words confused all those around him. Luckily enough, it was the last thing any of them got to hear or feel before they simply disappeared. Mephisto had let loose a small burst of energy from his core, which all but levelled the entire block. The purple ring of energy stretched from him, to the other side the block in two waving pulses. Not a noise was heard, not even a gust of wind, and when it was all over, in about a second and a half, not a soul remained.
"Hmm," Meph said looking around. "That'll do it."
He took one more glance around to make sure nothing, or no one noticed. There was no lightning bolt from the big cheese upstairs, and the ground didn't open up dropping him into the pits of Hell. It seemed as though everything was A.Okay. That was until he took a step forward and lost his balance completely. Mephisto reached out and propped himself up against the building. He wasn't sure what happened when he released the ring of energy, like where the souls went, or what happened to the people. He just assumed they either died, or he absorbed them. Whatever it was, he didn't feel too hot, which was weird because demons, by nature, were always hot - duh.
Somehow the smallest release weakened him, and he began to worry what might happen if absorbing the souls in the cemetery doesn't empower him, but weakens him. Springing off the wall, he shook loose the thought. It was different. He expelled the power from his body, which clearly drained him. He had to absorb souls, which could only make him stronger. He liked that theory better, and therefore it was the one with which he would stick. He just hoped that he could make to the

cemetery without passing out, so he lit up a cigarette. They make everything better.

# CHAPTER 17

The nether wasn't such a bad place after all. Sure it was dark, and a bit colder than they were used to, but ultimately there was a lot of space, or no space. It was hard to tell. Jort and Bort couldn't quite figure it out. Either way, they, or their souls anyway, were having a decent time rolling around, pummelling one another with nobody to yell at them telling them to stop messing about. They did sort of miss Mephisto though - he was like an abusive stepfather to them. He kept them around and even made them feel important and useful at times. But, as with most abusive relationships, there were a lot more bad times than good. Mephisto never did bring the boys to a ball game, or take them to the park - all things they wanted to do, but just couldn't find the words. They were both a little too dumb for language.

But, he did send them to the magical emptiness in which they now inhabited, probably forever. The only thing they didn't like was the seemingly endless swarm of...something... always in the distance. They could never quite get to it, for no matter how much they walked towards it, it always seemed to stay the same distance away. At first they thought it was the most beautiful thing they laid eyes on, but over time, which passed differently in the nether, it slowly terrified them. Something about it first unsettled Jort, but Bort wasn't buying it - he still found it prettyful.

As time crept on, Bort began to see how uncomfortable Jort was when they were facing it, and it soon infected him like a virus. He trembled at the sight of the orange swirling mass and its mesmerizing allure. He caught himself staring at it from time to time; it usually only felt like seconds, minutes at most,

but Jort claims he would be caught in its gaze for much, much longer. Since neither of them have any concept of time in the void, Jort could only estimate that he would stare for thousands of years - a gross overestimation. Still, it was probably longer than a few minutes.
The notion that it could grab the attention of either one of them only added to the worry they already felt, and so they made a promise to one another to always have their back facing it. Of course it was a terrifying thought to have their backs always facing the evilness that was the swarm, but it was for the best, and it worked. They began to feel better, and they were able to play and frolic freely, that is until one morning (one can only assume it was morning), when they awoke to be facing it. They were certain they didn't move in their sleep, and that could only mean one thing - the mass was moving.
Bort and Jort decided the only course of action was to move away from it. Always keep walking the other way. It was a great plan in theory, however the glob never seemed to grow in distance. Just as they walked towards it with no success, they walked away with the same result. The brothers barely had the brain capacity to know when to use the washroom, this scenario was freaking them the hell out.
Panic slowly set it in two them both, and they became paranoid, thinking the other one was in on it. It must have been the other's fault, right? Since they were sucked - or sacrificed - into the vortex, they hadn't seen single other being. No floating skulls, no ghosts, no zombies or demons. There was nothing but emptiness, and the swarm, so naturally who else could be at fault but either Bort or Jort. Their gratefulness for having one another had transformed into a pit of resentment, pushing them apart. If moving away from the ball in the distance made no difference in terms of proximity, it was super confusing that as the brothers fought, they found themselves moving further and further apart physically from one another.

Before long, Bort and Jort were just specks on their respective horizons, with the swarm being equal distance from them - which seemed impossible. For all intents and purposes, they were alone. Bort had the most trouble after losing Jort. He felt awful for being so accusatory towards his brother. Jort had similar feelings, but he was mostly hungry - which was a first, and if was honest with himself, Bort looked a tasty treat.

It wasn't long before boredom set it, and Bort especially wanted to rekindle his relationship with his brother. Jort too was bored, but the hunger rose up and overtook all of his thoughts. He couldn't go a second without thinking about food, or eating, or starving. It was especially weird - going seconds, or minutes, or even hours without thinking about anything was sort of his speciality. He prided himself on it. But the hunger, it was too much.

Bort could see his brother pacing in the distance. Of course he looked like nothing more than a flea on a dogs back from where he stood, but he could tell it was him. There was nobody else around. As Bort watched him like a game of pong, going left, then right, then left, he got a bit dizzy. Motion sickness was always a problem with him. He closed his eyes and rubbed them harder than he should have, and when he opened them again, all he could see were little spots of light, which happens when one rubs their eyes too much. Through the blinking dots, he could see his brother now at a standstill, and he could feel him watching him. It was a bit creepy. Just as the dots cleared from Bort's eyes, he saw his brother clearly on the horizon, and then in a split second, he vanished.

The hunger was too intense for Jort to handle. He could see his brother watching him in the distance, and no doubt he felt the same hunger. He must have been sizing him up to eat, it was the only explanation. He wouldn't let that happen, he would survive this time. It was dog eat dog, and he would be the one with the full belly at the end of the day. But first, he needed a little lie down. Jort hit the ground, or what he assumed to be the ground as everything around him was the same shade of black, devoid of anything.

Bort became worried, of course. But just as Jort fell from existence, he was overcome with a sense of sleepiness. It was stronger than anything he'd ever felt before, and before he knew it, he too fell asleep. He crashed to the ground, and slept like a rock. He didn't dream, he didn't move, he simply slept the deepest sleep he'd ever slept.

Unlike his brother, Jort dreamt feverishly wild dreams. He dreamt about the ball of whatever in the distance. He dreamt his brother was tortured, skinned, and cooked on a spit, spinning slowly over a flame. Where Bort laid still in a state of unconsciousness, Jort writhed on the ground. Arms flailing and crashing, his legs kicked in a fit of struggling making this sleep full of unrest and, in fact, it was rather exhausting. And then, just as quickly as he passed out, he awoke. But he wasn't alone.

Before him hovered the great massive swarm. It stayed about a foot off of his ground level, but it didn't emit any light, or heat whatsoever. It was like it was a being in and of itself, not a ball of light like the sun. However, he and his brother were right in considering it a swarm. It appeared to be a concentrated version of the vortex. It was orange, with skulls, and faces, and various other macabre and unidentifiable things floating, moving and swimming around its confines. Jort felt as though he should have been afraid, but he wasn't. Instead he felt calm and at ease - and hungry. His hunger intensified with every passing moment the thing floated above him. He could do nothing but stare at it. It made no noise, which was uncomfortable, but soothing at the same time. He suddenly didn't feel so alone. He wanted to touch it.

Slowly, Jort rose to his feet and brushed off his shirt, for some reason. Just as slowly he reached out toward the entity, which did not move. His hand hovered, his fingertips trembled as it hung just inches from the swarming mass. Swallowing hard,

Jort took the plunge and threw his entire arm at the thing. His hand went through a weird squishy membrane and into the abyss itself, and in an instance, he began to draw energy from it like a lamp plugged into a socket. He began to glow the colour of the swarm, and then it vanished with no warning.
Jorts arm still hung straight ahead of him, glowing. He looked around with his eyes and a slacked jaw, but despite the glowing, he did't feel any different, except for the sensation of being watched. Slowly he turned on his heels and glanced over his shoulder. Behind him stood an entity of an immense stature. He couldn't get a good look at it before whatever it was screamed in a pitch reserved for dog whistles, and forced itself into Jort's body. Now Jort felt differently.
Bort's uninterrupted sleep soon felt stale and no longer refreshing. He began to shift for the first time, his body felt stiff and painful, like he'd just run a marathon, despite not moving an inch. His muscles had begun to atrophy, which sent a message to his tiny brain that it was time to wake up. He slowly opened his eyes to the world around him, which was just has he'd left it - dark and empty, or so he thought. Rolling on to his back, he closed his eyes again to get a good stretch in, and when he opened them up again he was met by the gaze of his brother. Though, it wasn't quite his brother. An initial reaction of excitement quickly morphed into fear as he realized what stood lurking over him wasn't who he'd thought, but rather a monster not of this world, or any he'd known to have existed - and let's be honest, he didn't know much of what existed, or anything of his world let alone others.
Anyway, Bort went to stand if nothing more than to back away from this imposter, but he was blocked by Jort's foot to his chest. He fought and struggled, but he was too weak from his nap. Completely drained of energy, Bort succumbed and laid flat once again. He looked up with an expression of pure, unadulterated terror on his face. Tears began to well and

eventually stream from his eyes as he knew this wasn't going to end well.
Looking down at his brother, Jort tilted his head. The hunger was too much, he couldn't handle it. He needed to eat, and Bort was his only source of food. He smiled, and any semblance of what Jort once was had disappeared completely, being enveloped by that entity. His smile widened, revealing a mouth full of six inch long teeth. Rows and rows of razor sharp spikes lined his ever growing maw, and just when it reached its limit, Jort reached down and grabbed Bort by the shoulder. In flash he threw him into the air and swallowed his once brother hole. The circle of life; the food chain, whatever nature dictated in the real world apparently applied in the vast nothingness that was the nether.

***

While the time in the nether moved at an erratic rate, time in the real world chugged along at its normal pace, which Mephisto cursed. His entire body ached, he'd never felt pain like that before. He had a firm understanding of it and what it could do, but he'd not known it first had. The power that surged through him was becoming a burden, and he was beginning to think that he wasn't meant to wield such a force. Every step was agony, and he wretched in pain with every slight movement. Nausea hit him like a brick wall, but he'd never eaten, so there was nothing to throw up. It was a very complicated situation, and Meph didn't quite understand it.
On top of the pain, he was now confused, which in turn made his head spin and throb. He could just give up and absorb the souls and send them into the vortex right there, but he need to be as central as possible in order to get them all, and in his current state, he couldn't risk letting the necromancer revive a single corpse. He just hoped that after the whole thing was

done, he'd regain his strength so he could pop that bastards head like the pusy pustule it is.
"Ugh!" He groaned and fell to a knee.
"This whole pain thing sucks," Mephisto said to himself through gritted teeth.
With a deep breath, he pulled a cigarette from a pack in his pocket, lit it up, and trudged on like a trooper. He stumbled forward , clutching tombstones and statues as he marched on towards his destiny. He truly was a sorry sight.

As luck would have it, Chip and the gang arrived at the cemetery at almost the exact moment that Mephisto made his way into the sanctuary of the dead. Luckily enough, they entered from two separate ends, avoiding a prefight fight. Meph entered from the east, and Chip from the south, however, they both made their way towards the same location - dead centre. It was a convenient place for the meet up, and a suitable place to have a battle really.
The sky had changed from the glorious twilight hues to a dark and cloudy night. No lights lined the cemetery, making the walk more treacherous than it should be. Gravestones jutted from every which angle, the occasional gopher hole surprised the group, twisted ankles and bruised shins were inevitable. Though, if truth be told, if they escaped the night with a couple of bruises, that would be a win.
"Hold up, lads," Bill said, holding up his fist and punch Mort in the face.
"Ahhhhhhoooooooooow!" Mort yelped holding his nose.
"Sorry, son. Didn't see ya there," he said with a smirk.
"No shit?" He said through his cupped hands.
"Shush. It's too dark... we need some light," Bill said half to himself, half to the others.
"Ya think? Gaaaaawwwwd, it hurts so much," Mort said. Chip laughed.

"Hold a sec," Bill said. He reached up and grabbed a handful of beard hair, and in one solid motion, he ripped it clean from his face. Mort and Chip winced in vicarious pain. Bill held the hair to his mouth and whispered a few secret words, ending with a little blow. Instantly the hair ignited into flame and hovered in the air.
"That'll do," he said with a smile and carried on his way with the flame ball leading the way.
"Whoa." Chip and mort said in unison, and followed.
Chip sniffed the air after a few seconds. Something smelled off, but he couldn't quite put his finger on it.
"Hey, Mort," he said whispering, "you smell that?"
"Ha-Ha. Very funny," he said pulling his hands away from his nose.
"Oh sweet mother of God." Chip exclaimed, in reference to Mort's twisted, swollen, bloody nose. Really, it was gross. It looked like a corkscrew it was so twisted.
"Wh-what? Is it that bad?" Mort said with a nasally voice which whistled on every breath.
"N...no... Not at all..," Chip said turning away. He may have thrown up in his mouth a bit. "Hey, at least you can't smell that. It smells like...gross meat and burning...hair. Oh God." That's when it hit him. Bills burning beard smelled worse than Bill did. Chip definitely threw up this time.
The glow of the disgusting beard lantern shone ominously across the various graves and tombstone, throwing shadows to and fro, dancing across the ground like a ballet of the dead. The cemetery seemed peaceful and calm in the twilight, but in the dead of darkness, it rang eerie and disconcerting. The feel of something watching was never too far off, and the stench of wet grass mixed with the lantern made Chip throw up again, behind a grave marked *Marcy Davis: 1897-1907.* The poor girl died young, and Chip just yakked all over her resting place. He made a mental note *not* to reanimate her. It was the respectful thing to do.

As the three trekked onwards in the orange glow of Bill flame beard, two of the party member - it's obvious who - began to get anxious, like two kids in the backseat of a car on their way to grandma's for summer vacation. They wondered if they'd ever arrive, Hell, they wondered if they weren't just walking in circles. Everything began to look the same, and it was driving Mort slightly insane.

"I don't think we're ever going to find her, Chip," Mort said through a whistly nose.

"We will. Just keep following Fabian," Chip said pointing upwards. Mort cowered and carefully eyeballed the pigeon.

"I still don't trust him," he said quietly.

"Just, keep walking." Chip encouraged, looking back at Mort, who lingered a few steps behind. He wasn't even sure if he believed what he was saying.

"Just, keep your head up, okay?" Chip said, turning his head to look in front of him. Sadly, it was about a second too late as he crashed in a static Bill.

"Bill!" Chip explained holding his face. "What the Hell?"

"Look, lad," Bill said pointing ahead. "That's not something you see every day," he said in reference to a hummingbird darting back and forth just on the outskirts of his beard lamp.

"It's a hummingbird, Bill. Not the second coming," Chip said with snark.

"And when was the last time you saw one at night?" Bill asked.

"Well, I don't know. I don't think I've ever seen one in the day." Chip answered.

"And you don't find it suspicious that there's one just oh, patrolling, in a graveyard at night?"

"Fine, when you put it that way..."

"Good, then you agree that we should check it out."

"I didn't say tha-"

"Let's go, boys!" Bill said taking off into a light jog of excitement towards the hummingbird. Chip and Mort look at each other, and as the light from the flame gets further away, they decide it would probably be best to follow. The dark is scary.

"Uh-Oh. People." Alice said to herself in a squeaky little voice, pretty much what you would expect from a hummingbird. In the blink of an eye she took off towards camp, and the others.
"Mum! Mum!" She came shouting, as loudly as she could - which to be fair, wasn't very loud. She hovered in front of Ellie and Zed.
"Mum, we have company. It looks like three people, but I couldn't be certain in the dark." She explained.
"What did they look like?" Ellie asked standing up at attention.
"One was a fat guy with a big beard. The other two looked like normal guys, I couldn't make out any details." Alice said.
"Do you think it's them?" Ellie said turning to Zed, who was floating to her left.
"Possibly. I don't know. Didn't you say that Mephisto had two goons of his own? Did they look like goons, Alice?" Zed asked somewhat frantically.
"I...I don't know. I've never seen a goon before." She answered.
"Fair enough." Zed noted, "we should be cautious. I'll send Bruno over to check. If he doesn't come back, then we know something's not kosher." She added. Ellie nodded in agreement and Zed took flight towards Bruno's patrol area.
"You did well, Alice," Ellie said with a smile.
"Thanks, mum," she said turning and taking flight behind Zed.
Zed, followed closely by Alice headed towards Bruno's lookout, which was on the far side of the small camp they'd set up. The two spotted him marching in a straight line, back and forth in a very militarized fashion. The grass beneath his feet was completely trampled, as if he'd not taken a seat or a second off since beginning.
"Bruno!" Zed shouted from a distance. He stood at guard and aimed his pike in their direction out of pure instinct.

"Whoa boy, it's just us," Zed said coming to a halt at the tip of his spearhead. She came to a roost atop its point.
"Zed, what is the matter? Is the Earth Mother in danger?" He said sternly, with a hint of urgency.
"No. Well, maybe. We need you to check something for us. Alice spotted three figures, there could be more. We need you to intercept them. It could be the necromancer and company."
"Very well," he said snapping his spear to his side. He nodded and marched towards Alice's former post.
"That was easy." Alice said.
"Soldiers, they just listen without thinking. Really the perfect man," Zed said watching Bruno's ass end trot away. "Anyway," she said snapping out of her gaze, "you stay here and cover his post. I'll go back to Mother," Zed said. Alice nodded and perched atop a tombstone. Zed instantly headed back towards the centre of camp. She didn't want to leave Ellie alone.
Bruno marched towards his new post. He was surgical and emphatic with each and every step. He trod quick, but nimbly without making the slightest of noises. His training had taught him well - well enough anyway to survive the onslaught from The Butcher. Not many survived, which saddened him. But he couldn't help but think that if they trained harder, as hard as he, they would have lived, and ultimately defeated the horrid beast. But that was all in the past. He was the best of the rest, and arguably the best soldier that paradise had to begin with. He needed to focus on the task at hand, and with the slightest of head shakes, he focused on his current mission.
Before he reached Alice's former post, he took a sharp left off course. He spotted a lantern, or some kind of light source in the distance and dropped his head as low as he could get it. Every effort was made to blend into the various statues and monuments, and he hoped that he was far enough on their periphery that he could sneak up and confront them without being noticed. He took up residency beside a large statue and

watched the three approach. He would wait until the exact perfect moment to charge in.

"You see that weird horse man trying to be sneaky over there?" Mort said nonchalantly to Chip.
"Yeah, I spotted him a while ago. Whattya think he's doing?" Chip said just as calmly, which was weird as neither of them had any idea who he was.
"Think Bill spotted him?" Mort asked.
"Probably." Chip answered.
"Hey lads, ya see the centaur over there?" Bill stopped and asked them.
"Centaur! That's the name for those stupid things," Mort said in quiet excitement.
"Whoa, what's with the xenophobia all of a sudden?" Chip asked.
"Xenowhatia?" Mort asked, "Isn't that a videogame, with big robots or something?"
"No, you idiot. It means fear of new or foreign things." Chip explained.
"Ooh, mister word of the day over here. Fancy pants. Do you keep a thanasorous on you at all times?" Mort mocked. Well, he tried to, bless him.
"A what?" Chip said with a raised eyebrow.
"Ha, now who doesn't know things, and look who does know things. Chip, my simple minded friend, it's a book, that tells you words that can be used instead of other words. Duh," Mort said with a smile. Chip rolled his eyes.
"Ugh, come on," he said spinning, only to be met by the pointy end of Bruno's pike. He stopped centimetres from the tip. He opened his eyes wide and felt his heart race and sweat build on his brow.
"Whoa. That's one sneaky horse man," Mort said walking up slowly beside Chip. He reached out and put his hand on the

spear, lowering it, and pushing it back slowly, which got a nasty glare from Bruno.
"Bahahahahahaha!" Bellowed out from the darkness behind Bruno.
"Oh boy, you should have seen the look on your faces," Bill said, reigniting his tuft of floating beard hair.
"Excellent work Bruno," he said to the Centaur soldier who didn't respond, and resented the joke a little bit. However he did see merit in its practical training purposes. Once again, he snapped to attention and stood on guard.
"Bill, you clever sonofabitch."Mort said with a big ol' grin. "You really got him. Look, he's still in shock," Mort said pointing to Chip, who still looked like he'd just stared death in the face. His eyes wide open, sweat beading on his forehead, and heart racing.
"Oh come on, son. You faced worse than that already this week," Bill said with a chuckle, patting Chip on the back.
In Chip's defence, he'd been doing a lot better with the spooks and scares - it was becoming pretty routine. But there's a reason he doesn't watch horror movies, or play scary video games, hell, even hide and seek was a bit much for him. He absolutely hated the cheap jump scare. Something flashing in front of you out of nowhere, it was lazy, but ultimately effective, and for whatever reason he couldn't handle it. Balloons popping, car honking, what-have-you, it all shook him to the core.
In fact, in the 7th grade, Chip had a friend called Elmer. They were best of friends, until one day Chip was over at his house. They were doing things 11-12 year olds do, such as video games, trying to find the hidden stash of Playboys, being dumb, so on and so forth. Chip needed to use the washroom, so he did. It didn't take him long to tinkle, yet upon exiting the bathroom, Elmer jumped from behind a closet door sending Chip into a near catatonic state. That day Chip lost a friend, and they never did find the Playboys. Later Chip had heard

that Elmer's dad was gay, and ran away with his brother-in-law. It explained a lot, really.

Bill shook his head and grabbed Chip under the arms and began to drag him.

"Hey, Bruno, how about a hand?" Bill said struggling with Chip's stiffened body. With the smallest roll of the eyes, Bruno strode over and pulled up beside Bill.

"Very well," he said as Bill tossed the near comatose Chip onto his back. His rigor mortis yielded and he fell limp over either side of Bruno's horse end.

"Hmm. Interesting," Mephisto said to himself as he watched a proverbial changing of the guard between a Centaur and a hummingbird. Poor Mephisto lurched over a gravestone, holding his stomach in discomfort, the pain just wouldn't subside. He began to sweat; he didn't even know that he could sweat! This whole feeling mortal thing really wasn't working for him. He really couldn't wait to get back to his old self, which meant he needed to be pretty much exactly where that pesky Mother Nature set up camp. Seeing the bird take over for that giant horse man was a spot of luck.

Inhaling quite deep, Meph took to his stomach and began to crawl military style, wincing and squirming through the pain and nausea. He inched and crept closer to the hummingbird who sat atop a stone grave. She intermittently cleaned her wings or chest, but always seemed to have an eye out. She maybe small, but she would no doubt be quick. Meph had to act fast, something he was very ill prepared to do. Pausing in the grass and stone, Meph looked deep inside himself and asked, *do I really want to move anymore, or just fry her from down here.*

Seconds later, the Hummingbird known as Alice evaporated. Question answered. However, the shot didn't go without notice.

"The Hell was that?" Bill asked searching the distance.
"I do not know, Djinn, but it came from Alice's post!" Bruno said with urgency. He took off in the direction of the burst, literally leaving Bill and Mort in his dust.
"Who's Alice?" Mort asked.
"Did he leave with Chip still on his back?" Bill asked.
"I'm hungry," Mort stated. He looked at Bill and shrugged.
"Let's go. If we survive this, I'll get you whatever you want to eat," Bill promised. The two continued to walk at a fairly leisurely pace, not knowing the impending gravity of the situation.
Meanwhile, Bruno raced in full tilt towards Alice's station, running passed an equally concerned and curious Ellie and Zed. The two watched Bruno sprint by, and throw Chip to the ground at Ellie's feet. She barely noticed at first; she was too concerned for Alice, as she should have been.
"Oh hey, look who decided to show up...kinda," Zed said floating down to Chip on the ground. She poked his eye ball. He didn't flinch. Sometimes he can be a giant wuss.
"Chip?!" Ellie shouted in surprise. She knelt down beside his head, picked it up and began to caress it.
"Oh, Chip..," she said shaking her head.
"What's wrong with him?" Zed asked hovering his around curiously.
"I've seen this before," Ellie said with a small smile.
"You have? What, is he narcoleptic or something?"
"Nah. He was spooked. Jump scare."
"...What?"
"Yup. It happened when we were watching some shitty horror movie. A cat jumped out of a locker, he went wide eyed and nearly comatose for like 20 minutes. It was adorable." Ellie explained. Zed hovered dumbfounded.
"That's what happens when he's scared? Great. We're doomed," Zed said throwing her hands in the air.

"No no. Only sudden scares do it to him. Poor guy. He'll snap out of it in a minute." Ellie assured Zed.
"He'd better. Something tells me we'll need him sooner rather than later," Zed said looking into the darkness of the night. Something about the cemetery gave her chills. Maybe because it was a cemetery, at night, in the penultimate moments before a potential biblical battle. Or it could be something else. Nobody knows.
"Oh, shit, yeah. I forgot about Alice!" Ellie said jumping to her feet. Chip's head bounced off the dirt.
"Oops," Ellie said looking down.
Bruno continued his charge towards the burst of light. He worried for his little friend. She wasn't a soldier, but she was noble and loyal, and he admired her for it, but he still had a very, very bad feeling. Death has been an ever present entity lately, and he feared that it had just claimed another innocent life. He pulled up to the exact tombstone he'd left the little bird on, but she wasn't there. There was no sign of her, there was no sign of anything, except the faint smell of burnt chicken, with a hint of sulphur. It did not bode well.
He looked around into the black that surrounded him. The darkness was thick, denser than it rightfully should have been, and the atmosphere surrounding was off. He didn't like it. Slowly he crept beyond his track line and expanded his search. He readied himself for anything with his spear drawn in front of him. He lead headstrong peering around every corner or hiding spot. He checked the ground below and the air above, but spotted nothing. He was on more of an edge than he would liked, and he'd walked far beyond his predefined perimeter. He turned back, not wanting to venture too far from the base, in case it was a clever ploy to lure the only capable warrior from his position.
He really wished he didn't venture as far as he did. He really wished he didn't turn around. But most of all, he really wished that he didn't leave the poor hummingbird by herself.

Embedded into the back of the tombstone Alice had been sitting on was a shadow made of blood, in the shape of small bird. Affixed to it was a long pointed beak, which was left slightly a gap. Bruno knew then that she was no longer with them, and he nodded his head in grief.
"Aww, why the long face?" Mephisto said from the darkness. Bruno perked up and shot back into action, ready to attack at a seconds notice.
"Who goes there?" He said fiercely.
"What? No love for the horse joke? Pfft, you centaur's are so serious. Lighten up, will ya?" He said throwing a fireball in Bruno's direction.
With a swing of his spear, Bruno extinguished the flame.
"Silly demon, you just gave away your position." Bruno said tauntingly.
"See what I mean? Super serious."He said hocking two more balls of fire at Bruno's head, who easily dispatched them. Bruno said nothing, but he maintained his position. He would not be lured into a battle in the dark with a demon.
"Oh, come on. Don't you wanna hurt me real bad? After all, I turned that little birdy into a piece of KFC," Mephisto said with a taunt of his own. Bruno felt that one, but they were just words. He would not be drawn into his trap, nor would he be sucked into a battle of wits. He knew he'd lose that one... He was half horse after all. Sarah Jessica Parker could relate.
"Ugh, fine. Have it your way!" Mephisto said leaping from behind a large angel statue, which he thought was a bit ironic. Despite feeling like death itself was ripping into his soul, he still had enough energy to ignite himself in flame and reveal his true form, which was pretty spooky. Spikes spouted from his head, not like a traditional horn system, but they grew from every angle, forming a crown of horns upon his now bright red skinned head. The spikes intertwined with one another, much like the roots of a tree deep under the soil. They stretched to half a foot above his head, and atop them, a halo of fire ignited.

No longer did he look of a star soccer player who would spend more time posing for GQ than on the pitch. No, he more looked like a monster from every child's nightmare.
His chest puffed and swelled with muscle as his clothes tore away from his body, in fact, every part of him expanded so much so that he would make Arnold feel inferior. His hands were no longer human, but rather they resembled talons from a hawk. His face appeared misshapen, with bones morphing and moving like the continents on a very young Earth. But it was the teeth that were the most shocking. They looked just like normal, everyday human teeth. It was very off putting, like when people put dentures in a dog's mouth. See, spooky.
From his leap, Mephisto tackled Bruno, setting him slightly ablaze. In a swift motion though, Bruno wrestled himself free. The hair covering his body was flame retardant, but the sheer heat from Hellfire still managed to singe him. He looked at the small burn, and refocused on the enemy who stood nine feet tall surrounded by an aura of heat blur.
"You don't scare me, demon." Bruno said holding strong.
"Really? I don't?" Meph said in a gravelly voice. Bruno didn't answer.
"Perhaps you should reconsider. I'm really quite scary," he said lunging towards Bruno at a speed generally reserved for rockets. The two hit, and as tough and strong of will as Bruno happened to be, he was no match for a demon fuelled on nether juice. Mephisto expected to be weaker, due to the pain he was in, but he was using it, like an athlete fighting through injury. It was motivation for him, and the energy he absorbed added to his power. He couldn't quite understand how something so painful could give him strength and power, but it did. A very strange juxtaposition indeed.
Bruno soared through the air, crashing through stones and statues until he finally hit a mausoleum that halted his flight. He crashed to the ground an absolute mess.

"Is that it horse man?!" Mephisto bellowed all macho-like. He certainly was full of piss and vinegar.
Crashing, fire, yells, and all around commotion was witnessed from the centre of camp. Ellie and Zed shot up in a heightened state of attention. They stared off into the darkness, which was occasionally sprinkled with flecks of light, that is until what looked like a human torch flew through the sky before fizzing out. Concern crept onto the faces of Ellie and Zed, but it wasn't until they heard the shattering of rock, and the wet cracking thud of Bruno's body hitting the wall that they flinched in fear. Something was seriously wrong.
Speaking of seriously wrong, Bill and Mort wandered into the centre of camp behind Ellie and Zed.
"S-s-s-stop right there." A meek little voice said at Bill's feet.
"Ahhhhhhhhhhhhhhhhhh!" Mort shrieked like a little girl. Zed and Ellie jumped out of their skin and turned around.
"It spoke! Bill, the bunny spoke!" Mort said terrified. Rabbits scared the daylights out of him. No reason, really. He just didn't trust their cuteness.
"Yes, son, it did..," Bill said curiously.
"Mort!" Ellie shouted running over to him throwing her arms around him, "I'd never thought I'd be happy to see you again," she said hugging him tightly. Mort, not knowing what to do, put a single hand on her back. He kept one eye on the bunny.
"Ohmygod!" Ellie said in shock as she pulled back from Mort. "What the hell happened to your nose?" She asked, which was now about the size of an apple.
"Hmm? Oh yeah, this asshole punched me in the face," Mort said slapping Bill on the arm.
"You walked into it fist. Learn the hand signals," Bill said walking over to Chip, who was still catatonic.
"Christ, it looks painful. Does it hurt?" She asked.
"It did. But it's okay now," Mort said smiling, which knocked something loose causing it to pour blood down his face.
"Right," Ellie said taking a step back.

"Hey Ellie..." Mort started.
"Yup?" Ellie asked, watching the crimson faucet that was Mort's nose.
"What's the deal with that talking hopping rodent?" He said pointing at Frank.
"Oh, that's Frank. He's cool," she said nonchalantly walking back towards Bill, Chip, and Zed.
"Rabbit's are never cool..," he said to himself.
Mort, Ellie, Bill, and Zed hovered around Chip, who they all figured was just faking it by now.
"Have a nice little reunion?" Zed said sarcastically to Mort as he joined the circle.
"Yeah yeah, nice to see you too," he said back flippantly. She eyeballed him.
"How are we gonna snap your boytoy out of this? I think we're gonna need him sooner rather than later, as sad as that is."
"I don't know..." Ellie and Mort said in unison. Awkward glances were exchanged.
"Uhh, you field this one, El," Mort said shying back slightly.
"Yeah..," Ellie said slowly, turning back to Chip. "I think I might have an idea..," Ellie said leaning in examining her fallen boyfriend.
"Okay, everybody, turn around!" She said, being met by some weird looks from her audience.
"Seriously, guys, turn!" She emphasised. The group slowly shuffled and faced their backs to her. She took a deep breath, lifted up her shirt and stuck Chip's hand smack on her left boob. In a split second Chip shot up, ready for action.
"Hey, whoa! Yeah! Let's go do this!" He said in a ball of energy. Boobs, they work every time.
He didn't quite have his bearings yet, and spun around seeing all of his friends there, very confused. He'd be lying if the thought that he fell asleep during an orgy didn't cross his mind - it would explain the weird erection. But then he saw her, the love of his life, the queen of his castle, the girl that makes the

Mona Lisa look like a pile of poop - his Ellie. He smiled, and with great excitement - perhaps too much excitement, hugged her.
"Ellie!" He shouted, "I never thought I'd see you again. Holy crap." He began to shake a bit.
"Hey, Chip. I missed you too," she said softly in his ear as he hugged the living hell out of her, and continued to do so, and even longer. It was becoming uncomfortable for those watching.
"Chip?" She said.
"Yeah?" He answered, still clinging.
"Your boner's hurting my stomach," she said.
"I know." He replied.
"Can you...ya know, back up a bit?" She asked.
"Nope." He answered. She smiled and embraced him just a bit tighter.
"Okay, love bugs, we have some pressing matters to attend to," Bill said pointing in the direction of Mephisto and his burning glory.
"Right," Chip said clearing his throat. "What'd I miss?" He asked
"Dunno. But it looks like somebody messing some shit up over there," Mort said through a bloody face.
"Eek." Chip exclaimed at the site of Mort. "Uhh, I mean, okay. Let's do this thing," he said attempting to crack his neck and knuckles. Neither cracked.
"Bill," He said turning to the old Djinn, "Can you stay here with Zed and Ellie? I don't want them in this battle." He added. Bill cocked his head as if to say, *Boy, you be outta yo' damn mind.* But he was classier than that. Besides, he knew what Ellie was about to say. He's returning to full strength.
"Yeah, he'll stay with us, 'cause we're coming with you," Ellie said from behind Chip. His heart sank.

"What? No way!" He exclaimed, "You've been through enough. You need to rest and prepare for this ceremony thingy you have to do later." Ellie just eyeballed him.
"You done?" She asked.
"Yeah, I mean, I think. Did it work?" Chip asked.
"Not in the least. Now c'mon, let's go. Bruno needs us!" Ellie said raising her fist as a rallying cry. She rushed past Chip and Bill with, Zed, and Frank following close behind.
"What was that?" Chip asked.
"Oh, lad, you had to have seen that coming. We should go, and you should get summoning. 3 million corpses aren't goin' to raise themselves," Bill said with a wink before he turned and took off towards the action. Chip stood there looking like a lost puppy - a look he wore often and well. He sighed and broke out into a jog behind Bill.
The action in question had quelled slightly, what with Mephisto's only opponent lying in a heap on the ground. Bruno, though, had a lot of fight in his soul, and he wasn't going to let crashing into a wall at the speed of a train stop him from powering on. He just needed a minute, ya know, to catch his breath.
Every ounce of his being hurt, and he was pretty sure something in his back had been broken, but with the will of a million monks, he gripped his spear tight and began to prop himself up. With every shove, he anchored the handle in to the ground. He writhed and shook in pain and weakness with every inch he moved. Never give up. He hoisted and heaved until his knees straightened and stood straight once again. Mephisto stopped in his tracks and tilted his head like a curious dog.
"I thought for sure that you'd be dead," Mephisto said. He picked up his pace in walking over to the broken warrior.
"Not yet." Bruno coughed. Blood spattered from his mouth.
"Soon enough," Mephisto said lowering his head for a charge.

In a single breath Mephisto leapt and soared through the air with his horned crown aimed right at Bruno's heart. The attack was quick, and even if Bruno were at 100%, he wouldn't have been able to dodge the charging bull. He closed his eyes and accepted his fate. He thought of all his fallen brethren, he thought of his family and of the life choices he made. He thought about what the afterlife for creatures like him would be like, if there even was one. He thought about Ellie, and how he wished her well. He thought about how long he'd been thinking.

Mephisto charged through the air like a bullet. He closed in quickly on his target anticipating the gore that would be presented for him, and hey, it was a bonus that he was scorching hot so horse meat should be cooked to a perfect medium rare by the time he ripped through him. Delicious. The air around him swelled with pressure and energy, and then he made contact. A crash erupted sending birds in their nearby roosts into flight. Mephisto's neck bent back and his uppermost horn snapped off into the night.

"Oooooooooow, what the fuck was that?" He shouted picking himself from the floor.

"That was me, you ugly asshole." Ellie shouted. Not her best line.

"What?!" Mephisto said turning to face Mother Nature herself. With a grunt he kicked the force field she'd set up around Bruno in the nick of time.

He turned his attention back to Ellie, who was now backed up by Bill, Mort, Zed, Frank, and lastly Chip.

"You've done enough damage already. It's time to put you down like the dog you are." Ellie shrieked. Better line, still not great.

"Hmm, this is easier than I thought it would be," Meph said in a low gravelly voice.

"Let's get him!" Zed chirped in excitement. Everybody turned and looked at her curiously. She shrugged and zipped into action. Mephisto too sprang into action, and then everybody, except Chip launched an attack. Flame balls were flashing past everybody as Ellie's force field now protected the group. Bill teleported in behind Mephisto and threw out a lasso that he pulled form out of nowhere. He's a djinn. He's magic, leave it alone. The hoop wrapped around his ankles, and with a might crash, Mephisto's charge came to an abrupt end. Dust kicked up from the impact, and his face skidded across the grass and dirt.

Halting his progress it did, but only briefly. The heat emanating from his body burned through the magical rope, causing it to vanish into a wisp of golden dust. A fireball flew from the cloud of dirt towards Bill's head, however he managed to duck under it, but not before the hairs on the top of his head became singed. He warped back into the protective bubble.

Sniffing the air, Ellie turned to Bill, "Ugh, burning hair. Gross."

"Sorry, lass. Would you prefer well done face meat?" He said in retort.

"Fair enough. Got any other tricks up your sleeve?" She asked, holding the shield strong as fireballs began to rain down upon them again.

"One or two. But it won't be any of us who win this war," he said in reference to Chip.

Sitting back behind the action, Chip focused his attention and began to mutter the words that were absorbed into his very essence from that mysterious and gross book. The more he spoke, the brighter an aura of green sparkled around him. He uttered and repeated phrases, not knowing what a single word actually meant. He translated it roughly to be, *please, for the love of everything, bring bodies back to life to fight evil things. Also, please don't be evil yourself. Oh, and bring a sandwich for Mort.*

Of course, the actual translation was lost long ago. Not a soul dead or alive knows what the words were, as they were transcribed by the very first Necromancer, who's soul is not in any record books, nor in the memory of the oldest historian. Some say he fiddled with something deep, dark, and unknown causing him to be lost forever. Others tell the tale that when he came face-to-face with death himself, he destroyed the entity and became the grim reaper. All circumstantial reports, however. He's just as likely to have fallen down a well. Well's are notorious for holding on souls; peculiar.

Nevertheless, Chip continued chanting his mantra with his eyes closed. He felt the earth around him move, but he refused to open his eyes and break his concentration... and because whatever was happening on the other side of his closed lids was scary, besides he's had better luck lately with his eyes closed. Shifting Earth surrounded him, noises echoed through the night, and explosions of heat ricocheted all around.

The battle between Ellie and company and Mephisto raged on and on. Bill pulled a few tricks to keep him at bay, but ultimately he wasn't meant for battle. Frank did his best to survive and not get trampled upon, and Zed couldn't get close enough to Mephisto to be anything other than a minor annoyance. The heat radiating from his body charred her wings on every pass. Ellie and Mort were the only ones able to distract and keep the beast at bay.

Gale force winds were kicked up and concentrated at Mephisto as he trudged onwards. They were strong enough to make his progress slow and tedious, but ultimately it was a band-aid on a gunshot wound. It wouldn't last. Mort was creating fetishes out of everything he could see. Tombstones, sticks, branches, and the occasion statue met Mephisto at every turn, however they weren't very durable and were being crushed at most every swipe.

"C'mon Mort! we need something more. Chip isn't ready yet," she said glancing back at her cross-legged boyfriend.

Mort looked around for something, anything that might be of use - and then he spotted it. He focused all of his energy, and in a few seconds he had it under control. From behind Chip stomped huge stone feet, however he didn't look. Closed eyes equalled safety. The ground shook with every step, and everybody kind of stopped for a second. Bill turned and went slack jawed, Ellie wanted to look, but she was busy throwing wind at Mephisto, that was until even he stopped in his tracked and looked at what Mort had summoned.
Stepping around the group, Ellie finally got a glimpse at what it was. A gigantic statue of an Angel that had been erected as a monument to some poor soul called Elizabeth Granger, who died from syphilis, walked past. Lucky girl.
The statue in question stood at least eight feet in height and was constructed of granite. Mrs. Granger was a rich lady, apparently. The sculpture stood in front of Ellie's protection bubble with a stone sword in hand ready for action. Mephisto stared at the monument for a second. It brought back memories of the war, which only fuelled the fire that burned within him. He drew an incredibly large fireball and flung with the force of a fighter jet at the head of the angel. It exploded upon impact into a ball of smoke. Mephisto looked rather smug, but when the smoke cleared, the granite figure was unharmed.
"Balls." Meph muttered.
The statue lowered its head, and everybody who witnessed it would swear that she bowed and said a prayer. Spooky. She lifted her head, and there was a look of determination on her stone face. She lifted her mighty sword and struck down on Mephisto, who blocked it with his arm. The granite blade held strong and the statue continued its pressure a top it. Mephisto, clearly shocked by its incredible strength, began to buckle slightly under its power. He began to shiver mildly before falling to one knee. The angel crept forward gaining leverage over the weakened beast. She asserted herself over him as he

hunkered down trying to conceive a plan that would get him out of this pickle.
The statue was relentless with her dominance, and being made of granite, she was a big girl - big boned that is...Regardless, she weighed a lot, more than Mephisto was anticipating, and although he had the low ground, he couldn't find the energy to throw the blade from his own arm, but he had to do something. Gritting his teeth, he began to resist with an opposite force, using the might in his massively oversized legs to push back. However, the more he pushed, the more the blunt blade dug in, until eventually, a pop.
The sound and sensation was a new one to Mephisto. The stone had cut him ever so slightly. Sure, to humans wound looked horribly painful and deep - one that should be checked by a medical professional - however he was a demon, and medical insurance is hard to get. The premiums were mental. Prejudice jerks. Anyway, to him, it was nothing more than a paper cut, still, demons didn't get paper cuts. The only object in the universe that should be able to break their skin is steel forged in the heavens and blessed by the Archangel, Michael. This statue, although the shape of an angel, she was not one. It made little sense, but it pissed off Mephsito.
Upon seeing the cut, he looked up and met the stone cold gaze of the sculpture and grabbed the sword with his other hand. In one massive heave, he managed to break her mettle and stagger her backwards. He took his chance and launched himself backwards out of the angels reach. She was slow, which was something he could use to his advantage. She caught her footing after the shove by Mephisto, and began her march towards him once again. She walked like a soldier in an old Spartan army. She had purpose and poise holding her sword in front of her with two hands. Mephisto crept backwards, devising a plan in his head, but he could think of nothing.

Behind the action, everybody watched in awe, especially Bill and Ellie, who really had no idea that Mort had this sort of power in him. To be fair, he was concentrating ridiculously hard. Ellie had only seen him like this one, while playing a marathon of the Final Fantasy series. He was determined to beat all thirteen games in one sitting. It was impressive, actually. He developed an eating, drinking, and washroom routine that was quite ingenious. The effort he put into that was like nothing Ellie had ever seen, until now.

Sadly, that session only lasted a few hours, and he didn't even get through the first game. That worried her. She had no idea how long he could keep it up, and if he could, what would he be like afterwards. The night was cool, but he was drenched in sweat and shivering like a Chihuahua.

"C'mon, Chip. We need you," Ellie said under her breath as she watched the heroic Mort struggle.

Mephisto took step after step backwards until he was met by a mausoleum wall.

"Hmm." He uttered. That was when he noticed his opposition watching the spectacle behind the statue, and he soon picked out the one controlling the stupid thing. Speed and wit would win this battle, though he'll never admit he couldn't beat up an angel statue, even if it was really big and heavy. The plan he was attempting to draw up in his head finally connect the dots, and he knew what he would do. He thought back to Bort and smiled.

The angel approached with purpose. Its vigour just oozed from its body and just in front of Mephisto, she raised her six foot sword in the air and swung down at the head of the demon in an effort to decapitate him once and for all. The only problem was, he ducked. The sword went sideways into the concrete of the mausoleum and dug in about two feet, jamming it in there. Looking up from under his brow, Mephito smirked at the success of his plan and wiggled out from beneath the frame of the statue and watched it struggle to remove its sword in the

stone. Her energy was on loosening the blade, but her focus remained on Mephisto, who just chuckled and walked behind her.
He stopped right behind her bent frame, looked over his shoulder at Ellie and company, and began to dry hump the poor statue. He thrust with really exaggerated movements and motions to really drive the point home. Pure class. Just as obnoxiously as he started, he stopped and spanked its stony ass and walked away, heading towards the group. He walked in a slow, cocky saunter. He was victorious, and he wanted to flaunt it.
Not before mentioned in its entirety was the anatomy of a demon. Unlike their angel counterparts, demons, once they fell, became human for the briefest time. This, of course, sexed them. Mephisto was a male, and boy was he ever. Used mostly as an intimidation tool, the demon penis was massive and swung nearly knee low. His testicles were roughly the size of two baseballs placed side by side. Back in the olden days, when they spelt old with and e at the end, this worked wonders in small conservative villages on his terror missions. Now-a-days, not so much. It was kind of like the human appendix, sure it's there, but it's not really needed.
As he walked, it swayed back and forth, and the only thought that Ellie could think was, *poor angel statue* while holding her stomach. Bill was slightly envious, though he thought he could make one for himself if he wanted. He made a mental note of it. Mort was still in a trance, attempting to have the angel get the blade from the stone. Though, oddly enough his butt hurt a bit.
Mephisto approached their protective bubble and glanced it. He smiled and waved at Ellie, which creeped her right out. He ignored Bill, and turned his attention straight to Mort, who was completely unaware of what was happening. Mephisto tilted his head from side to side and glanced back over his shoulder. The angel still struggled, but it gave him an idea. He closed his

eyes and focused his energy towards his hands. Slowly a hilt of fire began to form, and shortly after that, a blade of flame took shape. The fire licked off the edges making the sword look menacing and powerful. He drew the sword high and struck down on Ellie's bubble. It made a thunderous crash, which shook everybody enough to the core. Chip still kept his eyes shut; Mort kept his composure.

Over and over he crashed down on the bubble, which, like when the Butcher did the same thing, it began to crack. Small spider web tears appeared all over the top of the shell, and Ellie and Bill looked at each other with a sadness in their eyes. They both had a feeling it was over, that they had failed, and doomed mankind in some way or another. Mephisto raised his mighty flame sword one final time. They knew that was it He was at the pinnacle of his swing when a crash erupted behind him. Mephisto spun and looked over his shoulder, that pesky statue broke free.

"Damnit all," he said turning his attention back to the bubble. Like Ellie and Bill, he too knew that the their bubble was about to burst. Quite literally, in fact. He raised his sword once again and with all of his might, he crashed it down on the bubble. In slow motion, the bubble shattered into millions of pieces of a glass like material, that slowly withered and dissipated into the air. Ellie, Bill, and Mort were left exposed.

Wasting no time, Mephisto reached towards Mort, who was still out of it. Ellie and Bill did everything they could to dissuade him, but none of their attacks did much. It wasn't until Chip, who came from literally nowhere and tackled Mort just before Mephisto's fist connected, which surely would have obliterated the poor witch doctor. Mephisto whiffed and lost balance, stumbling forward briefly. The tackle snapped Mort back to reality, and the second he gained his consciousness back, the angel statue stopped moving.

"Chip?" He said sleepily, "Man, I almost had it." He finished before passing out.

"You did good, buddy," Chip said in particularly poor grammar, "I've got it from here." He added.
"You have GOT to be kidding me!" Mephisto said standing up straight, "Seriously, how many close calls can you guys have?" He said charging towards the necromancer.
"Hopefully no more," Chip said smiling as he watched a body fling itself at the charging Mephisto. It didn't hurt him, but it threw him off for a second, causing him to stop in his tracks.
"Huh?" He said, totally forgetting about his reason for actually being here. He looked behind him, and beside him, and from the darkness beyond Chip came corpses. Millions of them. Row after row, acre after acre, bodies came piling towards him, and before he knew it, he had one attempting to climb up his enormous genitalia.
"What the Hell?" He said looking down, attempting to swat it off, but the more he swiped at it, the more it flailed from side to side. Chip laughed; it was even funnier due to the corpse being an old whore from the early 1900's. Something's never change.
"Screw it," Meph said grabbing his manmeat and slamming it against his shin, crushing the corpse. The distraction was enough, however as when he looked up, he was met by to huge burst of green energy, which broke through the heat shield Mephisto had around himself. They hit with such a force that it sent the great demon stumbling backwards, and with a little help from Bill's bag of tricks, he took a little tumble to the ground.
It took the surrounding corpses seconds, literal seconds to climb atop of the beast and begin to take bites, scratch, and dig at his hardened flesh. Hundreds at first, then seemingly thousands. Ellie and Bill climbed atop large statue and watched the scene from a Romero movie. Chip dragged Mort to safety as well, so he wouldn't get trampled. It was worse than Black Friday at a Best Buy.

The mound of corpses upon the former demon general grew and grew with each passing moment. The heroes watched in awe at the sheer volume of zombies with a single hive minded purpose piled themselves atop Mephisto all the while gnawing and clawing at his stone hardened flesh. Before long, there wasn't a single inch of him visible, and from Fabian's position, who had been watching the whole time from above, looked like a swarm of ants attacking an old lollipop on the sidewalk.
"You think that'll do?" Chip yelled over to Bill and Ellie.
"Yeah, it looks - " Just as Ellie was about to finish, a rumble could be felt radiating along the ground, from point zero. The corpse pile, which was now about six or seven feet high began to rattle and vibrate with the ones on the top sliding off. Bodies hit the floor with a thud, but instantly got back up and started to climb again. However, the shaking grew stronger and stronger, and more and more zombies tumbled down. A thought crossed Chip's mind. When he raised Victor, he seemed to regain his personality, but the near three million corpses meandering around the cemetery seemed lifeless – almost hive minded. It was curious.
"Uh-oh," Chip said to himself. "I think I've pissed him off."
A squealing could be heard from inside the dome of flesh which was soon accompanied by the stench of burning flesh. Chip crept backwards and watched as a pillar of flame shot from the side of the corpses. Soon after another shot from the opposite side. The sky lit up like a volcano, bright red and smoky, then from the middle of the pile burst out Mephisto, glowing red, completely engulfed in flame. He was indeed pissed.
He erupted from the ground like a bat out of Hell and landed right in front of Chip.
"You think you can best me with these puny beings. Is that all you have?"

Chip looked around - it was actually all he had, at least, it was the best he knew how to do. A corpse jumped on Mephisto's back.
"Oh, bugger this," he said throwing the body off of himself. Mephisto inhaled and held the air in before crouching into a ball. When he released the air and threw his arms into the air, an enormous ball of light went with it. The orange globe the size of public swimming pool hovered in the air above him. The light expanded and began to envelop everything around. It was beyond blinding, causing everybody to shield their eyes. Chip ducked behind a tombstone, and Bill and Ellie dove behind their statue. Despite the ball being exceptionally light, not an single degree of heat was produced, if anything it felt cold.
Lingering in the sky like a small sun, the brightness hit its apex, and in a flash, burnt out. Chip's eye took a while to adjust, but when they did he saw something he'd never seen before. An orange swirling mass hanging in the air. It spun and undulated as if it were a living thing. It was both awe inspiring and disturbing to the core, and despite it being absolutely terrifying, Chip couldn't look away. It was worse than a train wreck, it was as if he were looking the death of the universe in the face, and he wanted it to happen. He began to shake.
"What the Hell is that?" Ellie asked Bill, who was beyond sombre.
"Ellie, dear. That is a vortex to nothing," Bill explained.
"What...does that mean?" She asked.
"I don't know. All I know is that once entered, it takes you to a place not known by any being living or dead. God himself doesn't even have an answer for what lies beyond."
"It's a place beyond creation?" Ellie asked.
"It's a place creation forgot. It's a place beyond existence," Bill said with a hard swallow. Ellie followed suit.
Crawling to his knees, Mephisto managed to lurch himself up on a tombstone. No longer was he the fear mongering demon,

but he took the form of that snarky English bastard. His hair was a mess and he was completely naked, which produced far less impressive anatomy than his demon form.

"Ugh. I need a bleeding smoke," he said shaking his head.

Chip managed to crawl out of hiding to see the naked and vulnerable Mephisto. He approached with caution, readying his green balls of death in his hands.

"What is that? What have you done?" Chip shouted. Mephisto used what was left in the tank to stand and face Chip.

"You wouldn't happen to have a fag on ya, mate, would ya?" He said with a sly smirk.

"Shut up. What did you do? What is that thing?" He said pointing to the vortex.

"Look around, what do you see?" Mephisto asked, and Chip instinctively looked around.

"Nothing. I don't see anything," he said sternly.

"Exactly," Mephisto said.

"Ex...oh," Chip said realizing that all of his reanimated corpses had vanished completely. Mephisto smiled.

"What did you do with them?" Ellie said running in behind Chip with Bill.

"They're gone, luv. To a place where they have never existed. All the millions of souls here, vanished, completely gone forever," he said with a chuckled, which caused a cough. He covered his mouth and looked into his palm. Blood.

Ellie's eyes welled up, and the sky began to drop small drips of rain.

"You just wiped three millions souls from existence?" She said with a tear rolling down her cheek.

"Bingo. Now there's nothing stopping me from sending you in there with all of them," he said cracking his neck like a cool guy. Chip was jealous.

"Ahh, finally, my mission is complete and freedom will be mi-" A leaping punch from Mort connected right on Mephsito's

jaw, cutting him off midsentence. Everybody stood and watched in shock.
"Whoa, buddy. You were like a ninja!" Chip exclaimed.
"Yeah, well. He was annoying. And he fucked my fetish in the ass," he said pointing to the angel statue.
"Aww, buddy," Chip said throwing his arms around his best friend. "But wait, how did a punch hurt him? Isn't he a demon? Shouldn't your hand have like...melted, or something?" He added.
"I dunno. Maybe I'm more magicy than I thought."
"Or maybe whatever he used to create that thing made him mortal, or at least weakened him," Bill said stepping in.
"Speaking of that slimy bastard, where did he scurry off to?" Ellie asked. The rest of the group began to look around frantically.
"Over here!" A small voice in the distance cried out. Chip, Mort, Ellie, and Bill ran over to the voice, which belonged to Frank who was hopping alongside a crawling Mephisto, who just gave up when he saw the group. Frank thumped him in the face.
"Well, it looks like your plan backfired, there Mephisto," Bill said walking over and kneeling beside him.
"Oh, shut up, you hairy, oversized buffoon," Mephisto said with a slight hint of anger and exhaustion. "I'm far from mortal, I just need a little rest."
"Sure ya do," Bill said ruffling his hair. "it's time to send you back to Hell. Something tells me Satan doesn't know what you're up to, and he probably won't be please to see you back down there," Bill said.
"No, wait. We can work this out," Mephisto said hoisting himself slowly to his feet. "I can be a very powerful ally" He added.
"This outta be good," Mort whispered to Chip.
"You shut your pig face." Meph snarled at Mort. Mort looked hurt by that.

"Don't even give him the time of day, Bill. Send him back," Ellie said.
"Shut up, you bitch!" He snarled again. Any wit and charm he once had began to fade rapidly as his demise came closer.
"Bill," Chip said nodding his head.
"NO!" Mephisto yelled, loud enough to cause the ground to shake. The group looked around in confusion, and then another shockwave like force rumbled through the area.
"That's not Mephisto, is it?" Chip asked to no one in particular. Even Mephisto looked confused.
The vortex began to pulsate once again, and with every wave came a ground shaking rumble. Everybody, including the bad guy turned to look at the glowing sphere.
"This isn't right," Mephisto said to himself, "it should have closed by now." He looked around frantically for an escape, but he was trapped like a rat.
From within the heart of the vortex appeared a shadow, or maybe it was more like a silhouette. The specimen wasn't large, but it was still menacing. Shadows are spooky enough to begin with, and one emerging from the heart of nothingness was particularly disturbing. Everybody backed away from it slowly. The figure didn't seem to walk, but rather it floated to the forefront of the vortex, inching closer and closer, but never being illuminated.
The shape reached the threshold of the doorway between his world and the real world, and just lingered on the precipice like an unwanted guest refusing to leave. Everybody waited in anticipation for whatever it was to reveal itself. Ellie went to wrap herself around Chip, but he had already latched onto Mort. She rolled her eyes. Bill watched in astonishment as Fabian and Frank tucked themselves away behind his legs. Mephisto however was perhaps the most fearful. He'd just sent an unfathomable amount of souls into the abyss, surely anything coming out wouldn't be good news for him. He began to quietly panic.

The shadow stepped out from the vortex and revealed itself. Mephisto's eyes widened.
"Jort?" He said in relief. With a newfound confidence, he stumbled over to his former minion - or what he thought was his former minion, completely forgetting that he slit his throat and sacrificed him earlier that same day. Short memories were never beneficial to anybody, especially Mephisto.
"Old friend, how are you?" He said walking towards Jort, who seemed slightly different than Meph rememebered.
"About that whole sacrificing thing...Umm, I'm sorry?" He said shyly. Jort Didn't flinch, or show any signs of anything.
"Look, it was for the greater good. We got her," Mephisto said turning to point at Ellie, who rolled her eyes.
"Whattya say we team up one last time and take down this band of merry idiots?" He said with a smile. Again, the creature formerly known as Jort didn't speak. Not that he had a way with words before.
"Say, you look different. Stronger. Were ya pumping iron or something...Hey, you wouldn't happen to have a smoke handy, would you?" Mephisto asked. Finally, Jort turned and looked at Mephisto, though not with any recognition, or soul, for that matter. Mephisto began to feel uncomfortable.
Jort took a step forward, toward Mephisto, who in turn took a tiny step back. Something began to feel off about his old slave.
"You know, on second thought, I think I have this under control. Don't worry about the smoke, I'll grab a pack later." Jort strode closer, and Mephisto backed up, until he tripped over a grave mound and landed on his arse. Jort stood over him more menacingly than Meph would have liked. He began to scurry on his backside. Coincidentally, Chip and the gang did the same thing. It was weird; very *The Day the Earth Stood Still,* and they wanted none of it.
Mephisto's panic returned, and this time it wasn't quiet, but rather full force schoolgirl seeing a spider panic. He attempted

to stand up and run, but he was met by the bottom of Jort's foot, pinning him down. He struggled like a mouse in a trap. He shouted out for help, but of course, nobody felt inclined to lend a hand - can you blame them. He looked up one last time at Ellie.

"Damn you," he said, flinging *the* knife in her direction; it landed short, but it was worth one last shot. The knife landed at Bill's feet. He and everybody wondered where Mephisto pulled it from. He was naked. The boys shuttered at the thought. Jort reached down and grabbed Mephisto's head, threw him up in the air, and much like he did with his brother, swallowed him whole. Everybody watched in shock, and Mort threw up a bit on Fabian, which made him smile. The creature that stood before them was no longer Jort - they weren't sure quite what it was, but it was frightening, and it was looking directly at them. It stood in place and sized up the group, as if looking for one last meal, but it didn't make a move. It just stared at them.

"Uhh...Hi?" Mort said, garnering the sole attention of Jort. The being gazed not at him, but through him. He then turned his attention to Bill, and then Ellie. Ellie seemed interesting to him as he lingered his gawk on her slightly longer, but then he moved onto Chip. When they met eyes, something changed, Jort didn't seem like a faceless or soulless being any longer, but rather a spark of curiosity rang out.

"Necromancer." A voice echoed out, much like how people figure God would sound. Chip looked around anxiously.

"Ye...Yes?" He said nervously.

"You have a great deal of power, which you currently do not understand. It is a power imbued to you, and you alone. It is a terrible burden to carry, and an even more terrible curse should you use it incorrectly. More than you know rests upon your shoulders. You must harness your craft, and use it responsibly. The very fabric of the universe will depend on you one day soon. You mustn't fail." The voice ended. Before Chip could

respond, the creature turned his back to the group and stepped through the portal to the nether.
Spiralling in upon itself, the vortex squealed shut, taking Jort, and whatever was left of Mephisto with it. A communal chill was shared between the group, and everybody just starred at Chip with a sheepish look in their eyes.
"What?" He asked. Nobody said anything, and shook their heads looking at the dirt.
"Lad, are you alright?" Bill asked.
"Yeah... why?" Chip asked.
"You don't remember?" Bill asked, "Weird. I can't see your thoughts any longer." He added.
"Remember what? The...thing said a few words, but you all heard that, right?" Chip said looking around. Everybody looked down. "Right?! Bill?!" Chip said freaking out. Bill walked up to him and analyzed him up and down, trying to find a trace of anything out of the ordinary.
"No lad. Nobody heard anything," he said solemnly.
"Then...what happened?" Chip asked, quite afraid.
"I don't know, lad. You and him were locked into a staring contest for some time, and then this beam of yellow energy shot from his eyes into yours. We were all frozen. I don't even know how much time passed, but it was longer than it rightly should have been. The sun is coming up," he said pointing to the horizon.
"Wait wait wait," Mort interrupted, "how can we be sure it was a beam of yellow energy, and that thing just didn't pee on him from his eyes? Hmm, Hmm?" He finished.
"Ew, god. Mort, shut up," Ellie said.
"Yeah, please do," Chip said. Bill just smirked.
"What did he say, Chip?" Bill asked snapping back to reality.
"Something about me having a lot of power, and that I'll need to use it right in order to save the fabric of the universe, or something." The three others just blinked.

"Hold on, did you say sunrise?!" Zed yelled, zipping down from the sky.
"Indeed," Bill said watching as the faerie perched atop his shoulder.
"Crap!" She exclaimed, "Mum, come on, we have to get you back to Paradise. We need to prep for the ceremony," she said, shooting over to Ellie and pushing her on the back.
"Well, to be continued?" She asked. The rest nodded.
As the group meandered out of the cemetery, they each took a moment to reflect in silence. Not a word was said amongst the seven of them. They had each just experienced something life altering, like nothing they'd ever been a part of. It was a war, but not one that will be written about in any conventional history book. Sure, somebody might jot something down and throw it in the *Library of Everything Unknown*. But ultimately, nobody in the world will know the service that they just provided. Being a hero sure was a thankless job.
Chip couldn't help but think that Marco would have really enjoyed the battle - it sure would have been a hell of a lot easier with him around. However, he did his job and died saving countless lives in the process. Nobody who was a part of that battle will ever forget his service. That's the way he would have liked it, in his own strange humbly vain way. There had been so much death and destruction, Chip couldn't even comprehend it, and mixed with the message from that thing, he need some time to digest everything. On the bright side though, he didn't pee himself. He was definitely improving, not just as a necromancer, but as a human person, though it was hard to feel good about anything at that moment.
Mort pondered things himself, mostly he wondered if his nose would ever get back to its old shape, or if he'd look like Owen Wilson for the rest of his life - which he didn't think was an awful thing. Owen was a handsome dude. Maybe he could take up acting, or modelling. Or be an actor who models on the side. Or a model who acts on the side. The options were nearly

limitless, but then reality hit, and he, like Chip, had a hard time appreciating the upside to everything that had just happened. After all, he had no acting skills, and he photographed horribly.

The only person who knew what everybody was thinking, except Chip, was drowning in thoughts of his own. Bill knew next to everything about the universe, but he had no idea what came out of that vortex. He couldn't even be certain that Mephisto truly died. He didn't like when things didn't make sense, and this was one of those times where nothing made any degree of sense. He tried to piece everything together, but the pieces just didn't fit the puzzle. Something was amiss, and he couldn't enjoy the victory, either. As well, he worried for Chip. He lied to the young necromancer earlier, he knew the process of the renewal ceremony well, he just didn't have the heart to tell Chip.

Along the same lines as Bill's thoughts, Ellie worried for Chip. She had come to terms with what might happen after the ceremony was complete. She truly did love him, and though they weren't married, or even engaged, she thought that maybe one they would be. He was certainly the love of her life, and she wanted to be there, to guide him when he became lost, and let's face it, that would happen a lot. She couldn't bear to look directly at him, an overwhelming sadness swelled within her at the mere thought of him. Looking at his puppy-dog face would send her over the edge. She had an incredibly important job to do, and as much as she loved him, she had to fulfill her duty. Her survival was the upside of all that had just happened - she was their reason for fighting, and each and every one of them did their jobs so that she can do hers. She couldn't enjoy the moment, as she had a feeling it would soon end.

# CHAPTER 18

How do you disguise a 9 foot giant in New York City? The answer is quite simple; you don't. It may even be impossible. The need for inconspicuousness was a major proponent in Sharok, the Master of the Order, not often leaving the safety of the Order's confines, but now, he needed to make an appearance. He strode through the heart of the city with a purpose, and even the distracted businessmen leaving for work early took notice of him. Many of them on their phones, talking to wives, girlfriends, or mistresses simply dropped them to the concrete, leaving them slack jawed in the process. Sharok didn't care. He was dressed to the brim in battle armour, and the blackened leather of his tunic shimmered under the streetlights as the weather turned from a clear night to foggy dawn. His silhouette traversing through the fog was a terrifying sight, and heaven forbid you didn't see him coming. Many a shoulders were bumped, expect, when he knocked a shoulder with his lumbering frame, people died. Seriously, three people not paying attention, poof, just died from the trauma of the collision. He was a big, scary fella.

Of course, Sharok cared not for the people he had hurt, or the ones that have spotted him and thrown his video up on YouTube. They didn't matter now, and they'd matter even less when he got a hold of Mother Nature, who his spies have informed managed to kill Mephisto and were on their way back to Paradise. He considered cutting them off at the pass, but he was too curious about the hidden grove tucked away in Central Park - besides, he thought it would make for a more dramatic and meaningful kill.

Showmanship was a part of his M.O. He felt that through the right act, or stage he could strike fear in his opponents hearts, both present and future. Word would spread of his triumph in Paradise, and how he destroyed Mother Nature and a necromancer in one fell swoop on their home ground. Nobody would dare threaten his power again. It was a little known fact, but it was Sharok that suggest to Vlad the Impaler to impale his enemies on spikes near his boarders. It worked for him, however mortals are far easier to frighten.

The giant stomped through New York City alone, he did not want an army, nor did he want back up for this fight. It was his, and his alone. Along with showmanship, he was greedy. He would garner credit whenever he had the chance, sharing it with The Order or its members was simply out of the question. He'd been warned by several elders that it would mean his demise one day, but he didn't listen, and those who questioned him ended up as dust in the wind. There was nothing that he was afraid of, and in his mind, nothing that could challenge him. This was his moment to put a stamp on his authority.

He traveled through the brisk morning air with a sense of entitlement, and though he didn't take notice of many of the bystanders gawking at him, he did have a curiosity for the mortals. How could such a puny and incapable race of beings own the world? They didn't have any special skills, and even their brightest and strongest paled in comparison to the average member of The Order. It boggled his mind, and the more he thought about it, the more it angered him until he took a swing at a light post, lifting it from the ground and crashing across the road.

He seethed. He'd locked himself away for far too long, and to see the progress of the human race was too much for him to handle. He was certain they would have died off, or killed themselves by now, but here they are, thriving in the everyday

world. It just wouldn't do, which is why putting a stop to the renewal ceremony was of the utmost importance.
Onlookers stopped and stared, and a few screams and shouts rang out after he knocked the light post from the ground. He didn't notice at first - their voices were so annoying and he'd blocked out their tone centuries ago. Nevertheless, the volume at which they were shrieking broke through his ignorance. He looked around through the fog and noticed an audience surrounding him. They looked like nothing more than shadows on paper, or the man in the corner of a sleazy porn shop having a wank.
"What is you would all like?" He shouted, loud enough so that the people closest to him hunched over and covered their ears. "You all worship a God. I can assure you, your God has nothing on me!" He bellowed, throwing his arms to the air.
"Fag!" A voice shouted out.
"Huh?" Sharok let out, looking around in confusion. Why weren't they trembling in fear? They used to.
"Loser!" Another voice shouted.
"Yeah, you gonna pay for dat light, asshole?" Yet another voice yelled. The fog clouded his vision enough so that he couldn't see who it was exactly that was yelling. Before long an entire chorus of yells, slurs, and comments were berating him. He was beyond mystified at the sheer lack of respect being shown towards him. What had changed in the years of his solitude? Did people no longer fear a being of his stature? He planned on making them fear and respect him again.
From the fog he spotted movement, in one fell swoop, he reached into the mist and grabbed the poor sap who'd been biking past. The man was in a single piece leotard, bright yellow, and a bicycle helmet. He had headphones on and had no idea what the hell was going on - though he did wonder why a light post was lying across the street, but it was New York, nothing surprised him anymore, least of all being snatched from his ride by a 9 foot dude.

"What the hell, man?" He said in a high pitched voice.
"You. Do you not fear me!?" Sharok said through his battle helmet, complete with face mask.
"Well, I mean, no. You're kind of a weirdo though." The biker said.
"Hmm." Sharok moaned, leaning into the man, looking him in the eye for any hint of fear - none could be found.
"Very well." Sharok said looking into the fog. "This just won't do." He added. The mighty warrior turned king inhaled, filling his enormous lungs to their bursting point, and in one heaving motion exhaled violently, sending the fog in every direction, eventually causing it all to vanish. Now he could clearly see the crowd, and they could see him. It was the perfect sight line. He looked at the man whom he was holding in his hand, then back to the crowd. In one quick motion, he broke the unsuspecting biker in half.
In actuality, it was quite gross. Intestines and blood splattered everywhere, and the people standing closest were soaked. It took a moment for the people who were watching to realize what had happened, but once they did, shit went crazy. Many of the people fled whilst screaming for help. others stood in shock at what they'd just seen, a select few pulled pistols from their pants (Amurika!), and one fellow shrugged it off, muttered *I've done worse*, and continued on his way.
The people who pulled guns began to fire at the giant, but the lightning fast, red hot lead did nothing to penetrate his armour, or skin for that matter. He shrugged off the shells as if they were nothing and threw his arms to the sky yet again and yelled, "Fear me, for I am your new God!"
The gun shots slowly died off, turning the once bustling street into a ghost town. Not a soul to be seen, nor a sound to be heard. It was the sound of fear. It was the sound of respect. It was a sound that he could get used to on the surface world. There was but one last thing to do, and with the fog cleared, he could see his destination; it was beautiful.

# CHAPTER 19

Paradise had never looked better. The sun had just broken the horizon, and morning was in full swing by the time Chip and the gang entered the sacred grounds.

"Holy balls," Mort said looking out over the vast impossibility of what Paradise had to offer. From the outside, it seemed like nothing more than an outcropping of trees, and any mortal that walked through would simply enter exactly that; however, somebody with ill intentions would be rejected. But, those pure of heart would be allowed in to witness its splendour. Generally mankind wouldn't be allowed in, as very few, if any, were truly innocent and pure. The pope, for example, had heard rumours of such a place existing, and he came close to entering once, but he was just shown the forest through the trees. Clearly he's got a teeny bit of a past - let your imagine fill in the blanks.

"Classy," Chip said, admiring the view himself. Beyond the space being impossible it was gorgeous. The trees were full and vivacious, flowers bloomed from nearly everywhere, and of every colour. Critters of all kinds were wandering around, mostly with haste as the ceremony was fast approaching. The sky seemed to be bluer than it should have been for the time of day, and there was a smell about the place, fresher than a spring day. It was more like a freshly sprayed *Fabreze*, it was that clean. It was difficult to imagine a more perfect place on Earth.

"Mum!" A chorus of voices shouted out as an enormous amount of animals and previously thought to be mystical creatures rushed over to greet their queen. Ellie was

completely enveloped by the crowd, leaving Chip, Mort, and Bill pushed aside.
"What? Uh, rude!" Mort said, sounding a bit gayer than he'd meant as a bear blew past him. It was quite a sight to see, and Chip couldn't help but smile at the love and admiration that all of these things felt for her. Though, not a single one loved her like he did.
"It certainly is sweet, isn't boys?" Bill said with a smile.
"Definitely," Chip said.
"It looks like a furry convention," Mort said. Chip and Bill did their best to ignore it.
"You boys did well. I certainly didn't have my money on you," Bill said with a wink.
"Yeah, thank...wait, what?" Chip said.
"Nothing, lad. Just rejoice. The worst is behind us now," Bill said crossing his arms and sitting down in the lush, green grass.
"Yeah," Chip said while being overcome with a slight uneasy feeling in his gut. He looked around at the jovial nature of what was happening, and he couldn't help but feel like there was still something to go wrong. It's just thing have been going lately, so why would this be any different? He won't be satisfied until he sees this procedure through, and he's at home watching a rom-com with Ellie. Something light, maybe with Patrick Dempsey or Katherine Heigl. He smiled at the thought.
"Okay, Okay everybody. It's great seeing you too. But, shouldn't we get this show on the road?" Ellie said squirming free of her fan club. She glanced back at Chip.
"She's right, everybody!" Zed shouted. "It's time to start this. C'mon people, we have until noon! The sun has to be at its highest, you know that. It only gives us another couple hours! Mum, follow me," she said sternly, grabbing Ellie by the hand and dragging her away.
"Where are you taking her?!" Chip shouted out, but didn't receive a response.

"Relax, son," Bill said sleepily as he lay on the grass. "She's in good hands. Besides, this is the most protected place on the planet - nothing can harm her in here. Celebrate! You've earn it," Bill said closing his eyes and taking in the sun.
"He's right, buddy," Mort chimed in. "Smooth sailing from here on in."
"Okay guys, you're gonna jinx it with this super laid back *everything's alright* attitude." Chip snapped.
"Pfft," Mort said, "Nah. Let's just have fun," Mort added. It was nearly incapable for negativity and worry to crack the barrier surrounding Paradise. There was a little extra something in the air, and it made everybody who entered feel super awesome all the time. Everybody except for Chip, which was an anomaly, and may or may not caused an irregularity in the space time continuum, of course. What else would it be other than that?
Nevertheless, Chip decided that worrying wasn't going solve anything, and so he took a seat under the shade of a giant willow tree. The sun was bright, despite it being so early in the morning, but it wasn't uncomfortably hot, in fact, the weather was perfect, as it always was in Paradise. He watched the hustle and bustle of the busy creatures building what looked like a bed of twigs, and branches, covered in leaves, and rose petals. It was quite beautiful.
"Quite a scene, innit?" A small voice rang out above Chip.
"Huh?" Chip said searching the branches.
"Over here." The voice said. Chip looked over and spotted a butterfly perched on a low hanging stick.
"Oh, yeah. It's something else," he said. Nothing really surprised him, least of all a talking butterfly.
"Yup." The butterfly said floating down onto Chips arm. He raised it and looked at him.
"Why aren't you out there...doing...stuff?" He asked.

"In time, I'll my role to play. I'm just taking a load off until then." It said walking down to Chip hand. It left behind a poo.
"Sorry 'bout that."
"Uh...No problem," Chip said.
"Why aren't you out there helping? I mean, you have hands, with thumbs. I'm sure you can do something." The butterfly said very casually. Chip tilted his head at the odd little creature.
"Uhh... I just summoned like 3 million corpses and took down a demon." He answered.
"Oh. Okay." The butterfly said investigating his hand. "Well, it was a nice chat. But I must be on my way. This freedom thing is great - nice hand. I've got so much more to explore in the next couple hours. Take care." The butterfly said, taking flight.
"You too..," Chip said watching the strange little guy take flight. He didn't put much thought into what it was talking about. In actuality, he began to feel rather sleepy. He'd been up all night after all, and despite the turbulence in his core, he needed to take a little nappy nap. Before he knew it, his eyes were closed, and he was out cold.
The giant willow tree under which he slept seemed to grow long, with its branches making a small pillow for the unassuming hero. Everything was alive, and they knew the renewal was close. Another cycle of life was close by, and everything felt good, and kind, and loving. Word travels fast of the groups exploits, and all they've done to help Mum and get this whole demon thing out of the way. Even the trees wanted to make them all feel welcome and comfortable. It was rather sweet.
Isn't it funny how when you close your eyes for a brief moment, you tend to wake up 2 hours later? Everything around you is different. You blinked during an episode of the Simpsons, and wake up mid way through Seinfeld. It's kind of a pain in the ass, and that was the exact feeling Chip had when

he awoke from his catnap, with a little help from Mortimer, of course.
"Chiiiiiiiiip," Mort said slowly and creepily in his ear. Chip shuffled slightly and scratched his ear. Mort had to up his game.
"CHIP!" He screamed as loud as he could, as close to Chip's ear as possible. Mort's voice ripped through Chip's soul, and he woke up in yelping like a puppy. Mort laughed. Chip swung. Mort fell.
"Ow! Fuck. Some nymph literally just fixed that," Mort said holding his once again bleeding nose.
"Sorry. Reflex," Chip said rubbing the sleep crap from his eyes. "How long was I out for?" He asked, realizing that he was sleeping for more than a minute.
"A couple hours," Mort said climbing to his feet, "the ceremonies about to start." He added.
"Shit! Really?" Chip said in a panic.
"Yeah. I gotta go find that nymph. Ellie's over there," he said pointing to a crowd of critters.
"Okay," Chip said.
Stumbling from beneath the willow tree, Chip walked across the vast field, which seemed larger than before. It was still the perfect day with not a cloud in the sky. The sun shone down with as much majesty and grace as Kate Middleton waving to her adoring fans. Everything was perfect, but even after sleeping, he still couldn't shake the feeling of unrest. Something had to go wrong, right? His story couldn't end here, it didn't feel right. Not that he wanted something bad to happen; quite the contrary actually. He wished things would go smoothly for a change.
He approached the crowd of creatures, animals, and nymphs, and as he did the crowd began to split, giving him a path right to the middle, and what he saw choked him up just a tad. In the centre of the circle was a bed, the same one he'd seen being built earlier, but it was complete. Rose pedals lined an

intricately laced medley of vines being supported by oak logs and perfectly spaced branches. The green, red, and brown contrasted each other to perfection, but it was what laid atop that was truly beautiful. Gowned in a white dress, with a crown of leaves and the slightest hint of make-up was Ellie, Mother Earth. She looked akin to a bride on her wedding day, but there was an extra glow about her, and not metaphorically, but quite literally.

She had begun to glow slightly, as if an aura was oozing from her. It was nearly time, and Chip approached slowly.

"Hey, El..," he said sheepishly.

"Hey Chip," she said with a smile.

"You look...wow," he said in awe.

"Heh, I know. I look like a clown, or a hippie...Or a hippie clown." She smirked.

"Beautiful," Chip said, "simply beautiful."

"Thanks," she said blushing a bit.

"So this is it, eh? What happens next?" Chip asked taking her hand.

"Chip, I -" Ellie started, but was interrupted by a deafening crash near the north perimeter.

"The balls?" Ellie said gracefully.

"I don't know... Stay here," Chip said rushing off towards the commotion.

Chip only got a few feet away from Ellie when through the northern wall crashed a gigantic human being. In fact, it was too big to be a human, and Chip could only assume that it was another demon, or some other maleficent thing out to cause mayhem and fear. It was becoming quite typical. He knew something bad was bound to happen. It was inevitable. The smoke cleared, and Chip could clearly see the armour clad warrior giant looking to do what armour clad warrior giants do: start some shit. Chip took a running step towards him, but stopped the instance a centaur guardsman was turned to dust. Poof, again.

"On second thought..," Chip said to himself halting his progress.
"Bill!" He shouted.
"Yup?" Bill said from right behind him, spooking him.
"What the hell is that?"
"I don't rightly know. I can fathom a guess though," he said calmer than he should have.
"Well? Who...or what is it?"
"My guess? It's the Master of The Order, Sharok. In case you couldn't tell, he was a fierce warrior with unmentionable power. Most likely the mastermind behind all of this nonsense with Ellie."
Chip looked shocked, "Pretty specific guess," he said. Bill shrugged.
"Should we go over and...ya know, kill him or something?" Chip asked.
"I don't see another option, lad," Bill said.
"Right." With that, Chip took off towards the enormous warrior, who was literally flinging 1000lbs centaurs like they were ping-pong balls. Every once in a while it seemed as though he would turn one to dust just for the fun of it. Bill slowly meandered behind, he was getting too old for this crap. Chip pulled up in front Sharok, who looked down on him as if he were nothing more than an ant. In fact, he raised his boot to squash poor Chip.
"Whoa! Hold on a sec," Chip said, closing his eyes. He's batting 1.000 with the eye closing thing so far.
"Hmm. There's something different about you." Sharok said as a spear pierced his arm. He pulled it out and hacked it back in the direction from where it came, impaling a nymph guardsman on a tree. Chip swallowed hard.
"Different? No. Stupid, sure...But that's not really different, is it?" He said, rambling slightly. Sharok looked on curiously.
"Necromancer," he said, sniffing the air, as if he could smell it on Chip. And here Chip thought the smell phase was over.

"I still smell? Bill, do I still smell like death? Why didn't you tell me?" Chip said anxiously. Bill just face palmed.
"You're the one that's been ruining everything!" Sharok said pointing in his direction. He snapped. Chip closed his eyes and expected to turn into dust. Sharok, also expected him to turn into dust. Chip didn't turn into dust.
"What?" Sharok said quite angry. He snapped again, and again, and again, but nothing happened. Chip smiled.
"What is this sorcery?" Sharok questioned. "It matters Not! I'll tear you limb from limb, puny mortal!" He said lunging towards Chip.
Life works in funny ways. People blink in and out of people's lives all the time. Some live, some die, and some get sucked into a time vortex by a Cthulhu-esque creature. Sometimes, just sometimes in life, those people - the ones who got eaten by a monster from another dimension - pop back into your life just as quickly as they left.
From behind Sharok, a small tear appeared. It looked like a cat's eye, but suddenly ripped right open, revealing Ick riding atop the creature that had seemingly eaten him. Ick gave a little wink at Chip before the Cthulhu creature grabbed Sharok by the head, and pulled him into the tear in space/time. The portal closed as rapidly as it had opened, and everybody stood around confused as balls.
"Sure. Why not," Chip said matter-of-factly turning back towards Bill.
"Hmm. I didn't see that coming," Bill said.
"That's a first." Chip remarked, Bill narrowed his eyes at him.
"C'mon, we've got a ceremony to complete, and a world to save. I think. I'm still fuzzy on what this whole thing is going to do," Chip said patting Bill on the back.
For the first time since this whole ordeal began, Chip felt at ease. There was no lingering feeling of dread emanating from his core. He felt good. He felt whole. He felt at peace. Unless the Devil himself showed up, Chip couldn't even think of

another baddy that would attack, at least not in the next few minutes.
It didn't take long for Paradise to repair itself, though many were still confused, and worried about how somebody was able to break the barrier surrounding the grove. It had never before been accomplished. Regardless, it seemed to have patched itself, and was as strong as it had ever been.
Chip took Ellie's hand yet again when he walked up beside her.
"What the fuck was that?" She asked.
"Dunno. Don't care, really," he said looking at her and smiling.
She smiled back, knowing that he'd come a hell of a long way in the last couple of days. He wasn't the same boy she fell for when they first met. He was now a full blown grown-up, complete with battle scars and supernatural powers. What tween wouldn't love that? She kissed him, long, hard, and passionately. He kissed her right back, just as long, just as hard, and just as passionately.
A tear rolled down Ellie's face as they embraced one another.
Zed took this perfect moment to interject.
"Alright, alright. C'mon, I get it, you're young and horny. But bigger fish and all that jazz," she said guiding Ellie to her bed of foliage.
"Right," Ellie said wiping away her tears before Chip could see. It would just worry him.
"Let's do it," Chip said.
Ellie had lain down on the bed while two hummingbirds pulled a silken sheet over her body, leaving just her head. The crowd around them grew, as all of natures creatures watched with anticipation. The time was near, nearer than Ellie wanted it to be. Chip watched at Ellie's side. He went to touch her, but Zed slapped his hand away.
"Everybody, we gather here to bear witness to Mother Nature and the sacrifice she will make in order to keep everything that is natural, and beautiful, and clean as such. Without further

ado, let us all focus our energy. Positive thoughts, people," Zed said turning back, smiling at Ellie, who smiled right back.
"Sacrifice?" Chip muttered to himself.
A chorus of hums began to flow from all those in the crowd, it was memorising, it was hypnotic, it was flat out bone chillingly splendid. Chip watched with bated breath as the glow surrounding Ellie began to shine brighter and expand to encompass her complete. It was golden, with flecks of magic floating within. It was unlike anything else he'd ever seen, and he was totally captured by its resplendence.
Through the glow and the spectacle, Ellie didn't take her eyes off Chip, who watched intensely. It took him a moment, bless him, before he noticed Ellie staring right at him. When their eyes locked, he smiled, as did she. But her smile faded as the procedure continued. Unsure, Chip mouthed the words, *are you okay?*, to which Ellie replied *yes* with a simple nod of the head. She wasn't completely okay. Sure, she was saving the world, but she wasn't going to get to experience it with Chip. Hell, she even thought she might miss Mortimer.
She closed her eyes briefly letting tears stream down her cheeks. When she opened them again, all she saw was Chip, as if he were the only person around. Suddenly she didn't feel afraid. She felt comforted knowing that he was there. Nobody else mattered in that moment, and even though she knew the ritual was still happening, she couldn't physically see anybody else. She couldn't hear anything but the rapid beating of her own heart, and the quickness of her breath. Not being able to take her eyes off of Chip, who stood there adorably dorky, she squeezed out a smile before mouthing the words, *I Love You.*
Chip's heart sunk. He finally realized what was destined to occur. Ellie wouldn't make it. Perhaps he knew all along, but refused to accept it. Maybe he thought it'd be easier that way. He started this journey to save his girlfriend, not to save the world. The latter was a mere bonus. But if he could choose between the world and Ellie, he'd choose her any day of the

week. He may not have been able to find the courage, and gather the will to fight if it weren't about her. A tear rolled down his cheek, he mouthed back, *I Love You too.*
He began to sob, like, really ugly cry which made Ellie sad, but she couldn't help but giggle. For all the childish things Chip had done in their time together, he had never cried. It was sweet knowing that the only thing that could make his cry was her - or perhaps it was losing her. Regardless, it was charming.
Ellie took a deep breath, and began to float off the bed slightly, causing the silk sheet to drape over her body and hang down her sides. She looked like the most elegant possession victim ever. The crowd's chanting slowly came to a hush as she was lowered by an invisible force back onto her bed of roses. Hushed now, the only audible noise was a slight fluttering, like tiny wings beating in a rhythm. Chip looked around for the source of the noise, and then he spotted it. The little butterfly that shat on his arm earlier. What was he doing?
The butterfly slowly fluttered his way over to Ellie. He penetrated her golden aura bubble and landed on her chest. She breathed slowly, controlled. Her eyes closed, not fully conscious now, the butterfly flapped once, twice, three times with incredible force. On the fourth flap, Chip could feel the wind generated from it brush across his face. The air smelled like Ellie. He closed his eyes as if to embrace her one last time. When he opened them again, the butterfly flapped one last time, and in a split second, he and Ellie exploded into an infinite amount of golden flecks, no bigger than dust floating in rays of sun through a window.
The dust glittered and danced in the wind, blowing by everybody in the audience sending their hair, or feathers, or whatever they had backwards. Everybody took in the energy, invigorating them, sending a wave of euphoria through their very cores. The particles wafted farther and farther, up into the atmosphere, sprinkling its life giving energy to everything that

it touched. Flowers grew, tress sprouted, and leaves filled in. Everything was in bloom, and it was stunning.

All of the creatures in Paradise were feeling good, caught in their own ecstasy, everybody that was, except for Chip. His mission was successful, but he failed to reach his ultimate goal; protect Ellie. Sure, she didn't die at the hands of a Hellspawn, nor was she tortured to death by a demon, but she wasn't there, with him. It was a pyrrhic victory. What was the point of living on if he couldn't share it with the only person with whom he wanted it to be shared? It was a selfish thought, but it was one Chip thought that he'd earned. He strayed from the crowd and sat beneath the shade of that familiar willow tree.

He slumped against the trunk. He wanted to cry, but he was too sad to muster the tears, and so he merely hung his head and held his knees to his chest.

"Don't be sad." A hollow voice murmured.

"Hmm?" He said, looking up with red eyes.

"I'm here. I'm her. The grass, the birds, and the flowers, they're all me. I'm everywhere now." The voice said.

"Who's there?" Chip said looking frantically around.

"I love you, Chip." Ellie's voice, clear as day, rang out from the willow tree.

"Ellie?!" He shouted. No answer.

"I love you too," he said, smiling, looking to the sky. Maybe everything would be okay after all, he thought.

He leaned back against the tree trunk and looked out over Paradise, which seemed to be more vibrant and full of life than before. He didn't think it was possible. For all the selfishness in being sad, he did indeed miss the whole point of his adventure. He single-handedly saved the world... Okay, he had some help, but it was mostly him. The level of vanity was frightening, very nearly on Mort's level. But, the saving grace was, he began to feel happy for everything out there. Without Ellie's sacrifice, who knows what would have happened; it

surely wouldn't have been good. Besides, he knew he'd see Ellie again one day.
"Tehehehe," A cackle of laughter erupted from behind Chip, in the bushes. He swung around to see a foxy little nymph come trotting from a bush, behind her stumbled Mort, with his hair a mess, his shirt on backwards *and* inside out, and his nose back to normal.
"Oh." The nymph said surprised to see Chip.
"Chip. Oh, hey," Mort said, scratching his head and looking down awkwardly. "What's up?" He added.
"Ellie's gone. Ceremony's done. World's saved." Chip answered monotonously.
"Oh, buddy... I'm sorry," Mort said earnestly.
"Wait, it's done? And I missed it?!" The nymph shouted. "I waited 250 years for this, and I missed it cuz you thought my body was *weird* at the start? You asshole!" The nymph said punch Mort square in the nose, breaking it again.
"No! Wait! You can't leave me like this!" Mort said chasing after her, "I'm sorry! I don't usually take that long!" He yelled jogging past Chip.
Chip couldn't help but smile. Something's never change, and that's exactly how he liked it. He walked out from under the willow's canopy and looked to the endlessly blue sky and took a deep breath of the freshest air he'd ever had.
"It's gonna be okay."

# ACKNOWLEDGEMENTS

I'd like to acknowledge the support from the writing community, and all those who have given advice, or were willing to read this in advance for thoughts and such. That list includes, but isn't limited to, Barry Skelhorn of Sanitarium Magazine (who gave me my first ever writing job), Hans Heim, who offered up his editing services as well, and my old high school teacher, Sue Jackson. There are way too many people to individually thank for this, and just because there isn't a specific mention, it doesn't mean they weren't important – it was because of all of you – and you know who you are, that this is possible.

Thank you for giving me and my book a shot. It means the world to me that you would give a scruffy Canadian a chance at fulfilling a lifelong dream – eating pizza every day. No, wait, sorry, writing a successful novel that people will actually enjoy. That's better.
If you would like to contact me, you're more than welcome to – nay, I encourage it, nay, I demand it! Okay, maybe not demand, but you know what I mean.

Manufactured by Amazon.ca
Bolton, ON

45231664R00152